"You are exquisit
Arabic. He hoped
even as he fought to maintain a suave
exterior. Internally, his emotions churned
like milk being transformed into butter.

Had his mother given the dress Ranya was wearing
because she'd mentioned his name? Did Madame
Hala remember him? Ask about him? Miss him?

And then there was Ranya herself. He thought she
was beautiful earlier; it might have even been what
drew him to her plight in the first. But, standing
before him, in a dress *his* mother provided, she was
much, much more.

He could not afford to be smitten with a woman—
especially an inconvenient one who lived in Egypt
when he was set to sail to England on the morrow—
when the trajectory of his life path was set to
change in three months' time.

She is a complication, his mind insisted while his
heart and body demanded he ignore the dictum.

Author Note

I am fascinated (and, sometimes, horrified) by how complex global histories have happened around singular commodities while nuanced stories of the people affected by those histories are often essentialized or left untold. How can contemporary readers experience the trials and joys of people who lived (as the history textbooks might lead us to believe) only in relation to crops?

As a long eighteenth and nineteenth century (post)colonial literature student, it was the "white golds" of sugar and cotton that both formed my critiques and gripped my imagination. The history of sugar cannot be separated from the slave trade; and cotton, the commodity which Egypt is arguably most known for, has its own wretched history.

Researching the time period and reflecting on my family's stories of Alexandria and the Nile Delta helped me find evidence of people who had lived their lives unapologetically despite their circumstances. And, often, in defiance of the commodification that prioritized industry over humanity.

In many ways, Ranya is the embodiment of the determined Egyptian women who were my ancestors and it was an honor to pen this romance of hers. I hope you love her as much as Owen does!

HEBA HELMY

—

The Earl's Egyptian Heiress

HARLEQUIN
HISTORICAL

HARLEQUIN®
HISTORICAL™

Recycling programs
for this product may
not exist in your area.

ISBN-13: 978-1-335-72399-4

The Earl's Egyptian Heiress

Copyright © 2023 by Heba Elsherief

For questions and comments about the quality of this book,
please contact us at CustomerService@Harlequin.com.

Harlequin Enterprises ULC
22 Adelaide St. West, 41st Floor
Toronto, Ontario M5H 4E3, Canada
www.Harlequin.com

Printed in U.S.A.

Egyptian-born and Canadian raised, **Heba Helmy** holds an MA in English Literature and a PhD in Language and Literacies (both from the University of Toronto). A former high school teacher and current part-time university professor, her academic practice focuses on culturally sustaining narratives—and her creative one is all about storytelling that centers love. She lives far too much in her own head but you might find her online at hebahelmy.com.

Books by Heba Helmy

The Earl's Egyptian Heiress
is Heba Helmy's debut title
for Harlequin Historical.

Look out for more books from Heba Helmy
coming soon.

For my Earl and the Heirs and Heiresses
who humor our inside jokes.

May you forever have your happily-ever-afters.

Chapter One

Alexandria, Egypt, 1862

Ranya

People thought raw cotton did not have a smell, but Ranya Radwan knew better. It smelled of sun-scorched mud sipping from ancient Nile waters lured from their source. It whined with the flailing perfume of guava and orange, from the roots of trees hacked down to make room for it. Because the British always wanted more. And the Egyptian government wanted the shillings they paid for it.

Ranya inhaled the aroma of her childhood in all its complexity. Cotton was the livelihood of her people, but it had also driven her from her home. She wasn't walking the fields in Damanhour now. She was sitting on a large rock overlooking the harbour in Alexandria, watching as bales of it were being loaded onto ships that would cut across the Mediterranean. Its smell would be overwhelmed, transformed by the sharp salt of the sea, before it reached England.

If her brother were here, he might try to trick Ranya. She could almost hear Muhammad asking, *Which is heavier, a pound of gold or a pound of cotton?* But he'd only be teasing for he knew she had a mind for mathematics better than any accountant in their city.

'They are both a pound,' she whispered, to no one.

Were Muhammad here he might have laughed, but soon after he'd have got that look in his eyes. That far-off, dark one. As if he'd forgotten they did not live in the past any more.

Moments of lightness between brother and sister had been marred by how their lives had changed. Once they'd been the rich children of Damanhour's mayor, the Pasha, back when their father's business arrangement with the Malden Trading Company of England had been seen as foresight. But then the Egyptian government had sought control of all delta lands for their own cotton production trade, and unless Damanhour bought back their interest they would fall under central government dictates—that put less money in the pockets of its labourers.

Malden Trading was a family business, owned by the Earl of Warrington, an Englishman her father had once respected. But when Ranya's father had written to him, saying he wanted to invoke the exception clause in their deed, the man had completely ignored him.

Some people in Damanhour believed Ranya's father had lied about the deed's existence, but her father swore it was true. The Earl of Warrington had notarised the document in England and had kept it there, but its terms were clear: Damanhour could buy back the trading contract from Malden at the original cost plus a *halal* interest annually accumulated at a set rate.

As owner of the largest *izbah*, her father had become the mayor of Damanhour, but when the Earl of Warrington had completely ignored her father's requests and letters, people in the town had started to turn on them.

Muhammad had said he would make it right—force

the Malden Trading Company to pay attention to their demands. Her brother had vowed that even if he had to swim to England he would buy back Damanhour's interests and get the deed they needed to free themselves from a future of government control.

The landowner collective had cobbled together thirty-three thousand pounds—an amount Ranya herself had calculated—and entrusted it to Muhammad.

That had been a year ago. There'd been no word since. Her brother and the money were gone.

Her mama had died soon after, from a sudden heart attack, and now it was only Ranya and her *baba*.

And mostly only Ranya. Her father had been imprisoned by the city council as a way to lure his son back. If Muhammad didn't return in three months' time Baba would be sent to Cairo for trial. Exiled from his life-long home. Maybe to hang as a thief in lieu of his son.

Ranya was her father's last hope. And she had a plan. Not one she was particularly proud of, but the best she'd been able to think of in the time she'd been waiting in Alexandria for the Malden Trading Company's fleet to come and collect their cotton.

The plan involved the very coquettish dress she had just spent the last of her money on.

She kept on peeping at it, hoping to muster the strength to actually wear it tonight.

To be seen in it.

By *others*.

She reached her hand to the bag—except there was nothing there. The space next to her on the rock was empty!

Frantic, Ranya jumped up, searched around the rock. She prayed it had only fallen, or been blown a short distance away by a sudden too strong breeze.

Nothing. The bag was gone. Stolen?

Stupid thief!

Stupid her, for leaving her possessions unguarded and trusting others not to rob her.

But who would want a dress like *that*?

'*Harami!*' she shouted to no one in particular, '*Saraq minni shantiti!*'

People along the corniche paid attention. 'What did he look like?' they asked.

No one wanted a thief on the loose, lest they be his next victim. Ranya sprang from her spot, scanned the area, looking for a way to answer. She ran past an older woman, fanning the dark smoke coming from the corn cobs she was grilling, and a boy pedalling jasmine flower necklaces.

Ranya caught a flash of tawny brown and thought it might be the bag that carried the dress. The man carrying it looked as if he was trying to be inconspicuous.

'There! The *harami*!' she yelled, pointing at him.

He proved his guilt by sprinting towards the harbour, but he stumbled forward, crashing into the labourers loading the ships.

One, a handsome young man, met her gaze, and then, making the connection, dropped his bale and sprang into action. He was the first to reach the thief, pulling his arm behind his back and locking his leg by swinging it behind his own. Other labourers joined in, following the first one's lead. They circled the thief, trapping him.

Sand ran between Ranya's toes in her slippers, slowing her pace. By the time she reached them a larger crowd had gathered. People hurled insults at the *harami*, whose head hung in shame.

An English captain pushed past them all, blowing a whistle as if silencing dogs. 'There are ships to be loaded. I don't pay for distractions. Those not working—leave!'

Most didn't understand the man, but Ranya had spent

a few months learning English so she could put her plan into motion. She stepped forward, still fuming with desperation at how much depended on the dress in that bag. How close she was to losing it. And her plan.

'This man stole from me. Your men have been good enough to apprehend him.'

The Englishman's surprise at her skill with his language was a momentary triumph, but when Ranya turned around to face her now fully captured thief he'd pulled away from his captors a little. He held up the contents of the bag—the dress she'd intended to wear. In all its tasteless, inappropriate glory.

'I am saving the city from a whore!' the thief gloated in Arabic, playing the hero.

Ranya's face reddened as the crowd turned on her. But this was not the *izbah*—not Damanhour, where she would never live down the embarrassment of owning a dress like that. Everyone here was a stranger, and though she was grateful for that, she hated it that *anyone* should judge her.

Sensing the turn of the crowd's feelings in his favour, the thief held the dress against his body so the sea breeze wouldn't diminish the full effect of its bright red shade and the shimmering beads gathered at the pelvis. The material bunched at the waist. Its lack of sleeves. The cut meant for a full cleavage.

She could have sworn he leaned forward, so the others might imagine how a woman would look in it.

Ranya tightened the scarf around her head…covered her chest with crossed arms.

'A'ootho billah!'

Someone yelled an entreaty to Allah that they should be spared. As if Ranya were a devil. Fuming, she sprang for the dress, but other hands got to it first. One to the left, the other to the right, tugging and tearing at the material.

The brazen ripping sound opened the gates to people's disgust. One man spat at Ranya's feet, and a mother dramatically put her hands over her young daughter's eyes.

'*Sharmoota!*'

It was not so loud, but loud enough to make the mother shift to cover her daughter's ears. It was the ugliest word for prostitute—taboo for even the basest to speak out loud.

Ranya lifted her chin, refusing to give anyone the benefit of her tears. And she could only watch as the thief ran, pulled free from the grip of the man who'd first apprehended him.

The handsome labourer.

When his eyes met Ranya's, her blood seemed to boil with more than just anger over the insult to her. She chided herself. The dress wasn't supposed to make *her* feel inappropriate things—especially now it was gone. Besides, there was kindness in the downturn of the labourer's eyes, and his full lips were pursed sympathetically. She hated to see his pity, but she allowed his gaze to be a steadying presence amidst the vitriol.

Maybe he would see beyond the dress to the plan she'd had for it. How her intentions had been noble. It was not a dress meant to dishonour—it was a necessary tool to free her father and restore their family name.

She was still letting his face anchor her when the labourer looked away as the English captain moved to clear the scene.

'I said, get back to work!' he shouted.

I wouldn't want him to get in trouble, Ranya thought as she watched him moving away to fulfil his master's orders.

'Would you like me to fetch your…*item*, miss?' the captain asked with insincere courtesy, pointing to the sparkle of red now being battered by the waves at the hull of his ship.

Ranya managed a quick shake of her head before flee-ing back to the rock where the crime had been committed. She sank to its base, finding a small clearing between it and the other boulders around it to hide. It was like being cocooned in a large seashell, with the sound of the waves echoing.

Though she tried to stop them, the tears pricked too hot and she had to let them fall.

Ranya's plan was gone. She hadn't enough money for a new dress. Maybe not even enough to catch the train back to Damanhour. And she didn't want to go back like this. With nothing to show for her time away. No brother. No deed. No monies returned.

For months she'd been in Alexandria, planning for this night. Scrimping and struggling to learn English in prepa-ration. Never feeling sorry for herself. Now all she *could* feel was sorry.

She wasn't sure how long she stayed that way, but her tears had dried and the sun was beginning its descent when she heard a voice.

'*Afwan, annisa...*'

She looked behind her to see the handsome labourer who'd apprehended the thief sitting on her rock. His Ara-bic was heavy, and his 'Pardon me, miss...' said with an accent she couldn't place. Maybe he was from Southern Egypt, or closer to the Red Sea—come, like others, to Al-exandria, looking for work.

'I wanted to ensure sure you were all right,' he said.

She scrubbed at her face and brushed down her thick brows before standing.

He was handsomer up close, his eyes a shade of golden honey that danced with the darkest of greens. She'd never seen such a colour, and had certainly never before wanted to keep staring into a man's eyes like that in order to keep seeing it. His curly hair was a rich brown that bordered more on blond than black, and it struck Ranya that she had never before wanted to run her hands through a man's hair so much either.

It must be the loss of the dress making her think so foolishly!

Desperately trying to regain her composure, Ranya searched for a fault in the handsome labourer, and noticed that his skin was not as tanned as the others—as if he'd been avoiding the sun while loading the bales. Maybe he was avoiding work too.

'I'm fine,' she said. 'No thanks to you.'

His lips formed a small smile that made him look like a mischievous boy with a secret to hide. 'It wasn't me who ruined the dress.'

'You let the thief go.'

'But he did not get away with anything.'

'He could steal from someone else.'

He thought about it for a moment and then nodded. 'Yes, perhaps that was my fault. I think in the moment—do not consider the future.'

Ranya sighed in exasperation and sat down next to him. The labourers were still working, but the British captain was crossing the street to the fancy hotel that overlooked the sea. Maybe he'd left early to prepare for the bank's opening party. The one Ranya was supposed to attend.

But she wouldn't cry again. Not in front of a stranger. No matter how handsome.

'I am not a prostitute,' she divulged. 'That dress was supposed to beguile the man whose family have stolen from mine.'

He gestured to the captain. 'The Englishman?'

'Not him. Another… The Earl of Warrington.'

He cleared his throat. 'The Earl of Warrington died. Over a year ago.'

She knew that, of course. 'But his debts will be passed on to the next generation. Just as I must avenge my father, the old Earl's son should suffer for his father's actions.'

'I see…'

His tone was measured, and Ranya wasn't entirely sure he wasn't making fun of her, so she found herself blurting, 'I was going to catch his attention at the Anglo-Egyptian Bank's opening party tonight—make him fall in love with me and give me the deed his father held back from mine. In that dress.'

'I should ask more about this deed, but I cannot help but wonder what you would have done if the new Earl had wanted to take your honour *because* of that dress?'

'Steal his manhood!'

'Like a *harami*?' he joked.

His infuriating smirk turned into an outright laugh— the kind that had him holding his belly.

Ranya might have slapped him if they'd been better acquainted. Instead, she stared sternly—not at all as if she found him irresistibly attractive—until he spluttered and sobered.

Following a sheepish apology, he said, 'The Englishmen at the party will be the sort who don't respect Egyptian women. To get them to do what you want you'd have to act like one of *their* women. Cover up in the kind of gowns their women wear. Earls and their sons are only supposed to respect Englishwomen. And even then only if she is rich or comes from a noble family.'

I am a cotton pasha's daughter, Ranya thought, peeved, but she said nothing.

He reached a finger to a curly strand of her hair that had strayed from behind her scarf. He didn't touch it, but

Ranya's stomach clenched with the belief that he might. Then she found herself surprised by how much she wanted him to. He was arousing sensations in her she'd never before felt.

Probably because I am feeling vulnerable, she thought.

She had already lost so much, and today she might have lost her last hope.

'Iron your hair straight and pile it high on your head, so you look tall and intimidating,' he said. 'Some Englishmen can be fools like that…only respecting women who scare them.'

'How do you know so much about them?'

He shrugged. 'I have been watching them all my life.'

From minarets around them the call to the Asr prayer began. Deep and rumbling from a mosque in the distance, softer and sweet-sounding from the one a few metres away.

Ranya waited until the *athans* ended, holding her breath, irrationally wanting to keep the labourer next to her for longer. 'It doesn't matter now. Even if I managed to get into the party, I think the English captain is going. If he recognised me and then accused me of… *selling* myself.'

'Jarvis Larder is the man's name. Not a captain—only a taskmaster who wouldn't know the difference between us labourers if his employer was pretending to be an Egyptian. Trust me, *if* Larder is there, he will not know you.'

She wasn't sure she could trust him, but even if he was right… 'I have little money to spend on the type of gown you are describing. I have nothing to wear to this party that would be suitable.'

He stared out at the sea for a long moment before speaking again. 'Do you know the seamstress's shop at the corner of Firdous Road? A few streets from here?'

She knew he was asking her a question, but Ranya could barely manage a nod in response. He was leaning in conspiratorially, so close she might have tested the spikiness of the stubble scattered along his jaw and winding over the sharp peaks of his upper lip with her own cheek.

What was wrong with her?

Focus, she forced herself.

'Go there. Ask for Madame Hala. Tell her of the party. Say that you want to dress like an Englishwoman set to meet her suitors. She *may* help.'

Ranya hated sounding whiney, but countered, 'It would take weeks to sew such a dress, and the party is tonight— besides which, as I said, there is no way I could afford it.'

'No harm in trying. Maybe Madame Hala has one ready or one you can borrow. Tell her Iskander sent you, and if she asks for an amount, tell her Iskander will settle it.'

His name was Iskander. As pleased as she was to find out, she realised he hadn't asked for hers.

He was already standing up, making ready to leave.

'Why are you helping me?' she asked his retreating back, so quietly she was sure he wouldn't hear it.

But Iskander turned with that wry smile of his. 'It's the least I can do for letting that *harami* get away.'

Chapter Two

Owen

Even though her plight had personally touched him, Iskander was certain he'd never see the girl again. Best not to know her name. To forget her face.

No matter how beautiful.

It had been the hunted look behind her eyes. When she'd looked at him on the harbour he'd seen a desperation there that had felt familiar to him——stirred emotions he'd thought he'd tamed in himself.

He had learned long ago to move like a traveller in his own life. As if it were one long railway line and there were stops along the way where he chose to disembark for a change of clothes and a good meal before the next departure time. Never remaining long enough to even dream of settling or laying down roots.

Or taking the names of beautiful girls who admitted plotting to beguile him for a deed.

She didn't want it from Iskander, of course. No, the pretend labourer's given name was very different. For Iskander was, in fact, Owen Alexander Malden. And now his father had died, he had also inherited the Earl of Warrington title.

It was a title he had hitherto been ambivalent about, but this was the year Owen turned twenty-five. The Countess of Warrington was expecting him to completely take up the mantle her husband—Owen's father—had, in her opinion at least, never lived up to.

Owen was supposed to find a proper bride this season—the Countess likely had a shortlist of suitable girls prepared—and claim his estate's seat in the House of Lords. He and his new wife would take up residence full-time on the Warrington estate and live happily ever after, producing at least one son who would continue the earldom.

It would all be finalised after the annual Percy Ball in London.

But that was a stop in the railway journey of his life that Owen wasn't at all ready to disembark at—and certainly not the part of him who was Iskander.

He weaved around Cleopatra's obelisk. The towering stone needle engraved with hieroglyphs had been bought by England to commemorate their triumph over Napoleon's French fleet. It hadn't yet been transported, but a special ship had been built, and the needle's place on the River Thames secured.

Owen wondered if it would be sad to leave its home.

If I could buy us both more time, I would.

He crossed to the back doors of the hotel across from it and met the bellman he'd bribed when they first disembarked in Alexandria to let him pass no matter how he was dressed.

'A man is waiting for you in the lobby,' the bellman said, following him up the rickety back staircase. 'Mr Jarvis Larder.'

'Let the leech wait longer. I require a half-hour.'

'Very good, sir. Will you have your lunch now?'

The young woman had reminded Owen that there was

an event he was supposed to attend tonight, on behalf of Malden Trading. He might have skipped it altogether, but now he'd met her he decided he would go.

If only for the chance of seeing her again.

They'd probably have food at the event, but the bellman had been bringing him the most delicious local dishes, and even though Owen knew a place in London, here was the home of authentic cuisine. How often would he find himself vacationing in Egypt?

'Better make it a light one.'

Owen took the wrought-iron steps three at a time to the top floor of the hotel. He pulled the wide peasant-style *galabaya* over his head and ripped off his trousers as soon as he'd crossed into the privacy of his rooms. Both were made from a cheap cotton. Unlike the cotton they transported to England. He knew the poorer Egyptians kept the lower quality material for themselves. Fine if one didn't actually do any labour, but today's heavy work—the last major haul before the first cargo ship was set to sail—had Owen sweating and itching like a poodle with fleas.

He drew himself a warm bath, grateful for the option. This was the finest hotel in Alexandria, convenient in its proximity to the harbour and newly built with the most modern of amenities.

He stretched his naked form in the long tub, scrubbing away all outward signs of the labourer he'd been pretending to be.

If only it were as easy to separate who he was on the inside, Owen thought.

Iskander was a boy born to an English earl and the Egyptian woman he'd taken as a secret wife. A bastard, really, since his father's second marriage would have been considered bigamous in England and never recognised there, whereas a man could have four wives at a time in Egypt.

His father had rarely spoken of his Egyptian 'wife' after she'd left England. Owen had been a boy at the time. Over the years he'd gleaned very little about her. He knew she'd been a seamstress and a devout Muslim, who would only agree to be with his father if he converted and married her in a mosque.

Then, on his deathbed a few months ago, his father had spoken words Owen hadn't stopped hearing since.

'Hala laughed like an angel, despite her hard life. It's what I loved most about your mother...that laugh. I wanted to be her hero. Whisk her to safety. But I was her doom. I made her face Vivian's pain at my betrayal. Then Vivian's wrath. Instead of a hero, I was a coward.'

It had been a shock to Owen, hearing his father's death-bed confession. He hadn't shown it then, of course, because Vivian, the Countess of Warrington, had been in the room, and he hadn't wanted to further hurt her. Though she had never been affectionate, she was the only mother figure he'd had after his mother had abandoned him as a boy. And, amongst society she had, from the start, claimed Owen as her own. People might guess otherwise, but none could ever prove it nor dare to bring up the rumours in her company.

Still, after he'd buried his father, Owen had been possessed by the thought that he should like to know the mother who had given birth to him. To hear her laugh and wonder if it was still the same. Had not having her son with her made Madame Hala's life harder or simpler?

When the Countess had suggested Owen should oversee the Malden Trading Company's spring shipment from Egypt, he'd pounced at the chance. He'd visited the country with his father once, when he was eighteen, but Owen had mostly spent his time enjoying the Cairo night life. This trip would be a business one, according to the Countess, to 'get the Company's interests in order'.

In truth, Owen had no idea, nor even any interest, in what that meant.

If he had, he might have toured the Nile Delta, checking on the cotton fields, meeting suppliers. Then he would have had some inkling of the deed the girl had mentioned.

Instead, Owen had spent his days stalking his mother. Fuming over her life. Jealous that she had moved on to start a new one. As if she had forgotten him.

'The Pasha in Damanhour is a friend.'

Owen sat up so quickly at the sudden memory of his father's statement that water splashed to the floor. As he rose and began to dry himself, he wondered if he'd heard those words from his father on his deathbed too. Or had it been somewhere else? He couldn't remember—but what if the girl he'd met was from Damanhour?

She'd spat hatred for his father and, not wanting to expose his identity, Owen had brushed it off as an unfortunate mistake. Now, as he towelled himself off, spending extra time squeezing out the water from his hair, he regretted not defending his father more.

While Charles Malden's personal life choices might have been questionable, his success in business was undeniable. He had poured his heart and soul into it, building the Malden Trading Company even before he'd had the aid of the title he'd come into only because of the law that favoured distant male heirs rather than direct female ones.

More impressively, Owen's father had built his company without making enemies.

Nobody had anything untoward to say about Charles Malden.

'The girl is wrong,' Owen decided out loud, pushing away the prickle of doubt.

He wrapped the towel around his waist and examined his reflection in the looking glass as he prepared to shave off the straggly beard he'd let run amok for his time as Iskander.

He'd be sorry to let it go. He had quite enjoyed the cover it provided, and the smidgeon of savagery it suggested had turned out to be quite freeing.

By the time the bellman knocked on the door, with his lunch and Jarvis Larder in tow, Owen's hair had been slicked back, and the curls he'd inherited from his mother pomaded down. His pressed trousers and cufflinked shirt were donned and he was ready for the bank's opening gala that night.

He'd said 'light', but the plates being set before him were anything but. Fried sardines in a garlicky tomato sauce were served with a platter of bold green arugula leaves and sliced radishes. Then the bellman laid out a platter of yellow rice. '*Koshary*,' he named it, 'Alexandria-style—not find it in Cairo. Rice boiled with red lentils and only eaten on Fridays with the day's catch.'

Owen took a bite. It was mushy, but there was a slight sweetness to it that melted in his mouth. He decided it complemented the crunch of the fish very well. 'Delicious.'

'It must be because the Copts are forbidden eating meat on Fridays, but why should this matter to Muslims?' questioned Larder in a civil tone—so unlike the cruel voice Owen had, in disguise, witnessed him using towards the labourers all day.

Deception was a trait Owen hated in others, though he himself was guilty of it. The difference was that the essence of his character didn't change when he was either Iskander or Owen.

Owen was not a hypocrite.

The bellman's slight smile showed missing teeth. His English was mixed with a bit of French as he brought his hands together to answer. 'Us Alexandrians are hailing from south, west, east... *Tout le monde d'Egypt.* We not say *her Muslim* or *he Christian*. Others—foreign peoples—they come and try divide us. This no good. We want eat like family.'

'Hurrah to family!' Owen said.

He wrapped a sardine in a bite of the bread and sopped up the earthy tomato sauce, careful not to let it drip onto his white shirt.

'Larder—you sure you won't join me?'

'I like to keep to English mealtimes, sir.'

'You will not have much chance to get *baladi* bread there.'

Owen would miss the freshness of that the most. Even here, if the tasty bread used in lieu of a spoon wasn't eaten within an hour of coming out of the large clay ovens it was baked in, it wasn't malleable.

Speaking of spoons... Were he alone, Owen might have forgone utensils altogether and wiped the plates clean. But he allowed the bellman man to roll out the trolley with a polite amount left over on each plate.

Owen settled into his seat to hear the account Larder had been waiting to give.

'The warehouses in Mina El-Basal are emptied, then? And the loaded ships on schedule for tomorrow?' Owen asked, though he knew they were.

Larder answered him. 'There was quite a delay today, but I managed to wrangle it in due course. We are ready to sail on schedule.'

'Oh? What sort of a delay?'

Larder waved a dismissive hand. 'Turned out to be something between a pimp and his…lady of the night. Got a bit messy—and you know how lazy labourers can be…dodging work. I had to swoop in and save the day.'

Owen could barely contain his groan. 'Very good! Then I will see you tomorrow morning?'

'I was wondering how you fared on your trip to the Delta, sir? The cotton farms there?'

'Fine, fine… Spoke to the people I needed to.' Owen stood, meaning to usher Larder out. 'I have a party to attend this evening, but you should sleep for both of us.'

Larder rose, but his feet remained still upon the Persian rug. 'Party? Do you mean the bank opening, sir?'

Owen moved towards the door, throwing a 'Yes' over his shoulder.

'I could go, my lord. On your behalf. I know you do not favour such things.'

How could Larder possibly know that?

'You have me wrong. I quite like a party. It does not even have to be a good one.'

Larder nodded, but still didn't make a move out through the door. 'Let us chaps attend together, then? Practice for mixing with the ton later this season?'

'The ton?' Owen clenched his jaw.

He and Larder were certainly not 'chaps.'. He had only travelled with him because the fellow had taken over his own father's position in Malden Trading. The elder Jarvis Larder had indeed been a naval captain, and had regularly accompanied Owen's father on his numerous international trips. But the Jarvis Larder standing before him was only a notary who happened to be a convenient hire for this trip.

'Patter is the Countess of Warrington means to ensure your match this season. At the Percy Ball.'

'Is that indeed the "patter"?' Owen sniffled noncommittally.

'One hears things in London society.' Larder shuffled closer to where Owen stood, getting more brazen with each step. 'Maybe you have a lady in mind? Or maybe you're a rake? Our fathers were friends, so I assume yours told you, as mine told me, that a man can sow as many oats as he likes before he marries, so long as he marries right. Perhaps I could accompany you. Be your "first mate". Find myself a plain heiress or some other woman of means eager to fill her dance card.'

Owen gritted his teeth. Was Larder implying that Charles Malden had been a rake...that Owen was a product of his 'oat-sowing' days?

'Captain Larder was a valued *employee*.' Owen stressed the word, so Larder wouldn't think he could get away with exaggerating the relationship between their fathers. 'I expected him on this trip. But you and me...we are not—'

'I hope I was not a poor substitute for my father,' Larder interrupted. He lowered his head, tapped his fingertips between his pale brows. 'Things have been hard since his accident.'

Owen winced. He hadn't thought to ask about the reason for Jarvis Larder's retirement, nor considered the fact that he might have passed away. After the awkward silence that followed, he begrudgingly—guiltily—returned to the original topic, 'The Countess wishes to see me settled by my twenty-fifth birthday. For me to take up my seat in Parliament. Tend to the estate. Produce an heir—all of it. I should be resigned to it, but I would have liked to travel more...maybe vacation in Italy, India, China...'

Larder lifted his head and smiled gratefully. 'An English wife might stomach the European continent, but travelling to backwaters like Egypt might be hard on her delicate constitution.'

Even the staunchest awareness of decorum had its limits, and Owen had reached his. He opened the door, ushered Larder out with a sweeping motion. 'Get a good rest now. I will meet you at the docks in the morning.'

'And the event tonight?'

'*I* will be there, representing my father's company.'

Larder insisted. 'But I could join you in case—'

'I said I have it managed.' Owen put a hand on the man's back and practically pushed him out of the room. 'One of us needs to be bright-eyed tomorrow.'

When he was gone, Owen sighed with relief. He might have relented, but the girl had said she was scared that Larder would recognise her at the party.

Not that she would attend.

Owen was pretty sure he would never see the girl again.

He didn't think Hala the seamstress would come through for Iskander.

Even if she *was* his birth mother.

Chapter Three

Ranya

If she hadn't shouted Iskander's name, Ranya was sure the woman at the back of the shop wouldn't have heard and the boy at the front wouldn't have let her into Madame Hala's parlour. As it was, it made him open the door of the seamstress's shop after its closing time and brought the woman herself to stand before Ranya.

Madame Hala held a *fanoos* lamp in her hand, lifting it to her face and illuminating the display of dresses that hung in the dark behind her.

She might have been a beautiful woman once, but now she looked tired. Though her kaftan was well made, and her grey hair mostly covered with a coppery henna, the dark circles and frown lines around her eyes were deeply set. And the woman's hunched back spoke of too many years bent over needle and thread.

She clasped Ranya's hand almost desperately before sending the boy away. 'Stay with your father in the café until I come to you.'

He was much darker than Madame Hala, and looked nothing like Iskander, but the similarity was enough that Ranya guessed both were the woman's sons.

When they were alone, the woman didn't confirm it, only asked, 'How do you know Iskander?'

Ranya hadn't planned what to say. She hated to have come practically begging. Even if backed by a sponsor.

'I was robbed on the corniche,' she said. 'A dress needed for an event I must attend tonight. Iskander said you could help. That he would take care of the cost. And I will pay it back, certainly.'

'*Iskander* said I would help? *He* sent you to me?'

Both Madame Hala's tone and the look on her face were hesitant, hopeful, almost afraid. In that moment she reminded Ranya of her own parents when they had anticipated news of Muhammad.

It was odd, but Ranya replied in the affirmative.

The older woman seemed to want to say more, but she bit her lip and lit more lamps instead. Then she flipped through the dresses on the rack, each in various stages of production.

'What sort of event is it?' she asked, steering Ranya around like a doll as she held items up to her body.

'The Anglo-Egyptian Bank's opening.'

Madame Hala shook her head as if it was going to be an impossible task. 'When I started this business it catered to the English—their fashions. Now my clientele is mostly Egyptian women. Bridal gowns and wedding parties.'

Ranya fought a wave of disappointment. This was a waste of the little time she had before the Earl of Warrington sailed. She needed to think of a new plan to get his attention so he would give her the deed.

'Thank you for trying.'

Madame Hala put a hand out, barring Ranya from going. 'I cannot disappoint Iskander.'

Her eyes roamed almost frantically over the shop and landed on an armoire. She pointed to the top and muttered something to herself, before finding a crate and pushing it there to climb up. But she was too small.

'Will you try?'

Ranya wobbled on it as the seamstress crouched to steady the crate.

'Reach to the far back,' she directed. 'There should be a box…but be careful with the dust. It's been there for nearly twenty years.'

Ranya stretched her arms as far as they would go and found it. Gingerly, she pulled it forward, and handed it to Madame Hala before stepping down.

'Not so much dust… Issam's cleaning is worth his allowance.'

The seamstress took it to the cutting table and knocked away the bolts of colourful fabric there to make room.

'*Bismillah,*' she murmured, stretching her fingers before lifting the lid.

From beneath the tissue paper, she pulled a powder blue gown. She shook it out before holding it out to Ranya and urging her to try it on behind a screen she'd set up for the purpose.

Ranya did as she was told. The soft blue silk of the first layer of the dress was like butter on her body, and the delicate lacing of the second layer, with its white cross-stitch pattern, reminded her of cotton flower bouquets. The gown spilled from beneath her chest to the floor in a way that made her feel taller and more graceful than she had in a long time. She didn't have gloves, or decent enough shoes but she felt like an *amira* nevertheless.

'*Masha Allah!*' the seamstress exclaimed when Ranya spun for her. With a satisfied smile, she tightened the silk blue sash and explained, 'It was given to me by an Englishwoman who knew I could not wear it. I was too fat and short. The woman told me that a corset would whittle my waist and the full wire slips would lift the length of fabric off the ground. But us Egyptian women, here in Alexandria, we demand comfort from our clothing.'

Ranya perceived that Madame Hala and the woman who had gifted her the dress had not been friends, but the bitterness in the older woman's voice mellowed with her next words:

'There is always good in Allah's planning. This dress was waiting atop that armoire for *you*.'

She fussed around Ranya, sitting her down to style her hair, kohling her eyes with navy blue rather than a black blend, and dabbing a soft pink rouge to her lips. She found a lovely shawl that Ranya could wear around her head and arms too.

When the seamstress held up a mirror, Ranya barely recognised herself.

She'd not looked this pretty since the days when her father had still been a revered pasha.

'*Shukran,*' she said, but her gratitude could hardly be contained in that single word. 'Forgive me for not being able to pay you now, but I will…in a few months. And will return the gown tomorrow morning after the party and try my best to keep it clean till then.'

'It pleases me very much to help a friend of Iskander's, and I would not take your money. The dress will probably only return to its hiding spot.' Madame Hala lifted an eyebrow. 'But I can see you are a proud girl, as I once was. We shall negotiate a trade. You will keep the dress. When you are in a better position, return it to me, and I will charge you a fair price for the loan.'

'I have nothing to trade. No collateral.'

There was nothing fair about the deal.

'What is this?' Madame Hala held up the dress Ranya

had been wearing. The purple kaftan had used to belong to her mother. It was precious, but it had no monetary value.

'You are being kind…generous. But we are agreed.'

They shook hands and Ranya left the seamstress's shop feeling satisfied. Her plan had shifted—but for the better.

Now, she wouldn't have to feel guilty about cheapening herself in that first dress.

Plus, the thief had done her a favour by leading Iskander to her.

Madame Hala had said something that reminded Ranya of a refrain her mother had often repeated: *'Allah is the best of planners.'*

But there was work still to be done.

An earl to beguile.

The courtyard of the new Anglo-Egyptian Bank swarmed with a diverse crowd. Sheikhs from Arabia in their red-and-white-checked *gutras* were accompanied by wives decked in gold. European women with pale hair and white gloves walked on the arms of their husbands in top hats and tails. There were also many Greek women, and all of them strutted in outfits named after their queen, Amalia. A folksy velvet waistcoat over a wide-sleeved gown and a red fez hat with braided tassels. Perhaps it was a show of defiance.

In her time here Ranya had learned that the Greek community in Alexandria was extensive, and that this whole area had once been part of a consular club for them. But then Egypt's central government in Cairo had decided to let the building to the English. Where there was new money to be made, old friends meant nothing.

She settled near a date palm, waiting for Mr March, her teacher from the English school, to appear with their invitation. He was a bachelor who'd lived in Egypt since the days after the French occupation. Students called him *luti*, but if he took offence to the term for homosexuals, he didn't let on.

The school he ran was sponsored by English patrons and stipends for orphans. With her father imprisoned but still alive, and her advanced age of twenty-one, Ranya wasn't his typical student, but Mr March had said she could join if she helped him by teaching whatever she learned to the younger students. She had worked hard for him since the day she'd arrived in Alexandria, and, in turn he often abandoned his leisure time to give her extra language tuition.

She spotted Mr March with his bright orange silk cravat as soon as he passed through the garden gates.

'If it isn't my positively, absolutely, most fantastical, best student ever,' he greeted her jovially as she made her way to him. 'You look lovely, Ranya. Shall we have a good time while showing you off to our patrons?'

He took her arm in his own and pulled from his pocket the invitation required to allow them entry.

Ranya felt a twinge of guilt when she saw it. Once she'd learned that the Malden Trading Company was one of his school's sponsors, she'd suggested she should be here tonight, telling him that she could secure more donations. While she had no intention of actually helping on that front, her purpose *was* a noble one. And if Mr March had known he was helping free her father Ranya was sure he'd have agreed to let her come, regardless.

'I am happy to use the English you have taught me,' she said.

He smiled. 'How was your day at the docks?'

'I watched them loading cotton and I have many ideas to share with the Earl of Warrington that will be mutually beneficial to his company and to Damanhour, my city.'

Mr March pumped his free fist. 'A woman of industry!

First task: finding and wooing an earl.' He winked. 'For industrial purposes, obviously.'

They walked into the bright white building. The foyer had a sprawling chandelier hanging from its ceiling, holding at least a hundred candles, and surrounding adornments made their bright light flicker almost magically along the walls covered with artwork of English landscapes. Mostly they showed rolling hills and grand trees, none with fruit, however they were varieties Ranya did not know.

The bouquet of freshly brewed Turkish coffee beans and honeyed almond *basboosa* floated in the air, and staff with trays circled the crowd. Mostly they held soft breads with hard cheeses. The bright green cucumber slices looked the most appetising part, but even if she'd been tempted Ranya couldn't have brought herself to reach for anything.

Now she was here, she was nervous about meeting the Earl of Warrington. She'd practised being charming, but what if she couldn't hide the hatred she had for his father? The animosity she felt towards him for all that had befallen her family?

Even as she fretted over it, she found strength in Mr March. He was friendly with other guests, approaching those he recognised for short chats, circulating around the gathering with her on his arm. Ranya contributed to conversations whenever she was called upon, but many of the men were dismissive or only interested in flirting.

She imagined how much worse it would have been if she'd come in that red dress.

She remembered Iskander telling her to stand tall, saying that these Englishmen only respected women they were scared of. She searched the room for him, hoping to meet his gaze in the crowd as she had that afternoon, but, of course, Iskander wouldn't be here. This wasn't a place for labourers.

His warm smile was one she wouldn't soon forget. The way his curls swept around his face…how he had almost touched one of hers. He had been bold, but respectful. And Ranya had never felt so immediately attracted to a man before.

Before things had gone bad for their family, she'd had a couple of marriage proposals in Damanhour—her father was the Pasha, after all. With each suitor met, Baba had always given her the choice, but she had bolted from them, more repulsed than anything. Even if there was nothing physically wrong with them.

Her mama had used to say that when Ranya met the right man for her there would be an ease in her heart. An immediate feeling of attraction, yes, but also a desire to be with him that would feel irrational. A desire that would deepen the more time she spent with him.

Ranya *had* felt that initial attraction with Iskander, and *might* want to find out more about him. When her task was done, and her father freed, she could return the dress to Madame Hala and hopefully see him again.

You should be seeking out the Earl of Warrington, she reprimanded herself.

He was sure to be some surly type, with either a sickly ashy appearance or the robust complexion of a man who enjoyed his food too much. There was no in between in Ranya's mind. He was the spawn of a villain in her family's life and, as such, had to be awful on the inside and out.

A ringing bell brought everyone's attention to the podium that had been installed beneath the chandelier. Standing on it was a small man wearing a very tall top hat.

'Welcome to the grand opening of the Anglo-Egyptian Bank!' he boomed. 'I will be your ringmaster tonight!'

The crowd clapped politely, then laughed when he apologised for not having brought any elephants.

He went on to speak about the renovations they'd made on the building, and then conducted a short presentation on the bank's proposed activities.

'We have dedicated rooms where people may actually speak! The intention is to establish the Anglo-Egyptian Bank as a centre where projects are born and connections nourished between our two countries.'

People still seemed unsure, waiting for further direction, and the 'ringmaster' soon provided it. 'I will call upon some of you. You might already know each other, but humour me by pretending you do not! Come forward and I will allocate rooms accordingly.'

One of the first names called was Mr March's. When he left to answer, there was a jostling around Ranya. Though she tried to listen, to hear whether the Earl of Warrington would be summoned as well, she could not. She stood friendless as the other guests shifted towards the various rooms.

When she'd all but given up, Mr March found her again.

'Here,' he said, stepping aside to reveal the man walking behind him at a slower pace, 'is our prodigal Earl.'

Ranya gasped when she saw who Mr March was referring to.

He was freshly shaved and had waxed his curls. He wore a starched white shirt beneath a burgundy waistcoat that fitted his frame much too well, and his trousers were not the cheap labourer's *galabaya* he'd had on earlier. But even the change in clothing could not hide who he was. Standing before her was the man who had come to her rescue that very afternoon!

Iskander.

Iskander was the Earl of Warrington! How?

Ranya staggered with a mix of emotions. Shock, mostly. That would explain the flutter in her belly at seeing him looking so different, though still undeniably handsome.

Then came the horror-filled realisation she'd told him of her plan to seduce the Earl for a deed.

Ranya considered running, but her plan, her hopes—the spectre of both—kept her rooted for too long while he strode towards her. She saw the recognition in his eyes. The boyish smile. He had *known* she would be here.

Had he tricked her? What a cheating *ghasash*!

Her pride was pricked and that overtook all else—even her physical attraction to him. Which was, she decided, probably a good thing.

'Let me introduce you,' Mr March whispered.

Ranya shook her head, resisting, even though this was the introduction for which she had come.

It was too late, however.

Iskander stood before her, so close she could make out his cologne—a heady mastic and orange blossom enveloped in warm tobacco smoke.

'Ahlan was sahlan,' he greeted her.

Now Ranya could tell why she hadn't been able to place his accent earlier. It was because he was an Englishman pretending to be an Egyptian one!

Mr March said, 'It is a pleasure to have you visiting us in Alexandria, Your Lordship. Your late father was a favoured patron of our school.'

'Thank you for saying so,' said Iskander, glancing at Ranya as if to stress that his father had a *good* reputation. 'No need for the title. You may call me Owen.'

He turned to face Ranya completely. And her heart most certainly skipped a beat—first at the name, and then at the sense of him standing over her. The aura of him was like a charged magnetism. He wasn't that much taller, and the line of her eyes was on a level with his Adam's apple, but Ranya watched it bob and felt as if it was stuck in her own throat.

'And who might this be?' he was saying, while she was still stuck on his name.

Not Iskander. Owen.

Mr March answered. 'I dare say the best pupil I've had over my years in Alexandria! May I present Miss Ranya Radwan?'

'A pleasure to meet you, Miss Radwan.'

She knew she was supposed to curtsy, or hold out a hand to be kissed, or some such ridiculous English custom, but it was enough of an accomplishment that she could hold his gaze and not waver. Hold those half-golden-brown, half-hazel eyes that looked so beguiling, but also, she felt certain, as if they were mocking her.

'Ranya's father is a pasha in Damanhour—a Nile Delta city that supplies cotton for Manchester's mills.' Mr March tried to fill the awkward gap when she didn't say anything in response to the Earl. 'She has some good ideas about the trade. Is that not so, Ranya?'

Still, she could not lose the thing in her throat that wouldn't allow her to speak.

'Isn't that interesting?' said Iskander—no, Owen. 'There is an informal meeting on the cotton trade in the room I have been assigned to. Would you mind if I *stole* Miss Radwan for a while, Mr March?'

Was he insinuating her stolen dress? The man had no propriety!

'It is up to the young lady. I will make the trek to my own room and let her decide.'

Mr March graciously gave her an encouraging nod before leaving them alone. She felt even more guilty for using him, for not being more forthcoming about why she'd wanted to be here tonight.

Ranya needed to be more discerning and more savvy in her life outside of the *izbah*. She should not let her inexperience in the ways of men push her off course. She had a deed to get from the man standing before her, and he had been the one to trick her first.

He put one leg behind the other in a gallant movement, as if he were bowing before her. Then Iskander—*Owen*—turned up his right palm, offering his hand.

Damn her traitorous body for wanting to take it.

Chapter Four

Owen

'You are exquisite,' Owen whispered in Arabic.

He hoped he sounded charming, even as he fought to maintain a suave exterior. Internally, his emotions churned like milk being transformed into butter.

Had his birth mother given Ranya the dress she was wearing because she'd mentioned his name? Did Madame Hala remember him? Ask about him? Miss him?

And then there was Ranya herself. He'd thought she was beautiful earlier—it might even have been what drew him to her plight in the first place. But now, standing before him in a gown *his* mother had provided, she was much, much more.

The sleeves seemed to pour from her shoulders, exposing the tanned flesh along her neck and clavicle that shimmered in the light like an invitation. Owen almost couldn't choose whether to look up or down to take her all in. He chose down, since that direction would give him a bit of privacy while he caught his breath.

It was clear she wore no corset. The material fell freely, touching the floor, somehow too long, but not long enough to conceal the figure beneath. He was taller than Ranya by at least a head, but he had to push back the wholly inappropriate thought of holding her by the satin sash sitting above her waist—his hands would circle it if he stretched his fingers—to compare the length of their legs.

They're probably equal in length to mine.

When he'd composed himself, he let his gaze trail upwards. The shawl she wore draped lightly over her head and chest made her *seem* modest, but coiled wisps of her dark auburn hair fell from a high bun, hitting her cheekbones like wispy offshoots of forbidden fruit. He closed his eyes before letting them meet hers and inhaled.

She smelled faintly of the jasmine pedlars on the shoreline who would circle with necklaced cords of the small white flowers, hoping to sell them to lovers before they wilted.

Owen could not afford to be smitten with a woman—especially an inconvenient one who lived in Egypt—when he was set to sail on the morrow and when the trajectory of his life's path was set to change in three months' time.

She is a complication, his mind insisted, while his heart and body demanded he ignore the dictum.

When Owen finally met her eyes, he was almost sure the task would be easy enough. Ranya made a show of looking at his outstretched hand as if it were a dirty thing she'd never touch. He pulled it away, clasping his hands behind his back.

'What are you playing at?' she snapped.

Her English was nearly impeccable—nothing like his London-learned Arabic which he might have liked to continue practising with her, but doubted she'd agree now.

'Why were you pretending to be someone you're not, Iskander? Madame Hala couldn't have been in on it. Is she your mother?'

Ranya's barrage of questions sobered him. Reminding

Owen that he and she were not lovers, yet alone friends. He didn't owe her any explanation. *And* he wouldn't ask her how his mother had been when she'd heard his name.

'You were the one who told me you wanted revenge on me for the sins of my father. I merely helped by suggesting the sort of dress that would tempt an Englishman.'

Owen felt the shift in his tone as he spoke, heard the hardness in it. It was his Earl of Warrington mask being slipped over his head. And Ranya felt it too. He could tell by the way her chin lifted defensively. How those beautiful shoulders of hers straightened.

She made to leave him.

He might have let her go—should have, perhaps, since she was bound to soon enough. But he couldn't just yet.

Maybe it was because Owen had been too cowardly to face his mother since he'd come to Egypt. Ranya standing in front of him in a dress Madame Hala had provided presented a chance. Perhaps he could make up for that somehow—allow him to reclaim his intrepidness.

Or maybe it was the lie he'd just told her.

Because the truth was Ranya would tempt him in anything she wore. Or wearing nothing at all.

'Come, let us not quarrel. Your fortitude is to be admired. Demanding what was yours from a thief on the harbour. Your English… And Mr March says you have insights into the cotton trade. I am to meet with some of the men who oversee it. Join me. Share your ideas with us all.'

It was the right thing to say, and Owen was rewarded with, if not a smile, a lowering of that perfect chin.

'And after you will give back what your father stole from mine?' she asked.

'My father stole nothing. I am sure of that.'

'There is an agreement. With Damanhour. It would be dated twenty-five years ago. A contract that looks like a deed. It will say that our city can buy back the rights of its trade. And we need it back—otherwise the Egyptian government will swallow the cotton profits that should go to the people of my city. Money they desperately need.'

Beyond hauling bales of it when he was pretending to be a labourer on the harbour, Owen knew little of cotton. Certainly nothing about a hidden deed his father had signed before he was born.

'I will look into it—if only to prove you wrong. My father was honest. A good man.'

She huffed exasperatedly. 'We sent him letters—he ignored them.'

'He died.'

'It was before he died!' Her outburst was followed by a softer expression. 'I *am* sorry that he died, however. You have my condolences.'

Owen could only nod. The spirit of this girl was coupled with concern, vulnerability. He couldn't quite take stock of her, and he found himself wondering what Madame Hala might have thought of Ranya when she gave her the dress.

'Thank you,' he acknowledged. 'I am certain my father did not intend to do ill by your city and there must have been some sort of misunderstanding. Once I am back in London, I will solve it.'

She nodded slowly, then looked around, that curl bouncing along her jaw. Save for two women chatting beside the podium, and a waiter nibbling on leftovers, they were alone in the foyer.

'Shall we proceed to this room of yours?'

Owen pushed away the thought of what he should like to do alone with her in a room…

They found it easily enough. It was a fairly small one, with too many people smoking hookah pipes. Owen was greeted enthusiastically by the men inside, while Ranya was passed over as if she were invisible.

He was sure it would have been different were she an Englishwoman. He hated that what he'd told her about the sort of Englishmen here only respecting their own women had been correct in this instance. If this were England they might be aghast that an unchaperoned young woman was in the company of men at all.

If the lack of acknowledgement fazed her, Ranya didn't let on, heading straight for the shutters and opening them to let in the sea breeze.

One of the men drew his attention. 'I am surprised to see you tonight, Malden. I understood that your man Mr Larder would speak on the company's behalf.'

Owen stared at the man, a banker. He recalled meeting him on the docks when they'd first arrived, but couldn't gather his name now, and that was slightly disconcerting in front of Ranya. She would think him incompetent in matters of business. Not that she would be entirely wrong…

'Jarvis Larder is not my man,' Owen said. 'He manages the labourers…organises the ships' loading.'

The banker frowned, genuinely surprised by the look of it. 'I was under the impression that the Larder family and yours have a long history. That Larder's father was a naval hero who fought with the Countess of Warrington's brother before his untimely death.'

Even if that were true, the Malden Trading Company had been built by Owen's father before he had inherited the title and the estate that came with it.

That Larder had asserted a connection to seem as if he was in charge of the business irritated Owen, but he did not let it show. Where his school mates rowed or hunted, Owen used to spend his leisure time in admiration of stage productions. From his days in the theatre, he had learned that if one demonstrated comfort with silences other people might be compelled to fill the gaps and share more than they otherwise would.

As Ranya had with Iskander earlier today.

The banker continued, 'I was hoping to speak to him on our negotiations with the Egyptian government, who now dictate production from the cotton fields. I wish to act as a mediator between them and the mill owners in Northern England.'

'Oh?' Owen encouraged.

'Mr Larder said Your Lordship would be claiming your place in Parliament and that the Countess, your mother, would be overseeing the transfer of the company's stakes in Egypt. He claimed to be representing her because, if I remember his words precisely—' the banker pushed his spectacles up to the bridge of his nose '—you do not dabble in the business. The details bore you and you would much rather indulge your appreciation for the arts. Particularly those of the theatre.'

As Ranya came to stand next to him, Owen felt embarrassment fuel his anger.

He was angry with Larder. With the Countess. And with himself, for letting them conspire against him. His father had bequeathed the Malden Trading Company to *him*, and although he had run away from the responsibility of the business—just as he had the deadline upcoming on his twenty-fifth birthday—that did not give anyone the right to take it away.

He put on his Earl voice. 'I didn't catch your name, Mr…?'

'It is Gray, sir.'

'Mr Gray. I have indeed been occupied with preparing for my seat in the House of Lords—and what is Parliament if not a political stage?' Owen chuckled insincerely.

'Nevertheless, I can assure you that any decisions regarding the Malden Trading Company established by my father, and to which I am sole and rightful heir, shall be dealt with by me. *Solely*.'

'Then I am most happy to hear you say it, sir.'

Mr Gray moved a table forward, then reached into his waistcoat and unfurled a large parchment across it. He shifted through the room, gathering weights to anchor the corners. Two snuff boxes, a goblet, and the heaviest of all an arithmometer.

As Owen examined the map's details, he saw Ranya gravitate towards the calculating machine.

Mr Gray said, 'I was hoping to make you an offer to manage the trade routes and the supply from the Delta to liaise with the mills. The new bank would oversee it properly, extend credit so that monies would not be delayed at either end. If I may provide my proposal…?'

Mr Gray launched into the details of it but Owen could barely follow, preoccupied as he was by how Ranya's attention seemed to be torn between what Mr Gray was saying and the arithmometer she fingered like a child with an exciting new toy. Her brow was slightly furrowed, her lips dancing with what Owen guessed were silent numbers.

He beckoned her with a flourish, cutting off Mr Gray. 'Please meet Miss Radwan, a pasha's daughter in one of our holdings in the Delta. She has quite a deal to report from there. Brilliant ideas, truly.'

Owen had no idea what—he was only quoting her teacher. But the look on her face—questioning, hopeful—spurred him on. It was another trick he had learned in his theatre studies. *Trust your partner when improvising.*

'Tell Mr Gray why his *proposal* may or may not be a good idea for Malden Trading.'

When he'd invited her to share her ideas with the room,

he hadn't actually thought that the men would listen to a woman. But volunteering her now was a chance to fulfil his promise *and* get some much-needed insights himself. He might not know if the proposal was good for Malden, but he did have good instincts. And he felt certain Ranya would rise to the occasion.

She took a moment to carefully consider the parchment, and then quickly calculated something, as if the arithmometer was in her head.

'Mr Gray,' she started, 'if what you are proposing is to turn any true profit for Malden Trading, cotton production would need to increase by one hundred and twenty per cent. No—one hundred and twenty-one point three per cent. At the current average of one hundred and fifty thousand bales per harvest, and approximately four hundred pounds per acre, the available acreage might suffice—but what of the people's other needs? Corn? Wheat? Labourers cannot *eat* cotton. Now, while the American Civil War might drive the greed of the Egyptian government to increase production as demand increases, labourers will not see any profits. Never mind that the quality of the raw cotton would decrease. There would be more refining work to do when it did arrive in England, and I do not think the unions that represent the mill workers would stand for it.'

Ranya was a marvel! Well-informed. Passionate. Fiery. And, gosh, Owen was absolutely impressed by her.

Mr Gray, however, was not. 'What would a young Egyptian woman know of our unions?'

Owen was possessed by the need to jump to her defence, but Ranya spoke first.

'I read the English newspapers, Mr Gray,' she scolded. 'Granted, they arrive late, and their bias against the unions is outrageous, but what their leaders are fighting for—the justice in it—cannot be silenced. Unions make industry *right*. Were Egyptians able to do the same in the Delta our cotton would be the most valued in the world—and not further burden the *fellaheen* who already sacrifice much for it. In my opinion—'

'Unions fail and workers are easily replaced,' Mr Gray interrupted, spreading his arms as if the others in the room must all agree.

Ranya bristled, slapping her mouth shut, but Owen didn't want her to stop talking.

'Miss Radwan was about to enlighten us with her opinion and I am eager to hear it.'

Owen offered her a rallying smile, but she seemed to take it as some sort of challenge. And when she spoke it felt as if she was giving *him* an ultimatum.

'What if trading companies like Malden were to pay the people here more, to refine the cotton at source? An additional service directly mandated between the company and the labourers. It would be more expensive, yes, but it would arrive overseas ready for resale. That would mean less government involvement in Egypt, and the English unions would be pleased because it would be less harmful to their mill workers.'

Mr Gray scoffed. 'And therein your argument collapses. With machinery advancement comes less dependency on workers. I repeat that the unions will have no sway.'

Ranya pushed at the arithmometer. The corner of the map it held down curled up. 'The *fellaheen* method is sustainable. The quality of the cotton is superior. It is softer, yet longer-lasting. Handmade with care, not mechanised.'

'You are utterly losing the very *raison d'être* of the colonies. Her Royal Majesty's imperialist ideology is that *you* feed into *us* so *we* can process. You provide the raw material; we provide the manufactured products. It is how things have always been done.'

'Egypt is not a colony of Her Majesty, Mr Gray. And you speak of the future, yet hold on to the past like a dog to a bone.' Ranya's face reddened with anger as her voice rose.

'How dare you?'

It wasn't Mr Gray who spoke but another of the men, a portly fellow with a flask in his hand. Alcohol was illegal in Egypt—he would have had to purchase it by nefarious means, and it would not have been watered down. He stood from his chair, clearly drunk and ready for a quarrel.

Owen realised the indignation aimed towards Ranya might turn ugly, and he rushed to her, stepping in front of her protectively.

'Gentlemen, tonight is a celebratory evening for the new bank. We should save our debates for another day,' he said.

'My proposal!' Mr Gray protested, but Owen was already guiding Ranya out of the room.

His hand at the small of her back, he flexed his fingers with the rush of blood in his veins. Whether it was from touching her or the still-present danger that she might be harmed, Owen could not tell. He was only glad she didn't seem to notice his emotions, nor his hand there, huffing with anger as she was.

Owen followed as Ranya rushed past the foyer and the main doors, down the steps and into the courtyard.

He dropped his hand and watched as she paced there for a few minutes, could see that it was doing little to quell her exasperation.

She pointed at him accusatorily. 'I did not need you to protect me at the end nor give me permission to talk at the start.'

'What about offering you some warmth now, then?'

Owen unbuttoned his waistcoat as the night breeze, chilly from the sea, wafted around them. Her gaze seemed frozen on his chest, so that when he held it out to her she didn't notice.

Did she like what she saw?

He stepped closer. 'I am sorry not to have worn my coat, but take this—an extra layer with your shawl.'

In the scant light from the oil lamps around them she watched him.

Her voice had quietened, the anger fuelling it gone, but she refused his waistcoat. 'I want nothing from you except the deed.'

'You were magnificent back there. Your response to Mr Gray's proposal… The numbers you were spewing like the names of childhood friends…'

Ranya had been convincing, but the truth was that Owen didn't know enough about the business to know if she was right. It would have been easier to let Larder come, report the happenings of the night to the Countess. Sell if she thought they should.

He knew the Countess wanted him to take up the title of the Earl of Warrington fully, to be free for it. And though he'd committed to do it on his twenty-fifth birthday, he wasn't excited about that future.

But you've never shown much interest in Malden Trading either, chided a voice in his head which sounded oddly like his father's.

To defy it, Owen decided it was time for a change. He knew his father would have wanted him to take charge of the company he had built. But Owen had been avoiding it, believing he had time yet. With his birthday forthcoming, there was not much of it remaining.

'Unlike Mr Gray's bumbling one, I have a real proposal for you, Miss Radwan.'

It wasn't a fully formed plan, and Owen was sure she wouldn't agree. But he realised how badly he wanted to convince her to do so as he spoke. Ranya could buy him time. If his life was going to change on his twenty-fifth birthday, no matter what, then Owen had to ensure it was a change he could live with. A life he would want.

Even if he didn't know exactly what that life might look like yet, for the second time that evening his instincts told him *she* would be the one to help him decide.

The plan formed as his words rushed out. 'Sail to England. With me. Tomorrow. As a consultant. Teach me all you know about the cotton trade. In exchange, I will search for this deed you speak of. You can take it directly.'

He knew Ranya could tell him to send it if he found it. Hadn't he already promised her he would? She could tell him to learn about the trade from newspapers or books. She could say she was a young woman who wouldn't be safe travelling away from her home country.

Yet all she said was, 'How long would I be gone?'

'Three months.' It came to him automatically, having his twenty-fifth birthday and the Percy Ball in mind.

Owen had expected Ranya to do some calculations. He would enjoy watching her, as he had with the arithmometer. The furrow in her brow…the slight quake of her lips…

Instead, she actually smiled—not at him, Owen was sure about that, but to herself.

Was that a dimple in her left cheek?

'You promise I will be back in three months?' she asked.

'You have my word. Are we agreed?' He stuck out his hand, waited for her to shake it.

She didn't.

'Normally my father would not permit me to travel alone,' she rationalised. 'But he has been otherwise occupied with *izbah* matters. He gave me a set period away from Damanhour to pursue the English language, find my own vocation—a level of freedom, if you will.'

'That is very admirable. Young, unmarried English-women do not enjoy such freedom. They can barely move amidst society without a chaperone of some sort, a mother or an aunt.'

He hoped Ranya might say more about her life. It struck him that perhaps her father had given her a reprieve before he intended to marry her off. Maybe she was already engaged. Owen could not bring himself to ask for fear he would not like the answer.

She examined him with a wary gaze. 'A few consultations and that is all?'

Owen had already made her a promise, and that made him want to be honest with her too. 'You might have to deal my father's widow. She would need to be your sponsor, in order to protect your reputation so that your father will not be upset with us if his extension of your freedom is limited. Although please know that none except you know the Countess is not my real mother.'

He shook his head…knew he was meandering. He mightn't have said anything if he hadn't already sent her to Madame Hala. But now he couldn't seem to stop.

'The Countess of Warrington is still her title, though she will expect you to call her Your Ladyship. She would sooner sell my father's company than have me manage it. But being occupied with sponsoring you, a pasha's daughter come to learn English ways from a school her rich society friends support…? She will like that.'

Ranya objected. 'I care little for English ways.'

'Yet you have learned the language?'

'To beguile an earl! To take back what belongs to my family. Besides, it is the language of trade.' She waved her arm at the bank's doors. 'Commerce.'

'I did not mean to insult you, Miss Radwan. Perhaps consider it like acting on a stage. You would play the role of a cotton pasha's daughter—an heiress on a tour sponsored by the Countess of Warrington,' Owen explained. 'Is it so very different from what you were planning in that red dress? This role would be more aligned to your actual standing and position. Truer to who you are.'

She was still listening, so he went on. 'The Countess has the unfortunate circumstance of being born a woman in a man's world. But she has learned how to get what she wants even while society respects her as a lady of eminence. Back there, you were smarter than Mr Gray and any other man in the room but they refused to listen to you. I think, Miss Radwan, you might learn from your time with her.'

In the silence that followed his speech, Owen couldn't tell if he had convinced Ranya. He added one more thing.

'Plus, you would be doing me a favour. If the Countess is not busy with you, she will be busy choosing me a wife.'

At this, Ranya's eyebrows quirked. 'And you wish to marry for love?'

'I wish to choose for myself.'

Owen couldn't very well tell Ranya he would never fall in love. To be in love was to open yourself to abandonment. His mother had left him, and she'd also left his father—a man who had loved her with all his heart. Owen would never give anyone that power over him.

'Do we have an agreement, then, Miss Radwan?'

He thrust his hand forward once more.

This time, she shook it.

Chapter Five

Ranya

A chance to find out what had happened to her brother and to get back the deed? It seemed too good to be true. But when Ranya woke the next morning at the sound of the athan, she rejoiced. Her fortune had changed from one Fajr prayer to the next. In one day, she had gone from potential wanton to cotton trade adviser. Madame Hala had reminded her of her mother's saying that Allah is the best of planners, Ranya would never again forget it.

She packed her bag excitedly. It was the same traveling case she'd brought from Damanhour, fuller now because of the gown. Ranya had considered returning it to Madame Hala, but she still did not have the money for the loan of it. And although neither mother nor son spoke about the other, she sensed that Madame Hala would want to know about Iskander's life—*Owen's* life—in England.

Perhaps she could talk to her about him more when she returned. She would certainly learn about him over the next few months but at present he, and the circumstances of his birth, were an enigma Ranya didn't understand.

She made *wudu* in the small basin in the room she rented from the school and prayed two *rakats* solemnly.

She was soothed for the few minutes it took her to do it. The frantic plotting of the last few months, the frustrations and the worry…always the worry…faded.

Her struggles weren't over yet. They wouldn't be until Baba was free. But hope filled her. She had looked for Muhammad in Alexandria and not found him, but could almost imagine doing so in England, as he'd vowed to go there. Ranya hoped it was only a matter of him getting lost there, or feeling unable to return after learning that the Earl had died and then not being able to speak to Owen.

It was plausible. She knew Muhammad hadn't stolen the town's money for himself. Brother and sister would, in three months' time, return to Damanhour together to restore their family honour!

She'd said her goodbyes to Mr March last night—he was a self-proclaimed 'night owl', who refused to stir before midday—telling him that in addition to her advisory role, the Earl of Warrington had promised she could speak about the school, secure more sponsorships. But the lovely, sweet man had only said he would look forward to her return.

As she closed the door of her room, she realised she'd miss being there. Her love of language was something she'd inherited from her father, and she determined to visit the school with Baba one day. Restored as a proper cotton pasha, he too would love to be a patron of the school that had taught her so much.

Ranya passed the blind beggar who, six out of seven days of the week, would set up her busking station where the school met the main road. It consisted of an oud instrument, a tricorn hat that looked left behind from the French occupation to collect money in, and a bowl of olive oil to soak her fingertips between tunes.

The woman had an uncanny way of sensing anyone who

had ever paid for the pleasure of listening to her music, and greeting them with a cheery, *'Assalam alaykum.'*

This morning was no different.

'Walaykum as salam, ya hagga.'

Thinking to spread her good fortune before leaving, Ranya advised, 'You should play on Fridays. After Jumuah, people are most generous.'

The old woman's chuckle was as sweet as her oud-playing. 'We cannot work every day. Our families have a right to us too, *ya binti.'*

My daughter. It was a common endearment even between strangers, but Ranya's heart swelled to hear it. 'Then, may Allah protect your family and keep you safe for them.'

The woman offered another *dua* in return. *'Naharik gameel.'*

May your day be beautiful.

As she walked to the harbour Ranya saw it manifesting before her eyes. People bustled to start their day under a sky daubed in soft orange and pale pink by the rising sun. Boys on bicycles delivered fresh milk from tin pails, dodging others stacking eggs onto carts. The sour-sweet heat of bread from the bakery ovens mingled with the heavily brewed black tea and mint from the cafés. *Hantoor* bells jingled and horses' hooves clopped—cabs readying to take people wherever they needed to go.

Ranya arrived on the docks earlier than the time they had agreed to. She expected to wait, but then she heard her name being called.

'Miss Radwan!'

Owen stood upon on the same rock where she'd divulged her worries to Iskander. Ranya had to remind herself that they were the same person.

'This is early for you, Your Lordship,' she said.

'How would you know what time I wake?' But even

as he asked Owen was barely able to stifle a yawn. 'Very well… But you should know it's in your service.' He cocked his head towards the Englishman from yester-day, who'd been so domineeringly rude. 'Larder says we need travel documents before you're allowed aboard. He was ready to discount you, but I thought if we went early enough, we could get it done.'

He shaded his eyes from the sun just as Ranya noticed how the green in them sparkled, like the tips of the sea's waves on the horizon were wont to do on the brightest of days.

'I thought you might not come, after all,' he said.

'I said I would. If you think your word more superior than mine, you are mistaken.'

He jutted out his chin, then leaned closer. 'Do you have a passport or some proof of identity in order for us to have a travel document produced?'

She rifled through her bag to reach its secret pocket. It had been filled with the last of her mother's gold to pawn here in Alexandria, but now there was only her birth cer-tificate.

It occurred to Ranya to wonder, if her brother had gone to England, how he would have left. She'd anticipated needing her documentation for school registration, but was almost sure that Muhammad hadn't taken his.

She handed the birth certificate to Owen, then watched his face contort as he read the information aloud in Ara-bic. She had to swallow back the effect his speaking in her mother tongue was having on her. Ranya would admit that she was attracted to Iskander—but this man before her, the Earl of Warrington, was not him. How often would she need to keep reminding herself?

'Ha!' he whooped. Then, with a look of vindication, he explained, 'Larder said birth registrations were only standardised in Egypt in 1839, and that even today, in the year 1862, it is still only men who have them.'

'My father is a modern man. And my mother was a teacher.'

'*Was...?*'

There was a hesitancy in the word—one that made Ranya want to open up to him. 'She died last year, Allah have mercy on her soul.'

He placed a palm over his chest, and she had the distinct impression that he had wanted to reach out and squeeze her hand with it.

'I am sorry for you.'

His voice had thickened, and he cleared his throat before calling to one of the labourers to take her bag.

'We could take a carriage to the Consulate, if you would like, but it is only a short walk. And, if they are not yet open as it is still early, it would, perhaps, save us a longer, idle wait.'

'Let us walk.' Ranya surrendered her bag and silently followed Owen's lead.

'I love that about Alexandria—everything is along the sea and within strolling distance. It is a great city.'

Her pride swelled. 'It has always been a beacon for the world.'

She would have gone on to cite Alexander the Great's finding of it, but the translation of his name was Iskander. Owen's eyes locked on hers, as if he knew what she was thinking.

'A beacon and favourite of Cleopatra.' He cocked his chin towards her needle. 'Speaking of whom... I toured Qaitbey and there I had lunch with a cat so old I was sure it was hers.'

Ranya shrugged. 'If it were hers, she should have taken

it to her afterlife instead of Mark Antony. We Egyptians love our cats because they are more trustworthy than men.'

She tried to ignore the deep lilt of Owen's subsequent laugh. How the sound spread through her, reaching her extremities, putting them on alert. Her pace slowed, and when he tilted his head back to ensure she was well, it was all Ranya could do not to admit her swelling of emotion, because his was the most beautiful laugh she'd ever heard.

'The English prefer dogs. They're more loyal than cats.' He stopped walking until she had caught up. 'Your nose wrinkles, Miss Radwan. Do you not agree?'

'Dogs smell terrible! Mr March keeps one, and even the cockroaches are disgusted by it.'

After that, their banter became easy, cutting in half the already short distance to the Consulate, so that Ranya was surprised, and almost a little disappointed, when they stood before it. Indeed, it wasn't open, but there was already a line of people being watched by two British soldiers with long rifles holstered against their red coats.

The queue consisted mostly of labourers, like those on the docks, but there were a few Egyptians dressed more formally. Maybe they were students or business people. Ranya wondered if her brother had ever stood in line here...

For his part, Owen weaved his way towards the front of it, as if it did not exist.

'Good gentlemen,' he said to the soldiers, 'our ship is set to sail post-haste. Kindly let us in and inform the Consul that the Earl of Warrington seeks an audience.'

Ranya was sure the stoic men would dismiss him, but the first nodded to the second and he opened the gate wide enough to let her and Owen through. The first soldier pointed his rifle at the crowd, in case anyone got any ideas. She heard someone grumbling about the unfairness of it and knew the feeling acutely. Ranya might even have apologised for being the cause, but she had a mission and she couldn't waste time on sentiment.

As she followed Owen's decisive march into the building she marvelled at the way he acted when he put on his Earl persona. She'd noticed it at the bank opening party—the way it made others listen to him. How he exuded power. Owen wasn't much taller than Ranya, but with his broad shoulders, and the way his tailored clothes fitted him like a king's mantle, he might as well be a giant.

Further evidence was in the face of the Consul, who had clearly only been woken to meet them. He scurried to accommodate their request for a rushed travel document, his bald head glistening with sweat and his face flushed. The whole while he worked—asking for Ranya's signature in places or delving in drawers for seals and parchments—he spoke of his admiration for the Warrington estate.

'I have only witnessed it from afar, but it is a beacon, truly a paragon of how well things can be done. And you are to take up your seat in the House of Lords, you say? It has been awaiting you.'

'The Countess manages the estate formidably,' Owen agreed. Then, with a flourish, he said, 'And she still manages to find time for society activities. Miss Radwan here, a pasha's daughter, is to be sponsored by her this season.'

The Consul paid a little more attention to Ranya. Had he thought he was completing papers for a domestic servant, or perhaps Owen's personal prostitute?

'She speaks English, then?'

'I do,' Ranya answered, but still the man addressed Owen.

'Normally, we would require a chaperon for ladies who travel. A brother or an uncle or older friend. May I ask where Miss Radwan's father is at the moment?'

Ranya took her cue from Owen, and remembered the old way she'd used to walk in the world herself.

She stepped forward. 'My father sends me with his blessing and he trusts the Earl of Warrington, the son of one of his oldest friends. That should suffice. Then, when I arrive in England, the Countess is to take on that solemn duty.'

'Certainly, Miss Radwan. Let me finish this for you.'

When the Consul stepped away, Owen winked at her and whispered, 'We shall make an actor of you yet. You are a quick study.'

Ranya didn't respond, feeling confused as to why his pleasure should please her so.

The Consul returned, and after handing her the official travel document, along with her birth certificate, asked, 'Would the Earl of Warrington and Miss Radwan do me the honour of joining me for tea?'

Ranya could hear the noise outside, from the queue that must be even longer now. She prickled at the callousness of this Consul, who served his English masters while the land he stood upon was Egyptian and whose very position meant he was supposed to listen to its people's requests.

'We would not want to prevent you from attending to those waiting,' she said.

'They can continue to wait,' the Consul said with a shrug. 'Better they're out there than have them stow away and experience true discomfort when they dock in England and have to prove themselves there.'

Ranya didn't know exactly what 'stow away' meant, but in that moment she felt sure it was what her brother had done.

Owen answered. 'Our ship sets sail soon, and thus we must decline. But please be sure to call on us when you next return to England. I shall give you a full and proper tour of Warrington myself!'

Chapter Six

Owen

Dearest Countess,
I trust this missive will reach you in good health and
the gladdest of circumstances. My travel to Egypt
has progressed well, the details of which I will share
upon my arrival.

Please know that accompanying me is Miss Ranya
Radwan, a pasha's daughter from one of our hold-
ings in the Delta. She has interesting ideas to share
on the cotton industry with the board of Malden
Trading. Moreover, Miss Radwan has been a pupil
at Mr March's school in Alexandria and wishes to
learn more about English society in her three-month
visit to our country.

I have offered your sponsorship to her, knowing
you would be a mentor of the highest calibre. I trust
you will make her feel welcome at Warrington.
Yours, most sincerely,
Owen

The letter, he thought, struck a good balance between
making the Countess aware that he was going to pay more

attention to his father's business and his desire that she should be kind to their guest.

He sealed it and passed it to Larder. He wished he could force the man to ride with the cargo ship too, but instinct told Owen it was better to have him on this, their commissioned steam yacht, and not disrupt their initial plans more than necessary.

Even if the thought of being alone with Ranya was more enticing than it should be...

'Ensure this reaches Warrington as early as possible before we arrive.'

Larder nodded tersely. He wasn't pleased, but maybe he sensed he should not further rile Owen. He'd tried to find out about what had happened with Mr Gray, and then to dissuade him from bringing Ranya, but Owen hadn't budged on either. And although he didn't yet know how he would handle the Countess's conspiring with Larder, he had time to figure it out.

Normally, he would have dismissed it. Let the Countess deal with Larder and Mr Gray and anyone else who was interested in Malden Trading, but something had shifted in Owen last night. When he was a boy, after his mother left, his father's wife had swept in and claimed him as her own. Vivian had never felt like a mother in the traditional sense, but she had given him everything. Taught him how to be a gentleman. She had long said that Warrington would belong to him. And to his son after him.

Owen held her in esteem, even felt affection towards her. But there had always been a distance between them. He didn't believe it was because she blamed him for what his father had done, but perhaps she considered him 'tainted' by it. The Countess's most motherly moments came when she spoke longingly about the future. About

Owen's heir, to whom she would be a grandmother. How involved she planned to be in his son's life.

That was why she had permitted Owen his idiosyncrasies—his love of the theatre, in particular. His avoiding his estate duties had been fine by the Countess until now, but unless he married and fulfilled his promise she wouldn't get the heir she wanted.

Owen knew he owed her for claiming him as her own, and not letting any gossip around his Egyptian side thrive. But something between them had always been missing, and Owen thought that maybe if he reunited with his real mother he would find some resolution around how he felt about following the Countess's plans for the trajectory of his life. In that regard, it had been a failure of a trip. It had hurt to find his mother had moved on and made a life without him, whilst he had always felt stuck, avoiding living his own.

Owen might have just returned to England, resigned to what awaited him after the Percy Ball. But then last night, Ranya had been there. Wearing the dress *his mother* had given her. It had stirred hurts and possibilities in Owen he'd thought long-buried. And desires too. Because Ranya had looked stunning in it.

He had certainly wanted to stare at her and be close to her all night, but he had also wanted to listen to her talk, to protect her from those who didn't perceive her brilliance and dispel her anger by sweeping her up in his arms.

Which was a damned inconvenience—because if he was to follow the Countess's plans for marrying after the Percy Ball, falling in love with an Egyptian woman before it even happened would be a terrible reward for her patience all these years.

Besides which, nothing serious could ever happen between him and Ranya. A marriage arranged by the Countess would be convenient and mutually advantageous. That he could handle. But actually falling in love with a woman? He would not let that happen. He hadn't been obstinate over much in his life—but on that Owen was dogged.

He watched now, as Ranya stood by the boat's edge as they lurched forward and away from the harbour. A breeze rose, ruffling her kaftan, outlining the lithe, long body beneath. It swept around Ranya's face and she struggled to keep her thick curls beneath the scarf she wore.

When it calmed, Owen strode towards her. Saw how she gripped the hull, her knuckles pale with the effort. Her eyes welled with unshed tears, the way they had before she'd run from the crowd that had turned on her after they'd seen the stolen dress.

'First time away from home?' he asked.

She caught her lower lip with her teeth and nibbled. She was calculating something that wasn't numbers, he realised. Last time she'd done it, it had been just before she'd told Iskander about her plans for the Earl of Warrington.

Owen held his breath, anticipating.

His theorising soon proved correct.

'Alexandria itself was far from my home. Even in Damanhour we always stuck close to the Nile, only one time venturing to the sea.' Ranya smiled as if at a memory. 'My brother and I went swimming, thinking it would be the same as wading in the river. I almost drowned, the water was so deep. He was flailing too, but he saved me.'

'You have a brother?' Jarvis Larder startled them both. He'd clearly been eavesdropping. 'Not Muhammad Radwan, by any chance?'

Ranya turned, her eyes narrowed. 'You know him?'

Larder tittered. 'Don't all Egyptian males go by the same name?'

Owen was angry at the interruption. And at the insult to Ranya and to himself. He was half-Egyptian, after all.

'Larder, truly, your lack of decorum exasperates. Do not sneak up on people, nor share your ignorance so liberally.' He waved a hand dismissively, 'Go and make yourself useful and tell the chef to prepare us a meal. We must treat our guest amicably.'

Owen turned away, not waiting to see the effect, if any, his reprimand had had, but Ranya watched Larder retreat.

'Do you think he knows my brother?' she asked.

'I cannot imagine how he would. Larder is a small-minded man, and prejudiced. His sense of humour is base.'

Owen watched her face relax. She'd been riled. He was curious to learn more, but did not want to sound rude. The Consul *had* asked about a chaperon, and it was odd Ranya had no one to be hers. It was one thing to have a father allowing his daughter freedom of movement, but if she had a brother, surely he would have watched over her? Accompanied her on her travels.

He hesitated, then added, 'Larder might have perceived some sensitivity around the subject of your brother.'

Ranya stared at him in that way of hers—and, damn, but it was making his heart flutter and his stomach clench. This time, though, she didn't confide anything more.

After an awkward silence, filled by the slap of the waves on the ship's hull and the hiss of geese overhead, he remarked, 'Well, Muhammad Radwan must be a remarkable brother to save a drowning sister when he himself couldn't swim.'

It was the perfect thing to say. He knew it by the way her face lit up, which in turn lit up something inside him.

Something, Owen knew, that a man determined not to fall in love should not be feeling.

They dined on grilled meat and rice drenched in a thick tomato and onion sauce. Not exactly a breakfast, but at least their first few meals wouldn't involve fish.

'Because we will soon grow sick of that,' Owen said.

'Alexandrians never tire of it,' Ranya remarked between bites.

He was glad they were alone on the deck on a table set for two. He'd given Larder a menial task, made it clear he didn't want the fellow dining with them. Owen hoped it would set a precedent for the rest of the trip.

He felt joyful watching Ranya eating and wanted to bask in it alone. The way she dived in, with abandon. Slow but heartily chewing, sipping water between bites, like someone enjoying the taste but also appreciating how the food was sating her hunger. She didn't treat her food like an enemy, picking at it as if it were a weapon designed to split a corset.

Owen had loosed a few of those in his day and he'd always felt sorry for anyone who had to wear one. They were terribly restrictive. The Countess would likely fit Ranya with a corset…command she eat with the full range of utensils rather than savour the flavours. The thought sobered him, and he committed to ensuring that Ranya's strong will was not clamped down by her time with the Countess.

A sudden jump in a patch of rough water jolted the table beneath them, and had Ranya's face lurching close to his.

Very, wonderfully close.

'Oh…' she moaned.

Before Owen could revel in the sound, she threw down her spoon, clapped her hands over her mouth. She pushed back her chair and ran to the ship's hull, barely making it while the ship rocked over the waves.

Instinct made Owen rush to her, gently rubbing her back as her body was racked with convulsions. Concern for her kept him there, holding her shoulders until the worst of it had passed.

Rough waters carried away the bile, while the cold wind

whipped up salty sea spray. Ranya's head was hot beneath his fingers, damp with sweat.

'My fault for not warning you,' he said. 'About possible sea sickness.'

She leaned further forward even as his hands clung to her waist. She gasped at the water's iciness, but it didn't dissuade her from scrubbing her mouth and face.

When she was done, Ranya turned around slowly and Owen was forced to give her space. She looked a bit green around the edges, but it was the way her gaze lingered on his hands still at her waist that made his head start to spin.

'Thank you,' she said, after he'd dropped them.

'I should have warned you,' he repeated like a fool.

Her tone was light when she asked, 'Why did you not?'

'I forgot. I enjoyed watching you savouring your food.' Owen could barely believe his own honesty. He went on quickly, 'The first time is rough, but once you get over that initial hump sea travel is smoother, more pleasurable.'

As soon as he'd said it he recognised the innuendo, hoped she might not interpret it as such. Before he could tell her she'd started trembling, her teeth chattering. It was a normal reaction to being sick but it felt extra-violent. And the cold in the open air wasn't helping.

'Let's get you below deck.'

It was dark there—the lamps would be saved for the depths of night—but it was warmer at least. As they felt their way around, her shivering eased.

There was a small window over her bed that let in a little bit of light to the corridor. Owen took a banket off it and wrapped it around her shoulders.

'Thank you, again,' she said, her hand on the doorknob next to where he stood.

Owen couldn't bring himself to go, even if she *was* dismissing him. When he put his own hand on the doorknob,

she dropped hers. 'I shall leave when you're settled. In bed.
I do not mean to be anything less than a gentleman, but
would not see you be sick again.'

She huffed softly, but moved to sit on the thin mattress.
'Satisfied?'

'You should lie back. It helps with dizziness.'

'You should leave.'

'When you lie back.'

She kept her eyes on his as she lifted her legs and tucked
them beneath her. Leaning back, she lowered her head to
the crook of her arm. He imagined slipping off her boots
himself.

That would be a mistake.

Owen gathered the sigh in his chest and started closing
the door behind him. 'Someone will bring you dry toast
and a pot of ginger tea. If you need anything, my cabin is
the one at the end. Any time, any…need, do come.'

Owen stayed up for a long time, both hoping and dread-
ing that Ranya might require something, *anything*, from
him, but he remained alone until he finally fell into a sleep
as fitful as the waves beneath them.

Chapter Seven

Ranya

Ranya's queasiness soon settled, and she found what Larder called her 'sea legs', but her next problem was trying to minimise the intensity between her and Owen, which electrified the air when they were together—hard when they were often in such close proximity, sharing meals and conversations.

Daylight was best, because the presence of others made her more mindful of reining in her emotions, but every night the devil seemed to whisper in her ear.

Go to his cabin. Finish the game of chess you were winning. Remember his knuckle brushing yours as he moved his queen? Or ask him to read another chapter from the novel. Isn't his rich voice engaging? His reading of those beautiful words most transportive? Go! Let whatever might happen, happen.

Still, as much as her body might be tempted, her mind valued their time together. Owen listened intently to her talking about cotton, taking notes and often stopping her to ask clarifying questions or sharing his opinions for her to comment upon.

And that boyish, secretive smile of his! It was there

when he was right about something or wrong about something. More than once Ranya imagined herself bringing her lips to his, just to see if she could wipe it off. But then, she decided she rather liked it and wouldn't want to see it gone.

Besides, Allah knew she should keep her lips chaste and to herself.

They'd finished *Great Expectations* by Charles Dickens and were reading *Mansfield Park* by Jane Austen. Owen admitted they were his favourites for different reasons, but Ranya guessed it was because each featured characters being taken in and cared for—as he had been. But she didn't dare say it. Besides, that one time at the bank opening party in Alexandria, when Owen had mentioned in passing that the Countess had always claimed him as her own, he hadn't spoken any more about it.

It seemed he'd left Madame Hala and Iskander in Egypt. Which was probably for the best. Because if *Iskander* had been more prominent here, with his curls and earnestness, Ranya would have had a harder time staying focused on her goal.

Three months. Get the deed agreement so she could secure Baba's release. Find out if Muhammad had reached England and if so what had happened to her brother there. Advise the Earl on the cotton industry.

A three-pronged purpose that would usually have satisfied her mathematics-minded head, except now there was an added wrench: *Don't fall for the Earl of Warrington.*

As long as she separated Owen from the memory of him as Iskander, Ranya was sure she could weather it.

She leaned back in her chair with the warm sun in her face, the seagulls overhead like a chorus to Owen's reading. But then he stopped and her eyes fluttered open.

'Are you finished for today?' she asked.

'I thought you slept and did not want you to miss my favourite part, forthcoming.'

It must be about the theatre. He'd mentioned it yesterday and, remembering the thought she'd had last night, she said, 'I think Miss Austen uses the drama to show how vain the family is. How uninformed they must be to put on plays while slavery on the plantations across the ocean is what makes them rich. Sugar, cotton... It all means suffering for locals but white gold for the British nobility.'

Owen set the book on the table between them and steepled his hands beneath his chin. 'You often see past the façade to the truth, Miss Radwan.'

She didn't know if he was teasing her or if he was serious. His smile didn't help her work it out, and nor did the way he held her gaze. Huffing, she rose and moved to the boat's bow.

Owen followed her. It was as if he could sense her weakness for him and wanted to tempt her more. It almost made Ranya laugh to think of that red dress now. She wouldn't have been any good at acting the seductress in it for he was much more adept in the role of seducer.

She took a stealthy breath. Her goal. Her duty.

Remember what is important.

Ranya was stronger than any obstacle—or any man— who would stand in her way.

'Do you see there?' Owen pointed ahead. 'France.'

She took in the rolling hills, made out trees of green against rising brick towers. The waters were a pristine aqua, shimmering jewel-like from their vantage point.

Ranya had fallen in love with Alexandria and the Egyptian side of the Mediterranean when she'd first left Damanhour a few months ago. The sea there had a familiarity to it, a soothing quality. As if it would welcome all her troubles so she could be at peace.

But, although this was technically the same body of water, it felt different to Ranya…foreign.

A pang of homesickness pricked her heart. A deep loneliness. She watched his profile out of the corner of her eye. Did he miss Egypt like she did? Had he been Iskander she might have leaned into him, felt less alone.

'Where do you feel most at home?' she blurted.

He searched her eyes, as if the answer to the question was there, not within him. 'Warrington is where I grew up—the grounds of the estate are ones I know, and my room in the manor there holds most of my wardrobe. But I keep a flat in London, with other clothes. And my father had a townhouse there. Is home the place where you keep most of your clothing? I do not know. That is a hard question to answer for someone who has always felt somewhat unmoored.'

As two seagulls skipped and swooped near the yacht Owen frowned, as though he knew it wasn't the answer she had been hoping for. Still, after her struggles with the red dress, she agreed with a part of it.

'Home is where we keep our clothing.'

Owen stepped aside to answer a query from one of the yacht's crewman. When he returned, he informed her, 'We'll spend the night at a hotel, then travel the rest of the way by land—which is an altogether *other* method of torture than water. Mostly by rail, though.'

'That sounds fine.'

'I had planned to take the train to upper Egypt, visit Aswan and the Valley of the Kings. Alas, I did not get the chance when I was there. Have you been?'

He leaned on the railing, his knuckles brushing where her hand gripped. She felt her face flush at his touch and had to steel her breath as she answered.

'Only once. From a stop near our city when I went to

Alexandria. I learned that far too many people like to travel with angry caged chickens.'

She bristled with the memory of how fretful she had been then. 'Still, the fast covering of a long distance is wonderful for those without much time. As we don't have. Many days of our agreement have already passed.'

His jaw rippled. 'Travel time should not have been included.'

'You cannot go back on it now. Three months. Unless I am dead, I *will* be back in Damanhour.'

'Ba'd al shar.'

May anything bad be far from you. It was an Egyptian saying.

Ranya had tried not to encourage his speaking Arabic to her, but there were times when parts of his speech moved past her defences. When they did, it felt intimate, and not only because anyone in earshot couldn't understand. It was the way Owen said them. How he lowered his voice. Leaned in. How she had to fully concentrate to understand the words in their brokenness.

Before they knew it, the captain announced they were docking.

'Make sure you don't forget anything in the cabin,' Owen said. 'We must return the steam yacht and its crew to the French tour company we rented it from.'

After the ship had docked in the harbour and anchored, they disembarked. Owen hung back, offering Ranya his hand, but she kept hers on the railing, pretending she didn't notice. She needed to be more vigilant in protecting her emotions from the man.

The captain, cook and crew said their goodbyes to Owen and Larder, nodding politely in her direction. Ranya was glad for them that they would soon be returning to their families.

Testing her 'land legs', after being so long on the water, Ranya strolled behind Owen and Larder. It seemed a modest port, more recreational than commercial. Even the smaller-sized steam yacht they'd travelled in seemed huge amongst the other boats in the harbour.

They passed a marketplace on their way up a rolling hill. She spied jewellery made with beads and seashells on one table. Another was surrounded by racks of clothing, and most of the others were filled with all manner of baskets.

Owen sent Larder ahead with their luggage and lingered, waiting for her.

'This is not the main port at Marseilles,' he explained. 'We would have needed to travel upstream for a short while longer to go there. But my father found this place on one of his trips and made it a permanent part of Malden's itinerary. Chateau Canebière is named for the hemp fields that surround the area. He was very attracted to the large swathes of a single crop.'

'Like cotton.' Ranya felt a flash of affinity with the man she'd never met and had spent the better part of the last year despising.

Owen took a large step to avoid a snail along the path. 'We were opposites that way, me and him. I want to experience anything and everything. Gardens with a hundred varieties of flowers. Cities that sprawl with thousands of different building styles. Food with an array of flavours. But my father... Even though he was the founder of an international trading company, he detested travel. He would stay in one place for so long the Countess and I thought he'd never return. Then he'd hole up at Warrington until we thought he'd never leave again.'

'Maybe you are more like Madame Hala?' Ranya suggested, before thinking it through.

His face tensed. 'No. She only ever wanted Alexandria. You know she named me for it? In the end, her love for the city meant not even her son could keep her from it.'

Any apology she might have made was drowned out by Larder shouting from the chateau doorway, 'They require payment for the extra room.'

Owen had said all her services would be covered, but as he pulled out notes to take care of the unexpected expense Ranya felt ashamed. Her lack of funds, and not having her own spending power, made her feel helpless.

The feeling was pronounced when they passed through the hotel doors and she saw Frenchwomen, well-coiffed and finely suited, all better dressed than she was. She knew she smelled, and must look a mess, but the truth was that even if she bathed and detangled her hair she was already wearing her best dress and the only shoes she had brought from home.

Ranya would not take charity. She would work and earn her keep. Though her suggestions had only been casual thus far, perhaps she could ask Owen for a salary—an advance to be returned when she obtained the deed. Or it struck her that maybe she would find Muhammad, and her brother would produce the money he'd taken when he'd left Damanhour.

The possibility he had betrayed their people was one she'd resisted considering. But, at this moment, with Owen paying for her room, resentment made Ranya believe that maybe Muhammad *had* stolen away to England and ended up keeping it for himself.

'Take me to my room, please,' she told one of the chambermaids.

The girl either didn't understand English or would only take instructions from the moustachioed Frenchman who had taken Owen's money. He stood behind an ornate counter, elbows propped on it as he smoked a cigar so pungent she wondered how Owen could stand before him.

'See to it that the lady is taken care of first,' Owen directed, meeting her gaze as he said it and then switching back to French. He had told Ranya he knew the language, along with some Italian. *A gentleman's education*, he'd termed it.

Thus commanded, the chambermaid led Ranya towards a set of stairs, and then to a room at the end of the corridor. She gave her a quick tour, speaking in French. Ranya was too proud to say she couldn't understand, but she could tell by the young woman's smirk she knew.

Ranya bolted the door behind her when she'd left.

She drew herself a bathtub full of fresh water from the pump, used the complementary rose-scented soap until it was nearly gone and felt her skin almost raw with cleanliness. She took the opportunity to wash some of her clothes. She'd had a hard time doing it on the boat. Her kaftans were ill-suited for this country, but they didn't have to smell like sweat and salt.

After she'd used all her might to wring them out and set them to dry in the open window, she turned to sorting out her hair. Detangling the knots in it was a long and arduous process when there was no oil to help.

She'd barely finished when a knock came at the door.

Ranya knew it was Owen.

He'd bathed as well. His hair was still wet, the curls dripping without pomade to comb them down. She gripped the doorknob to resist reaching out to touch them.

'Sorry to interrupt…' Owen exhaled as he took in her loose hair, barely wrapped in the towel. 'I would have sent a maid, but I wanted to check on you as well.'

'I'm fine, thank you.'

'I had them find you this.'

It took her a moment to realise he was holding up a dress. It was a dark earthy brown, almost black, plain but finely made, with the most delicate lace around the pleated bodice and sharply defined waist.

'I'd have had them bring up a selection for you to choose from, but the nearest modiste is quite far away. This was all they could muster from a vendor at the port. Next is Paris. We can stop there to visit shops, or wait and choose from what London has to offer. I am sure the Countess will have things made for you when we arrive in Warrington.'

Ranya knew she should demonstrate grace and elegance, but her pride kept her from taking what Owen offered.

'Why would you think I need it?' Her tone was sharper than she intended.

He frowned. 'I only wished to be thoughtful. Something new after days at sea. Something more... *suitable*.'

'What I have is not *suitable*?'

He held up his free hand, tilted his head and tried to explain. 'This is Europe and there are expectations... *fashions*. Not any *I* care about, certainly. I think you are beautiful. Erm... that your clothing is beautiful.'

While Ranya processed the way his admission made her feel—had it only been his way of sidestepping his insult over the way she dressed?

Owen continued, 'Unlike a hired crew, we will travel in the company of others now—people we don't know. They can be rude... cruel. I only wish to protect you from being disparaged for an Egyptian woman's wardrobe.'

Emotion swelled with a memory of her filled closets in Damanhour before their house had been seized. The mauve silks, lime velvets... the bejewelled shoes and embroidered purses.

'Thank you.'

She snatched the dress from Owen, then closed the door, declining the invitation to supper he'd been making as she did so. She threw the dress on a chair without trying it on. With her pride bruised and her loneliness filling up whatever spaces inside of her were left, she stretched out on the bed. It was hard, but comfortable, a contrast to the rocking cradle of her bed on the sea…

Ranya woke before the sun rose, well rested and to the sound of a gentle humming. It was the tune of an Egyptian lullaby she knew. She remembered its words as the tune continued.

Go to sleep, go to sleep, little one
Let us lie on this straw mat
Sleep until the dark clouds pass
At dawn the rising sun will shine its light
Tomorrow your father will come home
With the money from the lemons he sold
He will buy you a coat and scarf
To keep you warm in the winter
My beautiful baby, with the cherry-picked black hair
Whomever does not love you, kiss you,
Does not know what they are missing

Ranya hadn't thought of the lullaby in a long while and she felt a pang of melancholy as the humming stopped. It was Owen, probably, in a room close to hers. She imagined singing it with him. Iskander would understand the words…agree with her that it was a sad song.

Ranya rose and slipped on the dress she'd been so hurt by last night. It fitted her well, and she decided it wasn't too different from one she might have had in Egypt. She opened the curtains and then studied her reflection in the mirror. She looked gaunt from her days at sea, but sun-kissed, her light brown skin flushed with a pink glow. Her dark hair had dried and was curling wild around her face.

She was just forcing it into a topknot when the knocking started at her door and grew more persistent.

She thought it must be Owen, like last night. She thought too that she would apologise for her reaction when he'd given her the dress, tell him she'd realised that he was right. Home was the place where you kept your clothes.

But it wasn't Owen behind the door, It was Jarvis Larder, who stumbled into her. The air around him smelled of a sweetened sour vinegar. Alcohol.

She could barely hold him up, and his nose was practically nestled between her breasts. She pushed him away, back out through the door. But he was heavy...stronger than her. He resisted, spreading his feet and gripping either side of the door frame with both fists.

'What are you doing here?' she shouted.

'You thought I was the Earl,' he slurred. 'I can pretend to be him. We'll have fun.'

'You are drunk.'

He widened his eyes and she perceived the mocking and cruelty there. For the first time since leaving Daman-hour Ranya felt fear. Knew what it was like for a woman alone in the world.

'One does not come to France and not sample the wine. They have the finest. Wine and women. That is what they are known for. The French. But I have an appetite for something *Egyptian*.'

He growled, moving the lower half of his body so that, try as she might to close the door, she couldn't. Her heart pounded as she pushed, and she wanted to scream for help, but the sound was lodged in her throat. She'd been looking after herself for months now—why should this be any different?

If Baba were here, he'd protect her. Kill, if he had to, any man who threatened to dishonour his daughter. Muhammad too. Her brother was just as protective. Ranya loved them both, missed them both. And she desperately realised that if anything were to happen to her at Jarvis Larder's hands, the knowledge of it would kill them.

'What the blazes are you doing, man?'

Iskander. That was her first thought.

But it was Owen. Barely awake himself, but angrier than she'd ever seen him.

There was no prim politeness as he tackled Larder, roughly pushing him back from the door frame and putting his own body between Ranya and the intruder.

'Get out of here, lest I carry you out to the water and throw you in myself.'

'You wouldn't be the first Earl of Warrington to act in such a way!'

She couldn't see him, because of Owen's back, but the fact that Larder had the audacity to sound insulted infuriated Ranya.

'What the hell do you mean by that?' Owen asked.

The drunk man ignored him, spun around to point to Ranya, 'She's no English rose nor French violet. She should be thanking me for wanting to—'

'Women are not flowers!' she fumed. 'You repugnant man!'

Owen gave him one last, hard shove, the force of which had him almost stumbling out of the room himself. Instinctively, Ranya wrapped her arms around him, keeping him near, *needing* him near. His heart pounded beneath her palms, but his final words to Larder were calm. Decisive.

'Go. Sleep it off and gather your wits before the Sûreté detains me for murder!'

Owen watched as the man made it to the end of the corridor, but Ranya couldn't look. Could barely lift her head from the comforting strength of Owen's back.

When Larder slammed his door, and the threat of him had passed, Owen's hands came to hers, squeezed gently. She moved to pull away, but he slowly turned, twisting to give her hands back to her and loosen her grip.

'I'm so sorry. It never occurred to me he could be a bad drunk. There's no excuse for such behaviour and I should have thought better on how to protect you from it.'

'Because you are my chaperon?' Maybe it was because she'd thought she'd detected Iskander in him earlier, or because she still felt vulnerable from Larder's threat, but she was confused. She needed to know that he was there only because of societal code.

'Because I *care* about you.'

He met her gaze for a long minute, and she saw the tenderness in his eyes. When he looked down, he caught the fact she was wearing the dress he'd brought her. He raised a timid finger to the material of her sleeve, barely touched it. Then he reached for a strand of hair that had escaped from its knot. Before he could touch it she blew at it, meaning to push it away from her face, but she blew on his finger and he shivered.

Without thinking, she clasped his finger like a baby chick in her palms. Then, embarrassed, she pecked it—a quick kiss. 'Thank you for being here. For caring.'

'Ranya…' His voice was thick.

Ranya. Not Miss Radwan, with its stiff-sounding English. *Ranya.* Said in the way Iskander would have said it.

He closed the distance between them, stared at his finger on her lower lip and slowly slid it from her grasp, exchanging it for his own lips. The warmth there took her by surprise, made her flush with anticipation, yearning. It wasn't a kiss exactly…only the promise of one.

A promise that felt like a punch when Owen withdrew. He bowed gallantly. 'I will leave. But rest assured, Miss Radwan. I would not see any harm come to you.'

Chapter Eight

Owen

As Owen downed the last of his bitter coffee, he stared out of the large window overlooking a herb garden surrounded by a patch of green-leafed hemp. Behind the Chateau Canebière there would be fields of it that crawled over peaks, each gradually getting higher until they met the mountains.

Perhaps Ranya would like to stroll after breakfast.

'We're ready to depart. The coach is packed and waiting for you, sir. And the driver says we must leave forthwith if we are to make the train to Paris.'

Jarvis Larder stood over him, and Owen wondered how the man had the gall to stand there as if nothing were amiss. He couldn't bear to think about what might have happened if he hadn't been stirred awake by the sounds in the hall. The sounds of Ranya's distress.

He pounded his fist on the sill and stood. 'How dare you show your face?'

'Sir…?' At least it sounded as if Larder knew now not to pretend they were friends.

'You were drunk. I had to pull you out of Miss Radwan's room.'

Larder started, staggered back. It seemed like an act—
an amateurish one at that. 'I don't recall… The wine…'
He stared at the door. 'That is why she was so cold with
me just now.'

'Miss Radwan has not come down yet.' Owen had been
watching for her.

'On the contrary, sir, she has been outside for a while,'
Larder said, already moving towards the door. 'I must
apologise to her.'

Owen stood in his path. 'You will and you must. However, immediately thereafter you will remove yourself from
our company. Take the next coach. Avoid us at the railway in Paris and go the Calais to London route because
we are to Dover. I do not want to run into you ever again.
Do you hear me?'

'I understand your upset, but surely there will be a meeting at Warrington to—'

'To allow you to report to my *mother*?' Owen hoped
Larder would fathom that this would be the end of that
relationship as well. 'No. You will be compensated per
our agreement, but any further business between us is
concluded.'

'I only mean, sir, that the Countess might be upset to
have you arrive at Warrington with Miss Radwan alone.
Two of us might make it more acceptable.'

'*You* dare to school *me* on the rules of social propriety?'

Before Larder could say any more, Owen brushed past
him.

'Give me a few moments alone with Miss Radwan before you make your apology.'

From the elevated position of the chateau, it was easy
for him to spot Ranya by the coach. She crouched at eye
level with a French girl and was putting something on her
lips. Even from a distance he could tell she looked stun-

ning. And as he went towards her, he marvelled at how she was able to make such a dull dress look so exquisite.

'*C'est tres belle,*' the French girl said, before running back to her mother's market table.

Ranya waved her goodbye, straightening when her eyes found Owen. Being on dry land had done wonders to restore her, and he had to tell himself not to gape at her coral-stained lips.

Ranya's beauty would not allow her to blend in with the French, no matter if she were dressed like one of them or not. And, as he had done last night, Owen determined to protect her. Especially from any louses who might fawn over her as being '*exotique*'.

If only he could control his own louse-like thoughts when she was in his orbit…

'Your Lordship,' she greeted him.

'Miss Radwan.'

He smiled in his examination of her, free to let his eyes roam because she wasn't looking at him as he did so. Was it shyness over the touching of their lips last night? Not quite a kiss, but he feared more dangerous, because a slowly simmering flame had just as much power to wear a heart down as a fire.

'Are you all right?'

'Fine. Thank you again. For coming…being there.'

He nodded, reminding himself to breathe. 'Larder wishes to apologise for his abominable behaviour. I thought to warn you—let you decide if you will hear it.'

'He ignored me earlier.'

'He claims he cannot remember.'

Ranya stared at him, perceived perhaps that he was not sure the fellow was sincere.

'I will hear it. For you.'

'You do not have to do anything for me. You owe me

nothing. I only did what a proper gentleman should. I have demanded he part ways from us.'

'But he is an employee of Malden.'

'So what? If anything had happened to you…' He fought an abrupt wave of apprehension.

Ranya put a hand on his sleeve. 'Thanks to God, and to you, I am safe. I only mean that I will hear him for *your* peace of mind.'

Larder once again interrupted, appearing like a literal thorn in his side just as Ranya dropped her hand from his sleeve. He rendered his apology, and said something inexcusable about being so long without alcohol, due to his time in Egypt, that his body had forgotten how to manage it.

Owen hoped they'd not see Jarvis Larder for so long that they would forget *him*.

It was early morning when the train Owen and Ranya had caught in Paris stopped in Calais. The first ferry across the English Channel would not leave for another hour.

The extended journey had taken its toll, so that both he and Ranya collapsed on the grass near the docks. The sound of the English Channel's rushing waters mingled with the birdsong hanging on the morning mist.

Owen leaned back on his elbows and extended his legs. He moved his free hand close to where hers was pushing at a blue cornflower. He felt as if he was in a dream with her.

'How are you feeling?' Owen asked.

Ranya looked at his hand, but didn't move hers. 'It is lovely to be free of both water and land. I cannot decide which I am wearier of.'

He picked the flower, then leaned forward to place it in her lap. 'We could have taken it more slowly. Stopped along the way. But your three-month time limit has lit in a fire in me.'

Owen didn't want to keep coming back to it, but he pressed her when she didn't respond.

'Will you be ready to take such a trip again so soon? People usually make these cross-continental voyages only once every few years, if at all.'

'I will be ready. Suffering comes and goes. We rest a little between, and then carry on.'

She lifted the flower to her nose, inhaled.

He sat up. 'As you wish, Miss Radwan.'

She didn't say anything for a minute, and then the horns started blowing nearby, signalling that the ferry was coming.

'You called me Ranya that night,' she said, as they stood to join the queue of those people wishing to cross the channel. 'I liked it better than "Miss Radwan".'

'You want me to address you by your Christian name?' Which was a stupid thing for Owen to say—because she wasn't Christian. 'It's not proper in England for a woman to be addressed by…' He clamped his lips before he said anything more tactless.

'I understand that I am a simple pasha's daughter who does not dress like a Frenchwoman or know the right manners that govern an Englishwoman's life. But my name is Ranya. When you said it, it reminded me of home. Of Iskander.'

Her impassioned speech scratched at the part of Owen which had never felt complete. Never English enough to feel truly at home in the Countess's society—not Egyptian enough to hold his own mother's affection.

'Very well. At least when we are alone, I shall call you by your name. *Ranya*.'

Chapter Nine

Ranya

Though the ferry crossing was surprisingly quick, when they'd disembarked on English shores and gone through the queue of government officials checking people's travel documents, it was to catch another train.

Owen had secured seats for them that were in a luxurious car with plush velvet furnishings, carts piled with sandwiches and pitchers of lemonade. They were not the only ones in the car, but there was space enough between the seats that their conversation could be private.

There had been an enquiry about the lack of a female chaperone for Ranya, but Owen had taken the porter aside to inform him that he was, in fact, 'Delivering this young woman to the Countess of Warrington, who is occupied with estate duties while I make my industrial travels to Egypt for the company.'

Owen hadn't named Malden Trading, but the porter had nodded as if he knew and it was a solemn duty of his to obey. He'd sat them down in fairly private seats and left them alone.

She stifled a yawn, but Owen caught it.

'This train will cut across most of England and take us

into the nearest station to Warrington,' he said. 'We are almost arrived.'

She would not tell him he was right about the prospect of the trip back to Egypt because her father needed her. He had spent a lifetime taking care of her, and she would not be thwarted by travel hardship.

'Travel is torturous,' she admitted. 'Once I am home, I will be planting my feet there for ever.'

She felt sorry to see the smile on his face drop at her words.

He is not Iskandar, she reminded herself.

He was an earl with whom she had an arrangement.

They didn't talk much after that. The landscape lurched by, and the stops were sporadic—some boisterous and loud, others calm and smooth.

At one point Ranya was embarrassed to fall asleep, waking with a start, her head on Owen's arm.

'Sorry…' she mumbled. 'Was I asleep for very long?'

'Not long enough,' he whispered, and she didn't know if he meant because he'd liked her near or if he wished more time had passed.

Either way, Ranya knew that he desired her comfort. And that was a heartening thing.

'You were humming that morning—just before Larder. I heard it through the walls,' she said. 'It was an Egyptian lullaby.'

He folded his hands in his lap, stared at them for a long moment. 'I know the one. The tune comes to me often. It sounds sad.'

'I could teach you the words if you like.'

He took a deep breath. Smiled. 'Perhaps someday.'

'Warrington, next stop! Warrington!' shouted the conductor.

They were the only ones to get off.

While the conductor offered her an arm to help her down the train's steps, Owen took her bag along with his own.

Ranya inhaled, and after the train departed noticed there was coach waiting for them. It looked fit for royalty, with its thick-spoked wheels painted red and a body with real glass windows. Two white horses waited for direction, as did a boy who ran to grab their luggage and load it on board.

Behind him, a middle-aged man in a formal black suit and top hat stepped towards them.

'Rogers, you are a sight for sore eyes,' Owen greeted the coachman. 'I thought we would have to go into the village and find a cab.'

'Welcome home, my lord.' The man bowed. 'The Countess wasn't sure when precisely you would arrive, so Boris and I have been taking turns to wait here for the last few days.'

'She is ever thinking ahead.' Owen laughed. 'May I introduce Miss Radwan, my guest.'

Rogers bowed again and Ranya did not know if she should do the same. She tried to recall the appropriate response from the books she and Owen had read, but could not before it was too late.

There were high steps to climb to board the carriage, but she felt too shy to take either man's hand and hoisted herself up. She stumbled clumsily into a seat and was sure she heard the young boy sniggering at her expense.

Even though she believed she shouldn't care, Ranya couldn't help but feel nervous about meeting the Countess. How was she supposed to act around her if she didn't even know how to conduct herself with her coachman?

'Decorum dictates I ride up front with Rogers, to protect you from gossip and the close scrutiny of people in smaller locales. My chaperon duties, alas, must be transferred to the Countess,' Owen whispered. 'But if you'd prefer me to ride with you just this once, then I can.'

'No, do not mind me,' she said. 'I will be fine.'

But as soon as he had closed the door on her, Ranya fought the urge to cry.

Owen knew this land. Its people. Here she was the one who was a stranger and that made her feel alone.

Still, as they rode towards the estate, he shouted down to her and pointed out spots he wished to bring to her notice.

'These are the meeting grounds for the annual harvest and spring festivals. Jam-tasting and flower-arranging competitions…picnics and hay-rides for the children.'

'See the promenade? Local people will stroll there a while, sharing gossip after supper.'

At a steepled building, Owen told her it was, 'The parish church. The pride and joy of the Countess of Warrington. During his reign, King George himself was welcomed there on his tour of the estate. It was a meeting place for his men.'

Then the coach took a sharp turn and Ranya had to steady herself.

She heard Owen asking Rogers, 'Why do you not have us arriving at the front?'

'Instruction from Her Ladyship, my lord. She said it would be more suitable, since she has prepared the cottage for Miss Radwan.'

'Surely there are rooms in the main house…?'

Ranya lost what he was saying after that, and soon the horses were treading on cobbles until they finally came to a halt. From the window she could see a small crowd of servants standing in a line, presumably waiting to greet them.

This time when Rogers opened the door and reached out his hand to help her down and out of the carriage, she took it.

'Owen, darling. Welcome home.'

The Countess stepped forward and opened her arms to her son. She hugged him kindly enough, but from Ranya's viewpoint she could tell that the woman was cold and stiff.

She was dressed in a rich forest-green dress that somehow both scraped the ground and yet looked cleaner than freshly mopped floors. Her silvery blonde hair was meticulously contained in a high chignon that made her seem taller than she was. She was well-endowed, but there was a thinness to her face that hallowed her cheeks and engorged her eyes.

Eyes that cut to Ranya even while Owen was still in her embrace and looked on her pointedly.

Owen made the introductions. 'May I present Miss Ranya Radwan? Miss Radwan, this is my mother, Vivian Malden, the Countess of Warrington.'

Ranya put out her hand, and would have hugged the woman and kissed her cheeks in a traditional Egyptian greeting, but the Countess barely budged. She gave her a once-over as she shook her hand. Hers was cold and stiff.

'You will find, Mother, that Miss Radwan's English is impeccable,' Owen said, giving Ranya an encouraging smile.

'Language skills aside, she will be a project, nonetheless. Really, Owen… There are only a few weeks before the season begins in earnest—how am I meant to get her ready?'

'I am sure you will manage it.' There was a soft scolding in his answer.

Ranya said, 'Might I be shown to my room immediately? It has been a long journey and weariness catches up with me.'

Owen was the Earl here. In his element. He'd introduced the woman standing before him as his mother, and whatever shred of Iskander she'd seen in him seemed lost. It was taking all Ranya's might not to burst out in tears.

She should be more gracious, she knew, but in that moment she didn't care. If she didn't find her brother, and didn't get the deed for Damanhour's cotton, didn't see Baba freed, it would all be for naught. Even if someone had offered her a way back to Egypt right then and there she would have run from it. A good cry and things would be different, she knew. She'd be committed. She'd see it through, no matter what. But now she only wanted to be left alone. To wallow in peace.

'Come to the main house and—'

Owen was hushed as the Countess put her hand on his arm.

'There is no room prepared in the house. With her duties as a "consultant", I thought it more appropriate to put Miss Radwan up there.' The Countess pointed to some trees beyond the driveway. 'She must feel free to join us for meal times, of course. It is but a short walk to the main house.'

Owen shook his head. 'You do not mean the cottage, surely?'

'It is large enough to be considered comfortable. And, yes, I thought it best. Miss Radwan will appreciate the privacy, will she not?'

Their quarrelling over her accommodation made Ranya feel like a burden. She moved away, towards the trees, not knowing where she was going but needing to get away.

'Let her go, Owen. I will ensure one of the kitchen staff sees to her needs, brings her things. After supper tonight, or even tomorrow morning, we can decide on a schedule for her...*proper* training.'

The Countess nodded gruffly to Ranya and looked anything but hospitable when she dismissed her with a wave, saying, 'Welcome to Warrington.'

* * *

The cottage was, in truth, quite lovely. Although most of the shutters were open, its mustiness indicated that it must have been closed up for a long while. But the sun seemed brighter here, and the walls were papered a soft lavender that matched the gardens that she could see past the high trees that had blocked the view from the coach.

'Will you be all right here, miss?' asked Rogers as he set down her bag.

'Yes, thank you.'

She heaved a sigh of relief when she was fully alone, pulling off the shawl she'd tightened around her head and slipping off her shoes and stockings to feel the wooden floor beneath her feet.

Simple furnishings filled the space. A Chesterfield and a tea table. A couple of chairs near a fireplace for warmth, most likely. A kitchen at the back had a sink and a stove, and a cupboard holding a few pots, pans, dishes and cups. The single bedroom door creaked loudly when Ranya opened it, startling her with its unoiled hinges. The curtains had been opened but the window there was still closed, so she opened that and felt the weak wind it stirred circulating through the cottage.

She set her bag as an anchor to the bedroom door and made a note to remember to keep it open—because she wouldn't be asking anyone to come and oil the hinges. This was a temporary dwelling place. Ranya would not be staying long enough to make it a home.

She noticed a blanket that had been folded and put on a chair next to the bed. It was sky-blue, threaded in white, with a geometrical pattern that reminded Ranya of the blankets in Egypt. It was cotton threads from the Nile Delta that had helped make this. Perhaps the late Earl had brought it over from there?

After spreading it over the plain white quilt, she moved to put her clothes in the armoire.

Ranya remembered how Madame Hala had reached up to the back of the armoire in Alexandria and brought down the blue gown. She took the chair and did the same, fully expecting not to find anything, but to her surprise—she did. It was a prayer mat! Very dusty, but not too different from the one she'd prayed on the morning she'd left Mr March's school.

Ranya sighed. That day felt like a lifetime ago.

Still, finding the mat felt like a sign. She washed, made *wudu* and then prayed. She wasn't sure of the direction of the Ka'aba. Nor of the timing for which prayer it was, but she knew God was all-forgiving. And her parents had taught her that whenever people remembered Him, He would be there for them.

With each prostration Ranya expected the flood of tears she'd been holding back to come, but there was only a trickle. More than anything, she felt a kind of calmness come over her. And a realisation. This place. The blanket. The prayer mat. Its location. She was sure Madame Hala had lived here once. Perhaps even given birth to Iskander here.

Ranya's heart seized for the young man she'd met on the harbour that day. She felt such an empathy for him. Felt that maybe he was as trapped in the body of the Earl of Warrington as she was in her duty to her father and her home. She wished, not for the first time on their journey, that she might be better friends with that part of Owen.

After she'd tucked the mat away, a knock came at the cottage door. She hoped it might be Iskander, but behind it stood a girl a bit younger than Ranya, her skin so white, the red blemishes on it were almost a relief.

Her mouth agape with a toothy smile, she said, 'Oh, is it

true you come from the pyramids? Cleopatra! And mummies! What are they like?'

She carried a tray loaded with a plate of bread and cheese, and bowls of almonds and apple slices. She thrust it at Ranya, then curtsied.

'Oh, beggin' your pardon, miss. I always be getting the order of things wrong.' She pulled the tray back, then sneaked into the cottage, spinning to find the table to put it on, before curtsying again. 'Molly, at your service, miss.'

'Molly…' Ranya extended a hand.

The girl pumped it heartily. 'Oh, my name has never been spoke thus. Oh, your accent is pretty.'

'Please call me Ranya.'

Molly's eyes widened. 'Oh, that's real bonny. Prettier than Cleopatra, because it ain't hard—all them parts with Clee-oh-pat-ra. Yours is just Rain-a.'

'Ran-*ya*.'

'Ran-ya,' she repeated, then clapped when Ranya nodded her approval.

'Eat with me,' she invited.

Molly hesitated, but then shrugged. 'Oh, no one will miss me in the kitchens—and it was the Earl himself who sent me here.'

Ranya didn't trust herself to ask for details on how that had happened, but the knowledge that he was in the main house, thinking about her, was comforting. He had not trusted the Countess not to send someone as arrogant as she.

Molly proved a good distraction. While they ate, they talked.

'Oh, I been obsessed wi' pyramids after reading one of 'em penny dreadfuls. Are they very haunted?'

'My home is in Damanhour, far from the pyramids, but my father used to go to Cairo sometimes. He took my brother once and had a tour. Muhammad—that's my brother—said to me that the pyramids are just empty tombs now, much of the treasure that was there taken by the government, and some offered to the British Museum. Even the ancient Egyptians who were once buried there are gone. Probably the souls from their preserved bodies had long been judged by God, but to be removed from their final homes… It is sad.'

'Oh, but they are not Christians. They'll be burning in hell for it.'

Molly said it in such an innocent way that Ranya couldn't take offence. 'I am Muslim. My people have different beliefs. It is our good deeds that matter to God.'

'Oh, but the vicar says all 'ave to accept Jesus as t' Lord and Saviour. He comes to the house sometimes, to preach to us. Mostly when the Earl's not here. For that reason everyone is happy to have His Lordship back, though they won't admit it.'

'Why would they not admit it?'

Molly's brow creased, as if she was considering how much to say. Ranya had used to attend parties in Damanhour and had always known when other girls wanted to share things. She'd often been privy to secrets: engagements before they were announced, or quarrels that would soon end in separations. People had understood that she could be trusted. Of course after Muhammad had left and Baba had been arrested no one had wanted to be friends with Ranya at all, let alone trade gossip with her.

Molly craned her neck left and right, as if to ensure they were truly alone. Then, 'The Countess has been prepping for the new wife coming. She's readied a nursery for a babe she calls "the new heir", and started interviewing nannies on the sly. All of us think the poor Earl should have a say and maybe put a stop to it. Besides which, the old crone will prob'ly be long buried before an heir is even grown.'

Molly stuck out her tongue and closed her eyes, mimicking a dead person. Ranya chuckled at her ridiculousness and the girl grinned, pleased.

Owen had told her he wanted her to distract the Countess while he made his own life decisions, but it sounded as if the woman had already started making them for him.

Molly was continuing. 'Oh, but I hope he gets a good lass, at least. He's fun—good like his da was. But those loyal to the elder Earl were oft sacked by the Countess. She tolerates Owen well enough…calls him her son to others.' She clapped a hand over her mouth. 'I talk too much.'

'People don't think she is his mother?'

Ranya's heart raced at the question, as if she was somehow responsible for protecting Madame Hala. Her gaze strayed to the armoire. The woman had given her a gown, been kind. And Owen had sent her to her. As Iskander, he had trusted her.

Molly scrunched her nose, wincing. 'There be gossip that the young Earl dinna come from the Countess. That the woman's womb be a shrivelled dry rock, and he being so handsome and looking nothing like her… It must be clear. But folk don't talk of it—leastways not in good company. There's rumours, though. That his real mama be a fallen woman from the old Earl's company excursions. Maybe she was the daughter of a pasha, like yourself!'

Molly's already reddish face burned crimson.

'Oh, miss, I din't mean to compare you with her, or say pashas' daughters are all fallen!'

Ranya squeezed her hand reassuringly. 'You did not insult me,' she said.

'Oh, but the idea of a pasha is awful romantic, innit? Is it very much like being an earl?'

Ranya didn't fully understand English customs, but she had picked up on a little of the differences from the novel-reading she and Owen had done on the steam yacht.

'In Egypt, the title isn't one you're born into. It doesn't pass from one generation to the next, like here. It's a Turkish word for any man in a high position. A pasha might own land, or he might be respected for something else. Often, he is a chosen man in a city—like mine. He promises to serve his people as best he can…relay their concerns to higher government. And pasha is a title just as easily stripped away as it is given.'

There was no need to tell Molly her father had been jailed as a pasha, but she could start enquiring about her brother.

'Have you heard of any other Egyptians coming to Warrington? A young man, perhaps, looking for the Earl?'

Molly shook her head. 'I only come here a few months ago from Liverpool. My aunt got me the job. All I could get, really. I was looking for a governess position, 'cause I know my letters, but there's not too many opportunities for those not finely born.' She shrugged. 'Who is this Egyptian fellow you're seeking?'

'My brother,' Ranya blurted, before she thought better of it. 'Pease do not tell anyone, but he left Egypt a year ago and we don't know where he is now. I am embarrassed to say that he might have run away from home. Perhaps as a…a stowaway?'

'Oh, on one of the company ships?'

When Ranya nodded, Molly smiled in a way that told her the girl would be sharing another secret with her.

'I have a fellow—Tom. He's a dock worker in Manchester. My beau.' She bobbed her head proudly as she spoke. 'I'll write to him—find out if he knows about any Egyptian stowaway. But please keep my Tom a secret. My aunt would kill me if she knew I'm risking a fine opportunity in service by loving...someday marrying.'

Before Ranya could give her word or thank her, Molly's name was shouted from beyond the trees in the garden.

'Oh, speak on the devil and my aunt appears! I'm in for a scolding to be sure.'

Molly dashed out and then ran back in for the tray. Ranya laughed and waved her goodbye.

Owen had sent her a friend.

Chapter Ten

Owen

It took every ounce of Owen's will not to stamp his feet as he paced in the hall. It wouldn't do to have everyone in the house knowing how angry he was with the Countess's insistence that Ranya be banished to the cottage.

The same damned cottage where his mother had been hidden away. Until she'd felt she had no choice but to leave England, his father—and him.

Owen wanted…*needed* Ranya to feel at home. Here. With him. The Countess would have to apologise…tell Ranya she had made a mistake. Issue a formal invitation to the house. Whatever it took.

The house was big enough that Ranya could occupy a whole wing and still not cause any disruption to their normal lives!

'I was informed you were waiting for me.' The Countess finally appeared. 'I assumed you would need rest. A hot bath. And certainly—' she twirled her index finger in the direction of Owen's face '—that needs to be shaved.'

She detested facial hair.

'Mama,' Owen started, knowing she disliked the word

even more than facial hair, 'perhaps I am testing the feel of growing a beard.'

He couldn't decide which was more liberating: the statement, or the look she gave him as if he'd gone mad.

Owen matched it with a look of his own. He had learned long ago that when a nobleman stood long enough without flinching people would be forced to comply with his wishes. It wasn't an act he pulled very often with her, but the Countess would *not* discredit his authority—especially when they were in listening range of others.

Sure enough, she marched to the study and waited for him by the large door that when closed would keep their conversation from the rest of the house. After shutting it, she turned to him:

'Your father used to be the same. His visits to savage lands would bring out savage behaviour. It would take weeks afterwards to ensure he'd relearned his manners. Pray you only take hours. By supper, preferably. We have guests.'

Owen had only ever known his father to be docile. He felt a surge of pride to think he'd had some backbone when it came to facing his wife—even if it had been short-lived.

Maybe he was still in love with my mother. Sad that she'd gone...that he'd let the Countess come between them and not fought for her to stay.

It was a childish thought. Vivian had been his father's wife, Owen's mother only recognised as a wife in Egypt.

'Your father betrayed me.' That was what the Countess would say were Owen to argue with her about it now.

He studied the portraits mounted on the rich mahogany wall behind what had been his father's desk. They were oil paintings of previous earls, each not very different from the others. Owen had never met any of them, but he'd had history lessons about most. The Earl before his father had died without an heir, after the death of Vivian's older brother, and the family had been forced to bring in the distant cousin who had inherited the estate.

Charles Malden.

Owen studied his father's painting. A thin moustache sat erect above the same mouth he himself had inherited. The blond hair, gone mostly white and thinning upon his brow, was nothing like the hair Owen had inherited. His father's eyes seemed to look at something in the distance. Something out of reach…something that made him sad.

Owen took a deep breath, remembering when he'd sat for the portrait. It had been Owen's fifteenth birthday. When the Countess had suggested he should sit for one too, his father refused.

'It took me this long. My son's turn can keep.'

'I want Miss Radwan here in the house.'

The Countess circled him, then took a seat—not at his father's desk, but the one beneath the painting. 'I have offered her the arrangement but the staff tell me Miss Radwan is quite settled in the cottage.'

'Cottage? It is barely a shed! I explicitly said in my letter—'

'A letter only received three days ago, Owen. This is the best I could do at such short notice. Never mind that you gave me no choice on whether I even wanted to assume her sponsorship.'

The image of Ranya being marched off to the cottage where he'd lived with his mother—a place he hadn't returned to at all since she'd left—shook Owen more than he cared to admit.

I'm not falling in love with her, he told himself. *It is only the place…the memories of what happened there.*

The Countess continued, 'And this ridiculousness about bringing her as a consultant to Malden Trading! You think me a fool that I cannot see you're using her as a distraction from your duties to this estate? There are only a few weeks left before you have to keep your promise. Your wife will be chosen and agreed upon at the Percy Ball. You will be taking up your seat in Parliament thereafter.'

'Why did you send Jarvis Larder with the message that Malden Trading's interests in Egypt might be for sale?'

Owen thought he'd catch her off guard—but if she was, she barely blinked in surprise. 'On my last trip to London some of the ladies mentioned the Anglo-Egyptian Bank was opening in Alexandria. Larder happened by whilst I visited my lawyers, and I asked him if he would make some enquiries.'

'You didn't think I could make my own enquiries?'

The Countess arched her back into the wing chair. 'You're hardly the epitome of good management, Owen, dear. We both know you traveled for a bit of fun. Maybe to take stock of the Egyptian theatre scene? Is that where you met Miss Radwan? Because I doubt you actually visited our landholdings or the cotton crops. Is she even really a pasha's daughter?'

The Countess knew Owen well. He *had* been acting when he'd met Ranya. But that meeting had prompted a desire in him to have more involvement with Malden Trading.

'She is—and she is brilliant too. A genius in mathematics, knowledgeable in every aspect of the cotton trade.' He knew he sounded like a smitten schoolboy, but he couldn't help expressing his admiration. 'I have learned much from her.'

The Countess stood, examining him from head to toe until he felt the heat of her glare.

'I should caution you that calling your latest conquest a *consultant* will not be believed by all. You are an earl, and while you might be excused for bad behaviour, no self-respecting woman will appreciate a man with a lover he flaunts as such. Your marriage cannot start happily on such a note.'

The jab felt personal, and though he could have turned on her, Owen kept silent. Her marriage had always been loveless. From where he stood, looking at his father's portrait, he could believe what he'd suspected all his life. That his father, Charles Malden, had only married Vivian because he felt guilty that, he, a distant cousin, should inherit the Warrington estate while she had managed it all her life when her father was the Earl. Maybe that was why Owen's father had gone on to build up Malden Trading so well—so that he could exist outside of this place.

'We are not lovers,' Owen said, wishing it were not the truth.

He thought of how much he'd cherished Rayna's nearness on the journey, how he'd often struggled not to go to her rooms in the dead of night, how he'd brushed his lips to hers comfortingly after Larder's deplorable intrusion.

'She is an honourable lady and I am merely trying to take up the reins of my father's company properly.'

It was as if he hadn't said anything at all, for the Countess countered, 'And if you truly want me to sponsor her, in the hopes of finding her an English husband so the two of you can continue the love affair you've begun under that guise, then you should know that you will be under scrutiny when you take up your seat in Parliament. Warrington, all the people who depend on this estate's livelihood, and your future heir will not endure any hint of scandal.'

He'd never heard the Countess being so crass.

'Enough!' he shouted.

She stepped back, throwing both her hands in the air as to seem the injured party.

Owen took a deep breath and sank into his father's

chair. 'It is only a couple of months—an exchange. Miss Radwan will teach me about the trade and we will treat her as proper hosts.'

'It hardly seems like an exchange—her coming all this way for a few months of hospitality. Don't lie to me, Owen. What did you really promise Miss Radwan?'

Though she had no say in his father's business, Owen saw no harm in divulging to the Countess that he was looking for a deed between their fathers—especially if it meant she would be kinder to Ranya.

'There is an issue between her city, Damanhour, and the central Egyptian government. Miss Radwan requires a deed her father signed with mine.'

'What kind of deed?'

'Apparently it stipulates that her family can buy back Malden's interest in their cotton production for a certain percentage.'

'And you are intending to give her this deed?'

'I have promised her, yes.'

The Countess threw up her hands. 'See—this is precisely why you cannot take over the business without training for it first! A lawyer will need to go over all documents, otherwise *we* might find we owe *them*…past profits or future ones.'

Owen gripped the desk as if it was the edge of a stage he was about to fall off. 'My father wouldn't have made any deal that damages Malden, nor one that fleeces anyone else. At least not the father I knew.'

'Which is precisely why you have to tread carefully. Anything you find has to come through me, and then go to our lawyers, Owen. Promise me you won't do anything to ruin us.'

There was a desperate edge to her voice he had never

heard from her before. The Countess was generally any-thing but passionate in her speeches.

'There is something you are not telling me,' he decided. 'Is it why you want me to offload our holdings?'

'I was not privy to the way your father ran Malden, par-ticularly in the early days...'

The Countess leaned over the desk and covered his hands, which were white at the knuckles now, with her own frailer ones, blue veins bulging. She slowly expelled a long breath.

Owen felt the shift in her—one more in line with the act they'd been taking part in with one another for the bet-ter part of their lives. She, the placating mother who pro-fessed concern for his best interests; he, the dutiful but spirited son who tried to please her even if it went against what he really wanted.

He loosened his grip on the desk and slid his hands from beneath hers. It was a familiar role, but one Owen was growing weary of.

'But it's true,' she said at last. 'I want to make the com-pany someone else's problem. A tour of Liverpool's docks or Manchester's mills would show you that the industry is crass—beneath the prestige I have always hoped War-rington will be associated with. You will manage the es-tate and you will also sit in Parliament. Move us closer to London if not in distance, then in spirit. The sale of Mal-den Trading will assure an easier transition.'

She swiped at a fleck of dust on the desk.

'I did things for your father...stood by him so that his past *transgressions* would not hurt our standing or this es-tate. His legacy is clean, and honourable, because of *me*.'

Maybe Owen's digging too much into the past *would* uncover unsavoury things about his father. Though she had been diplomatic about it since she'd agreed to come here, Ranya had initially implied that Charles Malden had deliberately chose to ignore her father's requests to honour their agreement.

'All my actions, Owen,' the Countess went on, 'from the day I brought you into this house, have been to secure *your* future. And your heir's.'

When Hala had left him as a boy, in the cottage where Ranya was staying now, it had been the Countess who had taken his hand and brought him to Warrington Manor with the promise of biscuits and a glass of milk.

'If I promise to focus on the estate over these next few weeks, will you promise to spare no expense with Miss Radwan?' he asked. 'It won't be for long—she has stipulated three months, travelling time included. She is counting the days.'

The Countess smiled. 'That sounds like a sensible plan. Know that I am not opposed to your giving her this deed. I only ask that when you find it you give it to me and our lawyers first. In the meantime I will bring Miss Radwan to my side, woo her with dresses and dance lessons, tea parties and luncheons. I will send word to my friends that there will be a proper sponsorship from me, the Countess of Warrington, to this pasha's daughter.'

'Very good.'

Although he wasn't entirely convinced of the sincerity behind the Countess's words, he would accept them and acquiesce in order to make his own independent enquiries *and* ensure Ranya's welcome in society.

'I will go and have that shave.'

She nodded approvingly. 'One last item, Owen... Whatever charms Miss Radwan possesses, you will not fall for them. You cannot.'

Chapter Eleven

Ranya

None of the novels she and Owen had read could have prepared Ranya for the massiveness that was Warrington Manor. From the back, where they'd arrived, she hadn't fathomed the extent of it. In the rear were housed the stables, carriages and gardens, but the buildings curved around themselves, belying the girth of the main house.

Rather than enter through the servants' entrance, she thought she would take an easy walk around to the front, but she had underestimated the distance. As she strolled past the rich red brick walls, saw the jutting fanlights built over the numerous large windows on the first level and the bonneted smaller ones along the second, Ranya measured the distance carefully in steps, converted them in her mind to yards, then miles.

Her feet were smaller than the average man's, even in the slightly large slippers that had been brought over to the cottage along with a few dresses. They weren't new, but there had been a note—signed by the Countess—apologising for that fact and promising to have some made to measure soon. The note had suggested that 'it would be lovely if Miss Radwan would deign to wear the lavender satin brocade'.

Ranya had done so, even though it was quite loose on her and looked grey and more suitable for a matronly woman than a young one. Luckily she had a veil from Egypt that complemented the colour well. But there was no mirror in the cottage, and the small lake she passed, while prettily populated with swans and water lilies, did not make for a clear reflection.

Owen's eyes will tell you.

The butterflies in Ranya's stomach proved her excitement at seeing him again. How had she managed to miss him already?

She reached to knock at the double doors—huge wooden things with copper details, which looked both intimidating and grandiose.

It was Rogers who opened it. 'Miss Radwan, do come in.' He pointed to a contraption on her left. 'For future reference, there is a doorbell there. You will press it and the butler will be called. We do not make use of the knocker— it is more decorative than functional. Luckily for you, I happened to be nearby.'

'Luckily,' she mimicked.

But as she passed him, Ranya was rendered speechless.

She took in the winding staircase and the collection of paintings on the panelled walls that led her eyes upwards to the landing, off which led corridors with a series of closed doors. Bedrooms—at least twenty of them.

Their villa was one of the biggest in Damanhour—because it not only housed the family, but also acted as the central government building—but they only had nine bedrooms, distributed over two levels. There the décor was simple—mostly empty space and brick walls. Here, even the expansive hall she stood in was flanked by chairs and tables upon which sat fresh flowers in exquisite crystal vases.

From a corridor to her left emerged the Countess, the smack of her heels against the marble floor indicating that Ranya should not take off her own slippers as she would have were she back at home.

'Your Ladyship.' She greeted the woman with a bow of her head. She did not want to curtsy to anyone unless she had to.

'Miss Radwan. Funny you should enter from here,' she said, in a way that stressed that it was not. 'At least you have arrived before the Parker family.'

She pointed to a grand clock, larger than the one near the pulpit of the Abu al-Abbas al-Mursi Mosque in Alexandria, which until now had been the largest Ranya had ever seen.

'Our time is for six. Do Egyptians not regard lateness in its fashionable sense?'

Ranya wasn't exactly sure what she meant, but the woman did not seem to want an answer anyway. Before leaving the cottage she had determined not to let the Countess's snobbery intimidate her, but when she circled her, in an examination of the dress, it was a challenge. She hated feeling like a doll for sale at the bazaar, but wasn't sure what else to do. She was in the woman's house. Wearing her clothes. About to eat her food.

It was an altogether terrible feeling.

'The dress is pleasant enough,' the Countess said. 'Although it does not fit right without a corset.'

'Does that not tighten the body? The gown is already loose.'

When Ranya tugged at the extra material at her hip, the woman shook her head in reprimand.

'A corset is a first order requirement. One of the maids can help—'

'Molly?' Ranya suggested.

'Who? Oh, the redhead from Liverpool? No, she is too new. Flighty.'

Before Ranya could defend her friend, the Countess lifted the edge of her scarf. She rubbed the silk between her fingers, then flicked it back as if it were made of burlap.

'I wouldn't normally allow the shawl, but I can understand the desire to cover those tight, unruly curls. I'll have a special iron ordered from London—and then that must go.'

'I wear a veil to cover my hair in the religious tradition of my people.' Ranya spoke as solemnly as she could.

'This is England. *Your people* do not exist here, I am afraid. You are a pasha's daughter, and I have agreed to sponsor you this season because of it. If we play our cards right, you will have much to write home about.'

'Perhaps Owen has informed you that I shall be returning home in a few months.'

The woman actually tutted. 'You must address him as His Lordship. Despite what he might have led you to believe, he cannot play games in proper society as he might do elsewhere.'

You do not have him right, Ranya would have said— but what if she were the one in the wrong? The Countess had known Owen for much longer, and he *had* mentioned a love of acting…

'Miss Radwan!' Owen called from the landing. 'Welcome!'

He leapt down the stairs, dressed in what must be the full Earl of Warrington costume. It was a completely black suit, its jacket adorned by a few colourful badges on the lapel, with a sky-blue dress shirt beneath. His hair was slicked back, and he'd shaved. His cheeks shone.

He bowed to Ranya.

She followed suit, because she didn't know what else to do with her body and because his presence—he was an earl—demanded it. Yet when he rose and caught her eye that secretive smile was still there. More magnetic than ever.

There was nothing of Iskander in his look, but Ranya could not pretend that the Earl of Warrington was not a very handsome man in his own right.

He kept his eyes on her as he brought the Countess into their conversation, 'To show Miss Radwan the Malden Trading Company's reach, I will arrange a tour of the factories and the docks east and west of us. Miss Radwan, the Countess will take you to functions in the village, and then to London. Shopping, tailors—so much to do before the Percy Ball and Miss Radwan's return journey.'

'We shall be busy, indeed,' the Countess remarked. 'And on Sunday, of course, the vicar will expect to see us for services.'

'In my faith we pray five times a day, every day. Is there a mosque nearby?' Ranya asked. 'Any other Muslims?'

'England does not contain such variety,' the Countess sighed more than said.

Ranya bit her inner cheek, and tried to sound pleasant when she countered, 'There are many churches in Egypt—synagogues as well. People of all faiths have places to fulfil their spiritual needs.'

'Actually, there is a congregational prayer space I know of in London—not yet quite a mosque, though I hear they hope to make it into one,' Owen provided. 'If you are interested, we can arrange a visit whilst you are there.'

She gave him a thankful smile.

'I was just telling the Countess it seems silly to have you in the cottage.' Owen looked pointedly at the Countess.

'Indeed.' The Countess nodded. 'There is much space here. We could have your things brought in.'

But Ranya did not want the woman looming over her—even if it meant being closer to her son.

'Here you will not be so lonely, so removed,' Owen added.

Ranya shook her head. 'I am happy in the cottage. Settled. And Molly is wonderful. She says she will visit me whenever she gets the chance.'

The last comment was meant to show her gratitude to Owen, but before he could acknowledge it a shrill ringing pierced the air. Ranya jumped at the sound.

When the Countess turned towards it, Owen moved to her side. 'That blasted doorbell is much too loud. Are you all right, Ranya?' he whispered.

She nodded, but her heart still raced. Was it the doorbell or his show of sentiment?

'The Parker party!' announced the butler.

A flash of annoyance passed over the Countess's face as she saw how near Owen was standing to Ranya. She pulled him next to her and the two moved forward to welcome their guests.

'Sir Henry, Lady Elizabeth, Miss Charlotte. How lovely to see you—and look who has graced us with his presence.'

'Your Lordship,' said Sir Henry.

Just as his daughter, a pretty girl with blonde tendrils falling from her flowered bonnet, happily declared, 'Owen!'

Was she allowed to address him as such? wondered Ranya. Why didn't the Countess reprimand *her* for doing so?

'How wonderful to see dear friends,' Owen said, and

proceeded to shake hands with the man and bow to the ladies.

Miss Charlotte took off her bonnet and shawl and looked a little embarrassed by her outburst, but the cut of her dress and the rouge on her cheeks had Ranya believing that the girl had already known Owen would be there. Or at least that she'd hoped he might be.

The Countess stepped aside to usher Ranya into the fold. 'And may I introduce Miss Radwan? She is the pasha's daughter I will be sponsoring this season. Her father had business dealings with my late husband, and I wish to reward years of loyalty.'

Ranya tried not to look at Charlotte as the woman was clearly studying her. From the girl's furtive glances between her and Owen, Ranya could tell she was trying to assess the nature of their relationship. And that she found it worrisome.

Maybe Charlotte was the Countess's choice of wife for her son.

Though it shouldn't, the realisation made Ranya feel she should be the worried one.

When the introductions were done, they made their way to the dining room for supper.

Without thinking, Ranya gravitated towards Owen, at the head of the table, but then noticed that each seat was indicated by a name tag in calligraphic script atop a gold-rimmed plate and knotted napkins. Owen found hers before his own and held the chair out for her. The others waited for him to take his seat. It was an awkward moment, not helped by the fact that he was on one end and she was a good two yards away.

Ranya's seat was surrounded by the older members of the party, and next to Owen were Miss Charlotte and her father. Planned, no doubt, by the Countess.

It was clear the woman deemed Miss Charlotte suitable for her son, and Ranya fought a surge of jealousy at the knowledge. And then the girl said something to Owen, leaning towards him as she did. When he chuckled in response, Ranya seethed.

What had she said to him? Why was he continuing the conversation? Did he like her? Find her pretty?

'You should smile more,' the Countess said under her breath. 'Small smiles…refined. Like this.' She demonstrated. But it looked stilted. When Ranya didn't mimic her, she inclined her head. 'Or try watching Miss Charlotte. She's perfected the expression required.'

Ranya wondered how she would survive pandering to this woman for the rest of her time in England.

Two men in livery attended to the diners, serving the appetiser—a tepid broth that tasted like something given to babies without teeth. In Egypt, such a soup would be the base of a main dish. Something to cook the rice in or soak the bread for a *fattah*. Not to eat on its own. Maybe that was why the English needed wine.

Ranya wasn't sure how to say no to what had been poured into her glass. She would need to keep reminding herself it wasn't *karkaday*. The dark burgundy colour was the same, and even the aroma was similar to the one emitted by the dried rosehips used in the popular Egyptian iced tea.

Sir Henry led the conversation. 'I trust it was a beneficial trip to Egypt, Your Lordship?'

He seemed jovial enough, but his wife was another matter altogether.

She talked over her husband. 'How ever did you bear the heat? You must be happy to be delivered home after such an arduous journey and being in barbarian company.'

'Not at all.' Owen's eyes sparkled in the candlelit shadows. 'Alexandria was especially pleasant. The sea air there was sublime. So many wonderful things happen on the harbour and the corniche.'

Ranya watched him as he spoke, and noticed how he knew her gaze was on him, how it felt as if his words were for her alone.

'The Egyptians themselves are warm—truly the most hospitable of people. The relief from protocol was welcome as well.'

'I'm sure gentlemen like to experience the positively barbaric at least once in their life.'

Lady Elizabeth laughed and squeezed the Countess's wrist, as if to reassure her and others in the room who might be offended by Owen's claims.

'My son was the same in his ventures to India. Thank goodness he's now settled in London, with his devoted wife and new daughter.'

Ranya gritted her teeth through the conversation that followed around British relations with India. Did these people truly believe they were better than everyone else in the world? Maybe they thought they were doing good, buying spices from India or cotton from Egypt, while offering language and education in places like Mr March's school or through missionary work. Yet for all their airs they did not realise how much they depended on the labour of those they termed 'barbaric'. Or that their assumptions about people who were not like them might be completely wrong.

Ranya wished she could call them out on their prejudice, but being a guest at their supper party stilled her tongue. Until the main course came in—a roasted pig. The skin was crispy and there was an apple in its mouth... How would people ever eat it? Looking like that!

She clapped both hands over her mouth to stop herself

being sick, then pushed her chair back, knocking cutlery to the ground. It was like the first day on the yacht with Owen, before Ranya had got her 'sea legs.' Except they were not alone so he could hold her head…stand at her back as an anchor. Solid. Warm.

'Apologies. Pig is forbidden in my faith,' she managed to mumble, after she'd calmed a bit. 'I am not accustomed to seeing it like this.'

Lady Elizabeth sneered. 'I had forgotten Muhammadans do not consume pork. And yet they don't have a problem with camel meat.'

The other woman's prejudice was too much for Ranya. She stood abruptly, backing away from the pig, refusing to look at it again.

The men stood too, out of decorum. But it was Owen who rounded the table.

'I'm sorry. I should have seen to the menu myself.' He stared pointedly at the Countess.

'Excuse my ignorance, Miss Radwan,' she offered. 'Pardon it this time and it shall not happen again for the duration of your stay.'

'Please…' Owen addressed one of the servants. 'Pass a message along to the kitchens not to serve any pork. Only lamb, chicken or duck.'

'Yes, my lord.'

'Also, please remove the platter to a side table and slice the pork there. You may serve it to our guests banquet-fashion, as at luncheon.'

The Countess made an objecting sound but said nothing as the servant complied, and in the bustle of the changes being made to the settings Owen led Ranya to a quiet corner of the dining room.

'I'm sorry. All this… A supper party… The customs…

It would be overwhelming even if the guests were not so rude and ignorant!'

His kindness made her tearful, and she had to bite her lip to stop the flood of emotion. She wished she could tell him that she had no problem with him. That in fact she wished they were alone, even though she shouldn't.

Behind his back, Ranya caught a glimpse of Miss Charlotte. Frowning. Fretful.

Then the dining room stilled, conversations ceased, and all stood over their filled plates—whether they were waiting for the head of the table to return or trying to overhear what he was saying to her, she could not be sure.

When the Countess called his name and Owen ignored her, his attention still completely on Ranya, she'd have been lying if she'd tried to deny how powerful it felt. How much it boosted her.

'They are waiting for you,' she said softly. 'Maybe I should excuse myself.'

'It is important to me that you feel welcome here. But if you would like to go you may, certainly. Molly will bring you a tray.'

She met his gaze. 'But you would rather I stayed?'

'Most ardently.' He nodded, and bit down lightly on his lower lip.

Ranya didn't know what daring possessed her when she saw that. 'Sit me next to you, then.'

He nodded before turning, and then moved to place a hand on Sir Henry's shoulder. 'Would you mind exchanging your place with Miss Radwan? I think it prudent to have her near me.'

She would have liked him to move Miss Charlotte instead, but it was fine. It was still a victory, being next to him and having him refuse to eat any of the main dish with her. Pushing away the wine when he realised that, too, was something she wasn't drinking.

Having the Earl of Warrington pay her such exquisite attention made Ranya feel as if she was flying. As if she couldn't be hurt or shamed by anyone else at that table.

But that didn't mean that there weren't moments when she felt as if her wings had been clipped and she was falling quickly…spinning, giddy. When his knee scraped against hers under the tablecloth, or the tip of his shoe nudged the tip of hers. The intimacy in the benign act of bringing his fork close to her plate to recommended or comment on the food.

'Try the Brussels sprouts dipped in the mustard dressing.'

Or, 'Doesn't the blancmange remind you of *mahalabia* pudding, but with vanilla instead of blossom water?'

With the contortions of the candlelight it was like seeing him anew. This version of Iskander that was Owen in front of others. It made her heart pound with the danger of it. And even though others tried to get their attention throughout the meal, it was hard to do.

Sir Henry had to ask twice if she knew the place where the Rosetta Stone was found.

'Yes, very well. The fort is central in the town named for it. We call it Rasheed.'

'The French like to claim they found it,' he said, 'but an old army friend of mine, whose father was with Admiral Nelson when he fought Napoleon's forces in Egypt, claimed one of his savants was led to it by a local peasant girl he had fallen in love with.'

'He's right,' Ranya agreed. 'According to local legend she was more than just a *falaha*. She was the siren *djinn* of the Nile, El Naddaha, who with her beauty and song could lure men to a watery death. It is said that the Naddaha would sometimes use her voice to possess a human body. And for as far back as any can remember she'd used the women of a particular family as vessels for her immorality. Maybe she fell in love with that savant—or maybe they drowned together. Neither was ever heard from again.'

'Fascinating!'

Sir Henry practically clapped, while his wife mumbled something that sounded like 'Hogwash!' to their daughter.

Ranya dismissed it as a reference to the meal they had eaten.

As for Owen, he only exhaled, loud and deep. A breath she felt in her own chest.

Chapter Twelve

Owen

After supper, the party moved to the drawing room, where, despite her contention that she would let Owen choose his future bride, the Countess did everything she could to settle him on Miss Charlotte. Owen ought to have been miffed, but he fancied that Ranya might just be a tad jealous and the possible reason why enthralled him.

Since he'd reached marriageable age and been permitted to attend social events frequented by single women and their mothers, who were looking for potential husbands for them, he had played the rooms like the keys on a piano, flitting from one to the next. Teasing, never serious.

Perhaps Ranya was punishment for his past behaviour. He couldn't imagine ever leaving her side if he happened upon her at any such event in future. And even though the Countess looked as if she would soon reprimand him for making a fool of himself in front of their guests, Owen found it extremely difficult to take his eyes off Ranya at all.

Her wayward curls fell to her neck…to the crook where it met her collarbone. She wore earrings he'd not noticed before, since her hair was usually covered with a shawl, but now the tiny gold hoops there didn't escape him. His imagination snagged on one lobe, her left. What would happen if he caught it between his teeth? If he nibbled there? Ever so gently...

The thoughts felt like punishment too. He knew Ranya would be leaving him. And, despite their developing relationship, and the journey they'd undertaken thus far, Owen understood that caring for her, *falling for her*, should still be as inconceivable as it had always been.

'Do you play any instruments, Miss Radwan?'

The question had come from Miss Charlotte.

'No,' Ranya answered, her voice throaty. As if she'd read Owen's mind.

'Sing, perhaps?'

'No,' she repeated, more forcefully this time.

'Egyptian women are trained in other arts, Miss Charlotte,' Owen said, loudly enough for her mother to hear and pull her daughter away. The girl was being condescending to Ranya, and it wasn't as if Owen had any scandalous arts in mind.

Until she said, 'I do dance.'

'Indeed?'

She blushed as she answered. '*Raqs balady.* But not in public.'

Owen knew exactly where he might take her so that she could show him in private...

Sir Henry reminded him that they weren't alone when he blurted, 'Isn't that belly dancing?'

His wife squawked in reprimand and the Countess spoke in a falsely cheery tone.

'Miss Charlotte,' she said, 'I distinctly remember you are wonderful at the pianoforte. Do play us something.'

It felt like a warning for Owen. He had agreed to be a better earl, and she might trouble Ranya if he were not a better host.

'Please do,' he echoed, putting on his most theatrical smile for the benefit of the Countess.

'As you wish, my lord.'

Miss Charlotte took her place behind the piano as the rest of the party found seats. The Countess pulled Ranya away from him and sat her between herself and Lady Elizabeth on the Chesterfield. After ensuring that Sir Henry was comfortable, he positioned his own chair so he would be in direct view of Ranya but still not look as if he wasn't paying attention to the tune.

The melody of Miss Charlotte's playing filled the room, but Owen's gaze kept flitting to Ranya. The Countess must have noticed, because when it was over and she suggested singing a duet he felt obliged.

Charlotte shuffled over on the bench and he sat down beside her, and the two of them flipped through the available music.

'My last singing lesson was at fourteen, so be forewarned,' he chuckled.

'I was there for it, my lord. I was younger then, and used to wait my turn after you at Master Maybury's in London,' said Miss Charlotte. 'Once, I waited so long—you'd been late, at a play at Covent Garden, and Master Maybury insisted on keeping you back. I was crying for fear Mama would scold me, but when I was finished you were waiting with a bouquet of tulips and offered to apologise to her on my behalf.'

Owen barely remembered, but it sounded like something he might have done.

'Yellow tulips to match the gold in my hair, you said…' She spoke quietly, as if the words were for him alone, but loudly enough that everyone in the drawing room would hear.

Ranya too. He felt oddly embarrassed to look at her,

wondering what she would make of his shared history with a potential bride, innocent as it was.

The Countess added, 'He has always been a charmer, the Earl, and has a way with the ladies—though he must settle soon.'

Eager to get off the matter, Owen pointed to a song. 'Miss Charlotte, do you know this one?'

He hoped she did not, and that would be the end of it. But the music was there, and she knew how to read it, and her playing was quite good, so he started singing. A thing made easier when Ranya looked down to her lap and the room's lights seemed to shine on him.

Performing.

Owen had performed in countless ways throughout his life and he was good at it. Now the lyrics moved in his throat and out of his mouth, evoking an image of a sparrow flying in pillowy clouds and through stormy winds. Free. Uncaged.

When they were finished the guests burst into enthusiastic applause. He chanced a look at Ranya. Although she too was clapping politely, her expression was unreadable.

Soon after Sir Henry insisted on taking their leave. 'The ladies will be staying on in the country a little longer, for the air, but my coach back to London leaves early tomorrow morning.'

'You must visit us while we are still nearby, Your Ladyship,' his wife said, kissing the Countess's cheeks in farewell. 'Bring Miss Radwan,' she added, as if Ranya had no say in her own schedule.

'You will be seeing us, I am sure.'

After they had left it was just the three of them, and although Owen hoped the Countess would take her leave she lingered—unwilling, perhaps, to leave him and Ranya alone.

'That wasn't the best of displays, but it is too late to go into the issues now. Shall I have one of the staff accompany you back to the cottage, Miss Radwan?'

'It is not necessary. I can go by myself,' Ranya answered.

Though he was not eager to go near the cottage that was the source of his most painful memory, Owen's desire to remain with Ranya as long as possible prompted him to say, 'It is dark. I will escort you.'

'Inappropriate, Owen,' said the Countess. 'We shall get one of the maids to do it.'

'She is on our grounds and it is the gentlemanly thing to do,' he insisted. 'Besides, I shall be back quickly enough to ensure Miss Radwan's reputation remains pristine.'

He made a point of gesturing to one of the staff waiting discretely behind the door for entry to the drawing room. They would want to clear it and conclude the evening. And the Countess would not argue with Owen within earshot of anyone else.

She gave a quick stamp of her foot before sauntering off.

'Can you show me the way out from the back?' Ranya asked. 'It was quite a walk around the front earlier.'

He disliked it that their route would be shorter, but did as she asked.

As they strolled, each step of his was slower than the last. Whether Ranya kept her pace to match his or if she too wanted the path to extend, so she could spend more time with him, he wasn't sure.

The chittering of crickets filled the silence until she broke it. 'You sing beautifully,' she said. 'I was not surprised, however. Your reading on the ship was as transportive. I have never been to the theatre, but when you perform, lift your voice, it is akin to hearing it in my own heart. You are a very talented man, Your Lordship.'

His breath hitched, and he felt her compliment sitting on his chest like a heavy brick. It was one thing to desire her, to want to be alone with her, but to have her appreciate him in such a way felt dangerous.

He stopped, took a deep breath, and tried subtly to steady himself so she wouldn't see how unnerved he was. Ranya stopped too, angled towards him so that the dim lanterns by the stables allowed her to examine his face too closely.

'You're so different from the boy I met in Alexandria, with his torn sandals and dirty *galabaya*, and an accent I couldn't quite place.'

'You liked him. I could tell immediately.'

'How?'

He reached for the tendril of hair that had fallen again from her scarf. Pushed it back, grazing her brow ever so lightly. Letting his hand linger there. Did she shiver or did he?

Ranya put her hand over his, wove her fingers between his.

'He almost did that then,' Owen whispered. 'You looked at him as if you wanted him to. Wanted *me* to.'

She laughed in a way that was a tad high-pitched. Or maybe it was his own heart's pounding that made him think so. She stared at him for a long minute before she lowered his hand from her cheek and let it go. He might have been sad, but at the same time she came close. Too close.

'Maybe,' she teased, 'I was calculating that there was more to you. An earl instead of a labourer. I do have a mind for numbers.'

Owen needed to put some distance between them. Get a grip on the pressing need to sweep her into his arms and kiss her senseless.

'And a mind for story-telling, apparently,' he said. Sir Henry was eager to hear more about the Rosetta Stone, but fear of his wife held his tongue.'

She laughed again, more openly now. And then they started walking again, the stars and the moonlight and the perfume of country roses guiding their path. Too soon, the cottage's silhouette appeared in the dark and Owen could not go any further.

'I should go back. The Countess is probably waiting to berate me for my behaviour tonight.'

'You were kind to me. Welcoming. Thank you.'

'She will say I was shamelessly ogling you. And she won't be wrong.'

'We have been companions on a long journey.'

'Companions?' he repeated, a little disappointed.

Ranya nodded. 'You could hide from her. Come inside.'

He understood it to be an invitation, likely for them to talk more. Or…

He couldn't let his imagination run too wild. No matter. There was no way he could trust his emotions to cross the cottage threshold.

Owen mimicked the Countess's haughty voice, 'And your reputation, pray tell?'

'I will not be in England long enough for it to affect me.'

It was a reminder that Ranya would leave him, just as his mother had.

Probably best to remember that when he felt weak around her.

'The Countess intends to show you off leading up to the Percy Ball. You will likely have your choice of gentleman callers. Perhaps one of them can convince you to stay.'

Owen watched carefully to gauge Ranya's reaction to that.

She scoffed, and he felt her breath warm on his face as

he angled his neck downwards and she looked up. 'How could he possibly do that?'

'You will fall in love with him, feel the hours are wasted and too long if you are not in his company. And when you are with him, even if you are doing nothing but reading a novel or playing a game of chess, you will wish the hours would go on. You will not be able to imagine leaving him for anything or everything in the world.'

God, but Owen didn't know what he was saying. Unmeasured words, from a cloudy mind. He found her hand in the dark, lifted it to his chest. She stared at it. Didn't pull it away, but didn't meet his gaze either.

'What of one's family?' Her tone was laboured when she spoke, her voice wavering. 'Loyalty to them? Duty? Should a man have the right to ask a woman to leave all that to be with him?'

'Yes,' he answered. 'If I am to be her man, then she should be my woman. I would only give her my heart if I was sure she had given me hers. Completely.'

His words might be muddled with his desire for Ranya, but Owen knew he'd never before articulated aloud what he truly felt about falling in love so well. And that was precisely why he should put distance between them.

'And if you had a daughter? Would you ask that of her? That she give up her father for a man?'

'Her heart should belong to her husband. And to her son.'

Their conversation had shifted into something deeper. Ranya was talking about her father. Owen of his mother. They both knew it.

Ranya pulled away, slipping her hand from his chest. She met his gaze.

'Your mother. Hala. She lived here once. I found a prayer mat she left behind.'

He turned towards the main house and away from the cottage. 'My recollection of it is poor. She left when I was barely five years old.'

'She hurt you,' Ranya said. 'But she is suffering for it.'

Owen winced. She was scraping at a wound he'd believed healed, but Ranya was proving that it wasn't. 'It is rarely the aggressor who suffers more than the victim. Hala left *me*—not the other way round.'

Ranya's voice softened, so light it seemed an extension of the air. 'You can talk to me about it. And I would like to tell you more about my family. My hurts.'

Before Owen could answer, a light came at them. Someone running much too fast. A stable boy, holding a lamp.

'Her Ladyship sent me, my lord. She thought Miss Radwan might need this.' He gave the lantern to Owen before taking his place a few feet away and adding, 'She insisted I escort you back, my lord. Bade me tell you that she will not rest until you return.'

Owen was almost grateful for it. Because he couldn't talk with Ranya about his mother in this cottage. He couldn't even go near it when it was dark, lest he turn into that sobbing little boy standing on an empty threshold once again.

He took the lamp and held it to her face before handing it over. Her eyes were downturned. The dimple in her cheek all but invisible. If he put his finger there, could he coax it to appear? Or would he need to use his lips?

She lowered her gaze even further, as if he had spoken that last thought aloud.

'Goodnight, Ranya,' he said. *'Ahlamik sae'eeda.'*

It was an Egyptian wish for happy dreams, and, although he knew he very much shouldn't, he couldn't help but wish hers would be of him.

Chapter Thirteen

Ranya

It would be two weeks before Ranya saw Owen again. He was busy with the managing of the estate and often came in for meals after the rest of the household had long finished.

He sent her a brief note before going away for a few days, saying he was meeting with some old employees of Malden Trading and making enquiries about 'that which we agreed upon'. Ranya knew he meant the deed, and it was then that she regretted not telling him that she was looking for her brother too.

She'd wanted to, the night of the supper with the Parkers, when he'd been so attentive. When he'd walked her to the cottage but held back from coming inside...

Every free moment since then she'd thought about what was happening between them. The attraction, mostly. But being so far away from home, from the culture and faith she'd been born into, brought on feelings of guilt.

If he were Iskander completely, raised in Egypt, he might have asked for her hand in marriage from her father and waited till their wedding night to act on his physical desires.

As Owen, raised in England, he could visit houses of

ill repute, but as an earl, he would need to marry a suitable young lady. Ranya was sure she didn't fit that description—even if she were being presented as a cotton pasha's daughter.

It was a good thing, then, that most of her moments were filled by the Countess's demands. Clothes fittings—and lessons in etiquette that Ranya absorbed quickly, thanks to her ability to turn them into complex mathematical problems: if three forks were used for two courses, and one small spoon was left after two courses were completed, what was the knife for?

A few times they went to tea parties and luncheons in Warrington village, or other villages nearby. Most were with older women, who ignored Ranya for the most part, but this latest luncheon was large enough that a party of girls her own age was in attendance.

Charlotte Parker was amongst them. She wore a ridiculous headband to match her lime-green gown, and as the other girls fawned over her, telling her how it complemented her golden curls, Ranya knew it would be a doomed luncheon.

'Speak to us about marriage traditions in Egypt,' Charlotte said with a mischievous smile, when there was a lull in the conversation. 'Will your father pay your dowry in mules and bales of cotton?'

If it was meant to be an innocent joke, Ranya did not take it as one. 'Egyptian culture is not as yours, where a dowry is paid as if a woman is being sold at a market. In Egypt a groom comes with his own wealth. As an *earl* has wealth. Unlike you, I should not like to be married to a man who only wanted me because I came with a dowry.'

At this hint of Owen and how he had favoured her that evening, Charlotte blanched. When she recovered, she asked, 'But surely you are promised at birth?' She said it in a way that sounded as if she herself had already been promised.

To Owen?

'Egyptians do not think of marriage as negotiation or strategy. What if a girl falls in love with someone her family has not decided on? Or a man decides to go against what his parents dictate? Best to avoid the embarrassment of it, since true love cannot be denied. Clever families in Egypt may make suggestions—arrangements, even—but even those are based on suitability. And they come from a place of love…a desire to see a son or daughter well settled. Happy.'

That last speech had been overheard by the Countess who'd come to find her, saying their carriage was ready. She didn't speak a word to Ranya the whole ride home, her disappointment clear. It was as if Ranya had been insulting her marriage to Owen's father.

The next day the Countess sent a note saying that she was feeling under the weather and Ranya should take her meals in the cottage.

Ranya was bothered by it, but also relieved. It meant that for a few days she spent more time with Molly, practising dances and laughing about the stiffness and stuffiness of the events which comprised the ton's Season.

Molly brought gossip too—about the strange sounds Rogers made in the middle of the night, and the distinguished country veterinarian who came to check on a pregnant mare and ended up staying too long because he 'couldn't stop drinking my aunt's lemonade. Oh, now, that would be a jolly wedding were it to happen!'

They talked too about Ranya's family in Egypt. About how her brother had disappeared after he'd gone to Alexandria to search for the old Earl of Warrington. Molly was surprised that Ranya hadn't shared the information with

able for some meetings today in Manchester. A mill tour, then union talks, and checking on the cotton supply that should have come through the canal by now and docked. Rather than your scheduled debutante duties.'

Ranya nearly clapped with joy. 'Really?'

He laughed, twisting his head so she could see his lifted brow. 'You must really be hating all the parties. Is it the little sandwiches or the watery tea? No, wait—it must be all the conversations about the weather.'

'Maybe it is the fact that my preferred chaperon has not been present.'

She did not tell him how she hung on every word from the others for word of him, and kept her gaze on every turn the carriage took for glimpses of him walking past. But now here he was, offering her his attention, and it made her...*happy*.

'Well, the Countess would say she is your chaperone now. Which is why we must make haste—before she gets wind of my plans to make up for lost time. We might need to stay away for a night or two, depending on the road, so pack a bag in case. Can you be ready in an hour's time?'

As she watched Owen leave, Ranya was certain she detected a skip in his step. She took less than an hour to bathe and put on the new dress she had chosen from a local shop herself. The Countess had said she should wear it with a corset—but it fitted Ranya spectacularly. With its flowing underlay of thick beige cotton and a sewn-on petticoat of rich blue, as well as its lace collar and billowy sleeves, it was both elegant and comfortable.

Although her pride had not decreased when it came to accepting things from Owen or the Countess, Ranya couldn't deny she loved this dress.

And maybe today was the day she'd start earning her keep. Or at least make progress on searching for her brother.

She and Owen would be alone. Visiting the docks where Muhammad might have come off a ship as a stowaway. It would be a perfect opportunity to tell Owen about him.

It was early enough in the morning that the Countess was probably still sleeping, but when she approached the carriage, she saw Owen was having a little battle of wills with Rogers.

'We're going all the way to Manchester. It would put you out of your way, I'm sure.'

'Not at all, sir. Let me inform Her Ladyship and I will be with you shortly.'

'Very well.' Owen shrugged, as if to say nothing could be done. But as soon as the fellow was out of earshot he called to another man, who seemed to be waiting for Owen's signal. 'Rogers will be gone for a long while, not wishing to disturb the Countess,' he explained to Ranya. 'I have left her a note, explaining that I've been pressed to attend a meeting at which your advice is required by the Malden Trading Board. Does that sound all right to you, Miss Radwan?'

When she nodded, he turned to the new driver, 'And you will not get in any trouble—I will see to it.'

'Much obliged, my lord.'

The coach they took was simple—not the fancy one she was used to taking with the Countess. Ranya had got better at climbing into them, but when Owen offered her his hand to help her up she took it. Just to test what it would feel like. Not a grazing touch, but a full hand-in-hand grasp.

She shouldn't have, though. The rush of emotions that hit her was almost too much to bear. All at once, she felt as if she'd fallen into a pit of fire and also waded into the Nile on a winter day.

She had barely caught her breath after sitting down when, expecting him to let go, she felt him squeeze her hand instead. She lifted her eyes to signal that he could release her, but he was preoccupied, staring at her cheek so intently that Ranya was sure there must be a spot of preserve left over from her rushed breakfast.

Finally, he did let go, and climbed into the carriage behind her, sitting opposite and saying nothing—lost, it would seem, in his own thoughts.

As the carriage began its trek, Ranya discreetly watched Owen, using the sides of her bonnet for cover. He wore blue trousers and a beige shirt beneath his coat. He was colour co-ordinated with her. She hadn't planned it, but it would be nice to stand by him, to present a united front in their meetings.

Perhaps sensing that she was watching, he flexed his forearm on the sill near the carriage window and, putting his head out to look up to the sky, squinted at the sun. Then, before she could look away, he caught her gaze and threw her one of the roguish smiles she'd missed over the last couple of weeks.

When he said, 'Beautiful. The day as well,' Ranya had to actually clamp her legs together to contain the flutter in her lower stomach.

What was happening to her?

He was the Earl of Warrington. And she was a woman on a mission. Find her brother. Free her father. Why were such simple priorities hard to keep straight when he was near?

Owen leaned forward and she caught a whiff of the cologne he had applied seemingly with the lightest of hands. That same mastic and orange blossom that was more suited to an Egyptian labourer than an English earl.

They watched each other for a few minutes—as if it were a contest. Ranya was too proud, too mesmerised to look away first, but then Owen mumbled, 'The Countess will be fuming by now. Going on to Rogers about how he should have stopped us leaving. Saying that we behave uncouthly. But I cannot be sorry for it, Ranya. To sit here with you, freely—it is everything.'

She blinked, and made herself very busy flicking an imaginary piece of dirt from beneath her fingernail. 'You embarrass me, my lord.'

'That is not my intention, forgive me.' His voice fell. 'Also, please call me Owen. Or Iskander. Either. Both. Just not by my title when there is no one around to hear the act of it. For it *is* an act. We are more to each other, Ranya.'

How much 'more' were they? Could they ever be? When he was supposed to soon be engaged to another and she to return home to her father?

Chapter Fourteen

Owen

'I have been working to take over the estate in a few months. The Countess bids me, "Check on the sheep farmer in the south of the estate. He says the animals are too promiscuous, not waiting for the right ram to impregnate them." Or, "Count the tithes from the collection boxes the vicar takes on Sundays against the taxes due from the tenants." It has all been quite time-consuming.'

'It is funny how you change your voice to mimic her.'

Ranya smiled, and Owen caught the flash of that left cheek dimple of hers. He wanted so much to keep it there.

'I will not assault your ears and tell you how the sheep affair went, but suffice it say it was singlehandedly the ghastliest experience of my almost twenty-five years in this world. And all that counting…and numbers.' He shook his head exaggeratedly. 'Your mathematical mind would have been welcome.'

Her laugh was finer than music—dizzying, almost. But it frightened him too. If he did something wrong, she'd be lost to him.

When Owen had asked Ranya to come to England, he'd hoped she'd be a distraction from having the Countess standing over him—and it was working. But to his chagrin the last weeks without the constant presence of Ranya had been infuriating. He'd been short with the sheep farmer... accidentally spilled hot tea on the estate's accountant. But after the moment they'd shared that night he walked her to the cottage he'd needed to put some distance between them and the unsettling feelings she was rousing in him.

'Do you like it?' she asked. 'Managing Warrington?'

He hesitated. 'The tenants I meet—they worry about the future. I can see that. I have not been present in their lives, and even my father was more occupied with Malden Trading then he was with Warrington. I believe that when he inherited it, he felt guilty. That it shouldn't be his.'

'I know the Countess had no right to it.'

He nodded. 'Such are British laws. My father tried his best to make amends, marrying her, letting her stay in the home she'd lived in all her life, for she would have been ousted otherwise. Most importantly, he permitted her power over the estate that she'd never had before. And it was my father's toil and Malden's profits that grew the estate. Made it more prosperous than it otherwise would have been.'

Ranya nodded. 'It is admirable, but you have not yet said that you *like* managing it. I can certainly relate to feeling that you must honour the burdens of your father and his pursuits.'

'I don't yet know. I can admit that some of the duties seem meaningless to me. Or at least that they can wait until after...' He didn't finish the sentence, but it hung between them.

Until after Ranya left.

Owen hated even to think about her going. He'd had women before. A few he'd known intimately—even enjoyed conversations with. But none had made him feel so time-bound or feel such despair as Ranya. It frightened Owen how often he thought of her. Of their conversations on the journey over, the books they'd shared.

Could he share with her now that it was her advice then that had prompted him to be more conscientious about the estate's upkeep? That the prospect of Ranya's approval had made him listen more to what the tenants at Warrington were saying? And Owen had found that he genuinely cared about them.

This was also why he was so excited to have her attend these meetings today. Everything she'd taught him about the cotton industry was at the forefront of his mind. Would it be enough to make him want to keep Malden Trading? Take its helm along with Warrington, and his seat in Parliament? Owen knew the Countess thought the sale of the company would handsomely fund the right choice, but he still wasn't sure it was what he wanted.

He had a feeling that Ranya would somehow help guide his choice. Indeed, no woman had made Owen feel as driven in body and mind and heart as she had. And, regardless of any impure thoughts he had about her, Ranya's effect on him, and on his future life choices, felt very pure. Being with her felt *right*.

But all this thought reminded him that they were on different paths. That the Percy Ball was creeping up on them…

'Did you know that there is a dimple that appears in your left cheek when you smile or laugh?' he said, finding he needed to change the subject, lighten the mood. 'I feel like a hero when it appears for me.'

He let his fingers hover near to where hers were clutched in her lap. Not breaking his gaze, he gently, slowly, unfurled her fingers while she watched.

He tapped his fingers there. 'Maybe you are ticklish?'

He imagined running his lips, his tongue, along the hills and valleys of her knuckles. Tasting her. His stomach clenched with imagining the other hills and valleys he'd explore on her body if she ever let him.

In a dream, maybe.

Ranya cleared her throat and looked down at her hands, then gently pulled them away. Tucked them under her knees.

'I am not ticklish. Not there.'

Then she smiled, very wide, and tilted her head to the right so her left cheek dimple was fully discernible.

Their first stop was for a tour of one of the mills that Owen's father had regularly sold cotton to. Owen had planned it because he knew they should be prepared before their meeting with the union, and was glad of it when he saw Ranya's excitement.

'I have read about these operations, but it will be good to witness them first-hand.'

When they'd disembarked from the carriage, Owen stretched to reach the notebook and pencil he'd brought for her.

'Yours. For notes or calculations. Though you probably use your mind for those,' he added, suddenly timorous.

He'd chosen the prettiest notebook in the shop yesterday, and had had a good time trying to guess which Ranya would love best. Like choosing the daffodils this morning instead of the daisies.

'I hoped you would like the celestial pattern. You seemed interested in the captain's sextant calculations on the yacht.'

'It is perfect.' She fingered the cover. 'But I have taken too much from you already.'

Owen would have given the world for her not to feel like

that, but he only said, 'Ranya, you are the cleverest person I have ever met, but those we meet today would easily dismiss a female with ideas. Having a prop is central to believability. Trust my theatrical experience on that!'

He took a ring from his inner pocket. A gaudy gold thing, with the Warrington crest—a raven perched atop a rowan—set within a topaz gem.

He slipped it on and showed her. 'See how I wear my earldom?'

He waved to a boy who looked as if he should be frolicking in fields, rather than taking a break from his mill duties. 'I am Lord Malden, Earl of Warrington, here to see the foreman.'

The boy led them around the huge, shapeless brick building with soot covered windows. They went inside and up a set of stairs. He rapped on the closed door of an office with a glass barrier that looked down on the floor.

'What?' yelled a voice from inside.

'Two people here to see you, sir. One an earl, sir,' the boy explained quickly, before rushing back to the mill floor.

Ranya watched his path, her eyes widening with what Owen could only describe as horror.

Usually, visits to the mill by members of the noble classes were planned, and workers told to be on their best behaviour with only the most basic machines operating. But this trip was impromptu—both to avoid the Countess's objections about him leaving Warrington in favour of Malden Trading, and to covertly bring Ranya with him.

'Apologies for the lack of a note, Mr Harris, and for this unexpected visit.'

Owen had taken the trouble to learn the name of the man at least. He'd impressed himself with how far he'd come since his first discussion with Ranya about the cotton trade at the Anglo-Egyptian Bank's opening. It was her influence, of course.

'Not at all, my lord. It is a pleasure to meet the heir of the old Earl, God rest his soul.'

The foreman was a gruff fellow, with a thick grey moustache and beard littered with crumbs from the oatcakes he had clearly been eating. He moved to bow, but Owen grabbed his hand and shook it before he could.

'My father always said you were one of his best customers.'

That wasn't entirely true—or at least not in any way Owen could recall. When he'd examined Malden Trading Company's ledgers, it had been the mill's proximity to the union meeting whilst being removed from the main hub of mills that had had him choosing it for a private tour with Ranya.

'May I present Miss Radwan? She is an advisor we have brought in from a cotton-producing city in Egypt.'

This time he couldn't stop the foreman's bow, and Ranya accepted it gracefully. She'd been paying attention to the Countess's tuition, but Owen twinged with sadness to see how stiffly she did so.

Was his bringing her to England pushing her into being someone she wasn't? Had his father experienced the same with his mother?

'To fulfil her duties Miss Radwan requires an understanding of how the cotton is produced at this end. How things work on the mill floor…the labour involved. That sort of thing. She needs a clearer picture before making her recommendations. Did I get all that right, Miss Radwan?'

'Yes.'

Ranya looked impressed with him, and Owen could barely contain his happiness at her approval.

'My pleasure to assist in any way I can,' Mr Harris said.

'Begging your pardon, but masks to cover your mouths and noses as you walk the floor are required…'

He offered them cloths, but while Owen took his, Ranya readjusted the veil beneath her bonnet to cover her mouth.

As they descended to the floor Mr Harris kept swiping at his beard, frowning as he pointed things out in a clearly embarrassed manner. But he did venture to say that the increase in demand was a way for some of the owners to try to punish the union leaders.

'That's deplorable,' Owen said. 'I wonder if it is possible that the trading companies could put pressure on the mill owners to scale back? Let the union have their say?'

The odour of dirt and sweat and general decay in the mill was nauseating. The din of the machines sounded like screeching geese being tortured, and the grimy muck they produced carpeted the floor. It was hard to see anything, considering how dimly lit the place was and how much fluff and dust there was in the stifled air, and Owen felt it twisting beneath his shoes.

They had to move slowly between the workers crowded on the lines. Workers who were mostly women and children. The boy who had ushered them inside seemed to be one of the older ones. The women were of all ages, a few were even pregnant. A good number were emaciated, their faces masks of depression, as if this were a prison camp rather than a place of industry.

He made out Irish brogues and a number of brown and Black people—Indians and Africans, Owen guessed. Slavery had been outlawed, and all workers would have wages, he was sure, but it was clear the conditions here were hurting the most marginalised in British society. None would be here if they did not need the wages to survive.

Ranya knew it too. She yelled questions to Mr Harris.

'What are the wages here?'

'Depends on experience and age.'

'The range, sir?'

'Between three to twelve shillings.'

'A day?'

'Begging your pardon, but I meant a week, miss.'

Then she asked, 'Why are they not wearing masks, Mr Harris?'

'They mention it inhibits their breathing during labour. Makes 'em hot and sweaty.'

Ranya took notes the whole time.

As if she is a reporter uncovering a scandal, Owen thought in admiration.

'May I speak to some of the workers?'

She pointed to a corner where a large machine was being operated by an older woman in a dirty apron. It looked as if it was spinning thread much too fast as two boys on all fours worked the pedals.

'I will stand there. If you could send people to talk to me in private it will allow them to be more open—without the Earl or their foreman listening. Only those who wish to need come, of course, but please assure them that everything they say will be in confidence and they should not fear any consequences. Tell them I am but a visiting woman whose people grow the cotton, and that I wish only to see how we can all work together to make its production easier...better for all.'

Mr Harris looked at Owen for approval, and although it was against his better judgement, Owen nodded. 'Tell them that I—Malden Trading—will make up any lost wages,' he added.

'Thank you,' Ranya said, before moving into position.

At least she was somewhere he could watch her. And watch her he did. For nearly an hour. People were hesitant at first, but those who came to her with frowning faces left her if not smiling then more at ease. She was empathetic, caring… Owen had experienced that himself—how much lighter he felt after confiding in her. How when he was at his most vulnerable, she could make him feel stronger. Filled with possibility. Hope.

It was foolish to allow himself to care about her so deeply. Ranya was leaving. She insisted on continuously making that clear. Yet Owen persisted in being hopeful that she would change her mind.

Why?

Even if she did, he couldn't fall in love with her…expose his heart to be broken as his father's had been, open himself again to the pain of abandonment. And what of the estate? His promises to the Countess? Even if he could convince her that Ranya could belong there, Ranya wouldn't agree.

Was that why he had brought her here today? To make her find something to care enough about in order for her to want to stay? To feel that she belonged here and was needed in order to make a difference in people's lives?

Owen was torn from his musing when Ranya started coughing. A racking sound, not as bad as his father's cough on his deathbed, but a reminder. In talking to the workers, she had lowered her mask.

He marched to her side. 'Enough. We need to go now.'

She pointed to the queue. 'There are more people who want to talk and I—' She couldn't finish the sentence through a fit of more coughing.

'I understand they have grievances, and that this is appalling, but I will not have you getting ill.' He waved to the foreman. 'Mr Harris, please offer our sincere apologies to those still waiting and assure them that Malden will cover their lost wages, nevertheless. I will direct my coach driver post-haste with the monies.'

While the foreman broke up the line of people Ranya hissed, refusing to budge. Owen had to tug on her arm and almost drag her outside into the fresh air.

He grabbed a flask of water from the carriage and insisted she drank. Then he sent the coach driver inside and told him to make sure to distribute the monies fairly amongst those the foreman had gathered.

When they were alone, and Ranya's cough had subsided, she turned on him.

'I was not finished.'

'You were dying in there.'

'It was a little cough.' Her eyes were wide as she paced around him. She was angry, nearly shouting at him. 'And they have to become accustomed to it…those poor people. What kind of barbaric society would allow such a thing?'

'It is deplorable—I utterly agree. But you wished for a tour.'

'*Tour?*' Ranya spat, and Owen felt her rage in the single word. 'Exactly the terminology of the wealthy and the privileged! How might what we just saw be described as a *tour*? A tour indicates leisure…vacation. The Countess's friends boast that they will "tour" the Paris shops for chocolates, and their daughters dream of continental bridal "tours".'

'Ranya, you speak as if I am to blame for the conditions.'

But even as Owen said it, he wondered if his own wilful life decisions—pursuing the theatre and avoiding his duties to Malden and to the Warrington estate—were part of the reason that these people were suffering. He had heard about the conditions in the mills but had never taken the time to bear witness to it. Now he had, he made a promise to himself that he would improve things.

'Because you *are*! Are you not a part of this "high and

proper" society?' she scolded, tugging at the material beneath her petticoat. 'This dress, and the hundreds like it, will be worn by the nobility once or twice and then discarded when a fashion changes. The Countess's friends… this way of life you all live…it disgusts me. And they call *us* barbaric? At least our labourers work in the fresh open air!'

Some of the words she'd slipped into were Arabic, and her voice was shaking with them. Owen hated to see her upset, and he agreed with all she was saying. At the same time, it was proving to him how different their worlds were. Maybe too much.

As much as he might try to make her *want* to stay with him, she was bent on leaving. And Owen couldn't get attached to a woman who would leave him ever again. He had to remember that.

'I will wait for you in the carriage, whenever you're ready to go,' he said, and then left her to her angry pacing.

Chapter Fifteen

Ranya

Even when she saw nothing of Iskander in him, Ranya liked Owen—truly. He was kind, only wielding his earldom when needed. But he was also self-absorbed, too willing to look the other way so he wouldn't have to see the injustices around him.

His father might not have been a cheat, but at the very least he had ignored her people by not supplying the deed when her father had requested it. Maybe Owen was more like him than he knew.

Was that what was behind her anger? Why she couldn't trust Owen? Or maybe it was guilt for her romantic feelings towards him?

She knew nothing could or should happen between them. It went against her upbringing, her very faith. If he were Iskander it might be all right—a pending marriage agreed to by her father. A passionate touch here, a sweet kiss there between two people engaged to spend their life together. But Owen? He was soon to marry according to his stepmother's choices. Take over an estate that Ranya was supposed to leave. Soon.

Perhaps she had been right not to tell him about Muhammad. It had been pressing on her during the two weeks when she hadn't seen him. Even Molly had made her feel guilty about it. Ranya could have sent him a note, but she hadn't, and maybe it was because she was afraid that an earl would not be willing to do all he could to find her brother.

It wasn't that she expected to be disappointed in Owen on the matter, but she realised that, were she to tell Owen about looking for Muhammad, it would mean she trusted him. And if she trusted him on that, then she was in danger of losing her resolve over fighting her romantic feelings towards him too.

She'd asked the people in the mill about him, but no one had heard of a Muhammad Radwan. Initially she'd been excited to see people of colour there, thinking he might have passed through. Had he been a stowaway, Muhammed would have needed wages. Although people in Damanhour might say differently, the brother she knew would never have spent their money. He would have worked to earn his keep.

As she was trying to do.

The Warrington carriage driver humming a tune brought her back from her pacing. Made her see that Owen was still watching her. There was concern in his very handsome face, but it was hard not to see how young he was too. He would be twenty-five soon, but he hadn't experienced hardship—not in any way that was related to poverty and suffering.

Still, when he held out his hand she felt the physical draw of him undeniably.

She cared for him. Liked him very much.

Yes. She would tell him about Muhammad. Was running out of time to do so. She needed his help. For her brother. For her own sanity.

They didn't speak for quite a time as the carriage horses sauntered onwards. It turned out that the mill they'd been to was probably one of the better ones, because it was smaller and in a rural location. They'd had to take a winding road to get there, and there had been some open space around it—a few trees, grassy area.

To get to the harbour they needed to move along the more industrial side of Manchester. Closely packed square buildings and concrete were everywhere. The carriage walls cushioned them, but the loud sounds of an industrial city pushed past them easily. Amidst the groans of iron machinery, market stall owners shouted their wares:

'Fresh pies!'

'Haberdashery for gentlemen's hats or those of their bastards!'

'Lilac and lemon verbena perfume for ladies!'

Ranya finally met Owen's gaze. She would have apologised, but he spoke first.

'I wanted you to look on the process from the inside so you could make your argument. And then, when I saw you suffering, I thought it was doing you harm.'

'I am not so soft as you.'

'You are a pasha's daughter.'

He said it so quickly that it pleased her. She couldn't help but start laughing. Her laughter became nearly hysterical, but then, rather than crying, she spilled her next words in a torrent.

'My father was an *eumda*—like a mayor who serves the city's interests. He listened to people's problems, interceded in their conflicts. And he employed as many as he could. During harvest we picked alongside others. I never would have left Damanhour if my brother hadn't gone missing. The villagers thought Muhammad had run to England to escape. The things they said about him were so ugly and—I don't know… I knew I needed to find him and confront him. To see who was deserving of my anger. Him or them.' She shook her head. 'I wanted to blame your father—or you. Anyone but those I grew up with. Anyone but my brother.'

When her tirade was over, Ranya buried her head in her hands, spent. It was the culmination of her thoughts while she paced, the desperation of her realisation that she had to trust Owen because time was passing. And that she would have to deal with the consequences to their relationship afterwards.

When he laid his hand over her knee, she experienced that same anchoring presence she'd felt when he'd stood at her back on the yacht. With her at the supper party with the Parkers.

'Your brother is here in England?' he asked.

'I think so. I haven't found him yet.'

'We must expand the search.'

We. The manner in which the single syllable pierced her heart and broke down her defences was astounding. Yet, as much as he might wish to help her, could he appreciate what it had taken for her to tell him the truth about Muhammad?

Owen could choose his battles. Hide behind the masks he wore at any given time. He could be Iskander in a *galabya* on a harbour with a group of labourers, or the Earl of Warrington wearing a signet ring, gaining entry into a mill and being treated like a noble.

But Ranya? She had failed at pretending to be anyone else but herself. She was a downtrodden Egyptian woman with a mind for numbers, yes, but she could not employ it in any meaningful manner.

'Thank you for today's visit, Owen,' she said. 'It was the

first time I have felt useful. As if I could hope to make a difference to people's lives.'

'I am glad for it—but also sorry that you are feeling this only today. Every day since that party at the Anglo-Egyptian Bank your lessons have had an impact on me, Ranya. Even in your absence.'

His smile was so sincere that she could detect none of its typical mischievousness.

They descended the carriage just in front of a complex of mills. It was wide—at least thirty times larger than Mr Harris's mill.

'Dicksons,' Owen named it. 'I have never been inside, but think it must be the biggest.'

'It is.' Ranya had read about it. 'The largest in England—probably the world. They have nearly one hundred thousand spinning mule machines in operation.'

Owen whistled. 'Impressive—although it cannot be good for Manchester's residents.'

Indeed, dark clouds of smoke hovered over the area. Ranya felt her chest congest, but she supressed her cough. She didn't want to worry Owen further.

'Fortunately our meeting is in there.' He pointed to a building in the distance. 'A warehouse office by the Bridgewater Canal.'

They had to walk along the canal and go over a footbridge made only for pedestrians. They made a small game of it, with Owen balancing on the edge of it like a tightrope walker. They were still laughing together when they heard their names being called.

Rushing towards them was Jarvis Larder, whom they had not seen since Owen had made him leave after his drunken intrusion in France. Ranya caught the twitch in Owen's jaw as the other man extended his hand. And he stepped protectively in front of her before shaking it.

'I am surprised to see you here, Larder,' Owen said, even as he steered Ranya around so that they might continue their route.

'I am a notary, my lord. My interests are wide.'

'But not in cotton, surely? The mills?'

Larder spoke tersely. 'As a matter of fact, I have a client with a vested interest in the trade.'

'Hmm…' Owen murmured.

Larder peeked at Ranya, and tipped his top hat to her. 'Miss Radwan… I trust your time in our beautiful England has been enjoyable?'

She nodded, but said nothing.

Unperturbed, Larder continued, 'You are the talk of the ton, according to my spies. They say the Earl of Warrington will announce his wife soon after the Percy Ball.'

'Perhaps they should tell me who she is as well,' Owen remarked, and then, he stopped abruptly, waving Larder ahead.

Ranya understood that his cold treatment of the man was indignation on her behalf, but although seeing Larder brought back a bad memory, it was one she'd all but forgotten—or at least had replaced in her mind with the first time Owen's lips had grazed hers.

Besides which, she would have liked to hear Owen's thoughts around this wife he was supposed to announce. In Egypt, he'd told her he wanted to decide on his own life path before his twenty-fifth birthday, but would he give in to the Countess's choice on this? Would he end up marrying Miss Charlotte Parker?

Ranya pushed away her jealousy as they walked up the steps to the door, where a gathering crowd of men in top hats and polished shoes were being allowed to pass. Owen waited until he was sure Larder was inside before turning to her.

'I'm sorry, Ranya, that you have to see Larder here. If I had known…'

'It is not a problem, Owen. Larder didn't hurt me. You were there. A noble chaperon.'

'You'll be at ease, then, having him in the same vicinity?'

'Yes.'

But it wasn't as easy for them to get in. There was a guard standing by the door.

'Sorry, sir.' He stood in Owen's path. Looked pointedly at her. 'I'm afraid that this is a meeting of gentlemen. No women are permitted.'

'Miss Radwan is an advisor employed by the Malden Trading Company.'

'No matter, sir. This is a closed-door gathering of mill-owners and trading company personages. I am under strict orders. However, the lady may attend the open meeting later, with the union.' He took out his pocket watch and showed it to them. 'That one starts in an hour.'

At the top of the steps, the vantage was giving Ranya a view of the canal's expanse, the large ships at the docks and the labourers working on them.

'I don't mind waiting,' she said, stepping away from the guard.

Owen followed. 'We'll go back to the carriage…take a tour of the city. A picnic, perhaps, until then?'

He kept on looking back at the door.

'What is it?' she asked.

'I do not understand how Larder got in. Or on whose behalf he has come.'

'Go in and find out.'

'You cannot stay here alone.'

'I will go to the docks…talk to the workers there.'

'By yourself?'

She felt she had to. Maybe someone here knew something about her brother. Maybe Muhammad had come through.

'I will pretend to be a reporter—a working-class woman who does not need a chaperon.' She waved the notebook Owen had gifted her. 'They may provide another view of the cotton trade. Help in my consulting enterprise.'

He leaned in close and an older gentleman tutted as he passed them.

'I am anxious about going in without you,' Owen whispered. 'It is as if they speak a foreign language.'

'Maybe Larder can help,' she teased.

He wagged a playful finger. 'Promise to be careful. I will come and collect you myself.'

When Ranya reached the edge of the footbridge she looked back and saw he was still there, waiting to see if she'd crossed. Only when she waved to him did he turn back and go into the meeting.

She wasn't sure where to start. The docks weren't very busy and there seemed to be a lull amongst the labourers, most of them sitting around eating lunch or talking in groups. She went up to the quietest ones and disclosed that she was looking for her brother, a man by the name of Muhammad Radwan.

'From Pakistan?' one asked.

'Egypt.'

He shook his head and went back to eating his food.

But the man next to him pointed to a wagon. 'There's a Muhammad who loads.'

Ranya's heart raced as she moved to the wagon, saw the figure there, hunched over a barrel. She told herself not to hope. What were the mathematical odds that she would find him?

Getting here from Egypt would have been intimidating. If he'd crossed the sea as a stowaway, the trading ship would have slowed in Liverpool and then come through this canal as a gateway to the rest of England. Muhammad hadn't had time to learn English, nor had he known an earl to support his trip, as Owen had for Ranya. He might have stayed here…thought it safer.

It wasn't her brother, though, who turned around. His name *was* Muhammad, and he spoke Arabic, but he was an older man from Mali.

He stared at the notebook in her hand and Ranya explained that she was interviewing people to get a better picture of the cotton industry—and also looking for her brother.

'We think he left Egypt on a ship he must have sneaked onto.'

When she said it aloud, Ranya knew it must be the truth. She'd suspected it from that day when Owen had taken her to the Consulate to get travel papers, and the more she thought about it, the more she could see it happening.

Ranya was a planner—a deliberator. Muhammad was the opposite. He jumped into situations without thinking. Ranya knew now that Owen's father had not made that last trip to Egypt before he became ill, and thought that if her brother had got a negative response from a Malden Trading official, such as the one she'd witnessed Jarvis Larder treating the workers to, stowing away would absolutely be a thing Muhammad would do.

He'd said it himself before leaving—that he'd swim to England in order to buy back Damanhour's rights to their own cotton, as per the deed between their fathers that Owen had yet to find.

He didn't know how to swim, but he might have hidden on a ship.

Muhammad the Malian wore a turban on his head,

even though it wasn't as hot here as it would have been in Egypt—or Mali, she guessed. It was a way to hold on to one of his customs.

'The English take our gold and diamonds and we follow, thinking there is wealth to be had, but there is little of that. Write that down,' he said.

'Why come, then?'

'It is America that I want. Better pay…stable job. Greener, even—like back in Mali.'

'You would go farther still? Cross a whole ocean?' she asked, disbelieving. 'Do you not have a family at home?'

'I left my home so that they wouldn't have to—like all the other Africans spread around Manchester and Liverpool.'

He told Ranya that his circumstances were similar to those of the others he lived with, all of them in a single room that they rented, taking turns cooking and sleeping in the shifts they had on the docks or in the factories while they scrimped and saved their earnings.

'Three years I will save, and then I will give my earnings to my son, so he can work a piece of land at home.'

Ranya closed her notebook. She'd been taking furious notes, but that last comment reminded her too much of her father. If he could have, Baba would have done anything to trade places with Muhammad…with her.

'It sounds hard.'

The old man sighed. 'It is *marhala intiqalia*.'

A transitory time. Temporary.

Like her having to go back after three months. Three months that were nearly gone.

Muhammad the Malian told Ranya that she wasn't the first to ask about a Muhammad Radwan. He pointed out a boy as if he were a nefarious thing. 'He is nice enough, but you never know with these British men. I think his name is Tom.'

It must be Molly's beau!

Ranya thanked the man profusely, wished him and his family all the best. 'I will keep you and your family in my *duas*,' she said.

He nodded kindly. 'May Allah reward you for listening. I was happy to share my story.'

As for Tom, he sat all alone, eating a white bread and jam sandwich. He was tall and lanky in his overalls, but handsome in a hundreds of freckles sort of way. Ranya made a note to tease her friend about how she might spend her life trying to count them and always come up short.

Tom stood and shook her hand heartily when Ranya introduced herself. They talked for a while, with him earnestly eager to learn of Molly's news.

He blushed when he said he hoped to have enough saved to marry her soon. Or at least to secure a job that would bring him closer to her vicinity. He rushed away for a minute and told her to wait for him, then returned with a tin of sweets.

'Will you take them to Molly?' he said. 'She's like a burst of sunlight, my girl. None like her in the whole wide world. Every time I'm bone-tired, I picture her giggling and want to do a jig.'

'Molly has been a wonderful friend to me. You are a blessed man.'

'Don't I know it? Knew it when we was childr'n. She were the sweetest girl in plaits and knickerbockers…drove the schoolmistress bonkers. Seems I've loved her me whole life.'

Then Tom's face sobered. He said that ever since he'd got Molly's letter about Ranya's brother he'd been searching for news of anyone who matched the description.

'One of the older men who bunks in the same house as me says one of two things happens to stowaways. If there's a shortage of labourers, they'll be processed at the docks and put to work. Others who can't speak or have some other ailment are sent to debtors' prison, where they await a trial. They're left to wallow there or sent on to other colonies, depending. There would be records kept as to who went where.'

'Where can I check these records?' she asked.

'The Old Bailey in London. But an officer comes once a week. Checks on ships in the canal with landing records from Liverpool. Every ship has a manifest he goes over.' He cleared his throat before continuing. 'Begging your pardon, Miss Radwan. Some stowaways don't make it this far. Some die at sea and are tossed overboard when found. 'tis easier that way. No officials to answer to nor bodies to bury.'

She wouldn't believe it. Muhammad…dead at sea?

It couldn't be.

Her face must have betrayed her emotions for Tom awkwardly put a hand on her elbow, his sympathy triumphing over any lack of familiarity.

Ranya's mind raced, thinking of what she had to do. Search for records of Muhammad's arrival. Possible prisons. And… Well, Owen would have to help her with any graveyards.

As if thinking of him had summoned him, when Ranya looked up, he stood over her.

Chapter Sixteen

Owen

Something clenched in his jaw when he saw Ranya wasn't sitting at the docks, waiting for him to retrieve her, but was with another man, deep in conversation, a tin of sweets between them. The man had a soft expression on his face as he spoke to her. His hand was gripping her elbow.

Was it jealousy he felt?

The man looked much too young and poor to be competition for an earl, but Owen recalled how Ranya had opened up to him when he was Iskander, apparently also young and poor, in ways she had difficulty doing with him now.

The fellow rushed off when he saw him, mumbling a quick goodbye to Ranya. *Coward,* Owen thought.

'Who was that?' he asked her.

Ranya seemed disorientated, confused.

'The boy you were just now speaking to?' he repeated.

'I… I should not say.'

Owen had never been a curious man—his life had been built around the idea of letting people be, so long as they did the same for him. Minding his own business while they minded theirs. Not prying if people didn't want to talk. But now he forgot all that.

'Ranya, tell me. Did he upset you?'

'Tom? Yes.'

'He hurt you?'

She frowned. 'Not in the way you are thinking. He is a gentleman.'

Owen didn't correct her misuse of the word. He pointed to the tin. 'He gave you that?'

'Sweets for Molly.' She clapped a hand to her lips. 'I should not have said that.'

'You can tell me anything.'

'Tom is Molly's beau.'

He nearly laughed with relief, and the way the *something* in his jaw loosened was…enlightening.

Surely a man not in love with a woman would not have felt jealous.

He pushed away the inconvenient thought.

'Molly is afraid of losing her job.'

'She needn't worry on that. In fact, if she wishes, I could give him a position at Warrington as well.'

Ranya stood and smiled, scrutinising him. 'You are a good man, Your Lordship.'

'I want to be—for you.' He didn't know where the words came from. There was vulnerability in them, but also the truth.

They were interrupted by a blaring, trumpeting sound. The canal bridge was lifting on loud hinges as a ship slipped into its docking space. When it had passed, he said, 'The open meeting with the unions is about to begin. We should be going.'

He hoped it wouldn't be as utterly useless to her as the previous meeting had been for him. They walked together, but when they reached the stairs of the warehouse that was the meeting place Ranya stopped and pulled him away from the gathering crowd.

She took a deep breath before speaking. 'Molly wrote to Tom about looking for Muhammad…'

'Has he found him?'

'No. But… What do you know of records? The ships' manifests from the cotton containers? If he sneaked on board and was discovered en route to England without travel papers Tom said there would be records—a manifest submitted to the officers checking from London.'

Owen was sorry he'd have to tell her he had no clue. 'Larder would know,' he offered.

Although he wasn't eager to ask *him* anything. He'd been annoyed with him since Egypt, and even in the meeting with the owners the way he'd insinuated himself so eagerly, as though he were more than a notary, bothered Owen. He hadn't actually named anybody as his employer, but Owen couldn't shake the feeling that the other owners thought Larder was with Malden Trading.

There were actors who knew their starring roles and bit players who didn't. Larder was in the second camp. And that night in France had made him look very unsavoury one as well. But Owen would not hesitate to put aside his dislike of the man if it meant Ranya would be reunited with her brother.

'Will you arrange an interview with him after the union meeting?' she asked. 'Otherwise my only other option is to search the graveyards.'

'It cannot come to that.' He tried to sound reassuring, even as his chest constricted at the possibility of what she might suffer. 'I will, of course, speak to Larder.'

They made their way inside the warehouse. Before, it had been nearly empty, but now the guard who had prevented Ranya from entering the first meeting was nowhere to be seen and it was much more crowded. The meeting with the union representatives would be much more chaotic.

The foreman Harris had said the mill owners used tactics to spread discontent between the unions and their workers. Owen wondered if this was one too. He'd heard these meetings could get rowdy, dangerous…

He put a hand on the small of Ranya's back. 'Stay close to me.'

The pungent odour of sweaty bodies mingled with the soot that permeated the clothing of the mill workers. Only a few of the mill owners who had been present earlier remained, this time surrounded by burly fellows who, Owen guessed, were hired for bodily protection. Nevertheless, the union representatives, men wearing bright yellow ribbons on their lapels to distinguish them, seemed to have things in hand. They worked to direct people, telling them where to sit and keeping order.

There were two other women in the room. They had seen Ranya and were waving her over. One, Owen saw, was wearing a yellow ribbon on her collar. Maybe Ranya would be better off amidst other women. If matters got out of hand, surely they would be respected.

Ranya must have felt the same, because she pulled away. He would have liked to be nearer to her, but took the seat Larder had saved for him. The man still displayed no shame over his drunken behaviour in France and Owen's banishment of him. And, though he would rather disassociate from him, he needed to enlist Larder's aid in finding Muhammad Radwan.

Plus, this seat would give Owen a good view of Ranya.

She found his gaze over the heads of others, and smiled to show she was content in her place.

A bell rang and the meeting was brought to order by one Mr Tisdale. He was black-haired and grave-looking, wearing an Inverness cape despite the warm summer weather. Owen had heard the fellow's name earlier. The mill owners insisted he was a fair fellow, with a history of employment in the top levels of their companies. They trusted he would have their interests at heart. But Mr Tisdale was also well-liked by the union members as a mediator.

Owen empathised with Mr Tisdale's position; he knew what it was to be caught between two camps. But who would the mediator actually align with if taking sides became necessary?

'Dear union members, while I am mediator for the next hour, I do not welcome this role and am more comfortable with the title information gatherer. I will make introductions to the unions' case, and ensure that all will maintain decorum,' Mr Tisdale explained. 'We will also hear from the mill owners and their representatives.'

The owners around the table clapped genteelly, while those who came from the factories shifted, a few grunting loudly as others whistled.

'Even amidst the Civil War in the United States of America and the difficulty of garnering supplies from disparate parts of Her Majesty's imperial colonies across the globe, the mills have shown record profit...'

Next to him, a man held up a canvas showing painted charts and numbers that Owen—like most of the others—did not consider too closely. Ranya, on the other hand, leaned forward and strained to see them all. Owen watched as she scribbled in her notebook, her beautiful fingers wrapped tightly around the pencil. He imagined unfurling them, wrapping them between his own...

Owen rubbed his palms across his trousers to shake the thought from his mind. He was awed by her. Ranya was worried about her brother, looking for him, but at the same time she hadn't forgotten her mission to the trade. To the people of Damanhour.

'This means that, singularly, it is the workers who are

most to thank for these results. Yet the mill owners do not listen to them. Do not recognise them. They are not paid enough, and their long-term health after achieving such productivity is not prioritised. The turnover for mill workers is high when opportunities open for them elsewhere. Once the American War settles we expect many more will leave English shores. It is a sorry state indeed that our methods are so archaic when we have been at the forefront of innovation up until now. The system cannot sustain itself. Unless mill owners are willing to come to the table and redistribute profits to their workers, all will suffer—them included!'

Owen felt a rush of gratitude for Ranya. If it weren't for her he might not have attended, would never heard the arrogance of the mill owners' arguments. And when another man talked about the lower quality of cotton that had been found hidden in the bales because international growers had rushed the harvest and taken steps to meet demand, Owen thought of Ranya's idea to refine the cotton at its source.

He looked at her to see if she'd mention it now, but instead one of the women beside her stood.

'Women need a stronger voice—we need to be heard too if we are to speak about salary increases or the dangers posed to children in the factories! As mothers and wives, we have no one listening to our voices we and demand representation in the union.'

Mr Tisdale put up a hand and said, 'Thank you, Mrs Johnson. As you know, union management has agreed to listen to the women's committee headed by your esteemed self, and we shall meet with you in London on the morning of the twenty-seventh. There was no need for you to travel all this way. I am a man of my word.'

Mrs Johnson nodded and said no more. It was a polite

dismissal of that section of the room, so whatever Ranya might have said was lost.

Owen fumed at that. But, if she agreed, he would ensure that she was at that meeting with the women in London on the twenty-seventh…that Mr Tisdale heard her ideas.

It occurred to Owen that that was only three days before the Percy Ball. He would have to adjust their schedule until then. Maybe not return to Warrington at all. He'd practically run away with Ranya, and knew the Countess would be more vigilant in future. And then there was the matter of finding the deed he'd promised her. If it was still in existence.

Owen was sure it must be in Malden's London office or at the family residence near it. He had to find it, keep his promise to Ranya, even though he had always known it would be the thing to send her home.

The conversation at the meeting volleyed back and forth, with neither the union nor the owners committing to a solution, only agreeing a deadline for one. A deadline that, unless, he could somehow convince her to stay, would be past Ranya's departure.

A departure Owen found was increasingly worrying in its undeniability.

As the meeting was adjourned and the setting sun behind a poorly closed curtain caught the shimmering honey in her brown eyes, another undeniable fact dawned on Owen.

He was falling in love with Ranya Radwan.

After he'd spoken to Mr Tisdale, and the latter had confirmed that he would listen to Miss Radwan at the meeting for the women's representatives in London, Owen ushered Jarvis Larder towards Ranya. She stood near the exit in her primed stance—one he was starting to know.

Straight-backed, but angled proudly, as if she were a match ready to touch flint. One task done, primed for the next. He'd begun to read her like a book, and enjoyed predicting what was to come as he turned the pages of the cotton pasha's daughter.

'Miss Radwan and I have some enquiries around certain records and require your knowledge on them, Larder.'

'What kind of records?'

'Ships' manifests,' Ranya said. 'Any records kept on people who stowed away in ships coming from Egypt in the past year.'

She'd taken him by surprise with that. It was hard for Owen to pull his attention from Ranya, but he was glad he managed to just then, otherwise he wouldn't have noticed the quick change in Larder's face…how his put-on airs slipped.

He was hiding something.

Chapter Seventeen

Ranya

It was too late in the day to visit the records offices, according to Larder—or, Allah help her, the graveyards to look for markers—but Owen had planned on their staying overnight. That was why he'd asked her to pack a bag. As it turned out, it might be for longer than one night…

Owen had secured rooms for them in a nearby inn and sent the Warrington driver home with the carriage and a note to the Countess telling her that they would be taking the train into London, to attend another important meeting there.

'She would keep us both under lock and key were we to return home,' he explained, 'and object to you travelling without a suitable chaperone, even whilst the average person in the larger cities would not spare us a second glance. As you said yesterday, you appear as a working-class woman, and I have put away my Earl trappings.'

Ranya's mind was too preoccupied for her to engage in niceties with Jarvis Larder, so she had supper sent up to her room. The way Owen tolerated him for her sake alone, however, warmed her heart, since his dislike for him was obvious.

Before she turned in for the night, he told her privately that Larder's notary status would allow him quick access to official records.

Owen also told her to 'sleep reassured'. Ranya knew he meant that he would protect her from Larder intruding upon her in a drunken state.

And she slept well, for the most part. She woke with the birds chirping from the perch of a leafy tree outside her window. Rested, but still weary.

Her mother had used to say that Allah's blessings were there for the taking in the early morning, but Baba had found her next to him in bed one early morning dead. And here Ranya was in the early morning, about to look for her brother. Would she find him dead too?

Owen was waiting by the entrance to the inn with a flask of coffee and a scone, which he all but forced into her hands. 'I gleaned that you would not be amenable to a leisurely breakfast.'

He had woken early for her, and understood what she might be feeling.

'Thank you…for being here.'

'Nowhere I'd rather be. I would have gone with Larder, but I did not want to be absent when you awoke.' Owen shrugged sheepishly.

Ranya nodded, took a bite, and tried not to compare the floury clumps to the smooth and crispy layers of her mother's *fatayer*, dipped in honey. Failing, she bit back tears.

She shouldn't be thinking of her mother today of all days. Ranya wasn't superstitious, like some back in Damanhour, and wouldn't even know what omen might be attributed to remembering the dead when awaiting word on someone who might also be also gone, but she was having difficulty remembering that.

Owen was looking around discreetly. He must have

seen that they were alone, in a private corner of the inn, for he touched her cheek tenderly, then let his hand drop to her shoulder.

'Perhaps Larder will discover good news and we will not have to go to the cemeteries at all.'

But when Larder finally appeared he was shaking his head. 'A wasted effort, I'm afraid. I looked through the manifests for the last two years. No record of a Muhammad Radwan from Egypt at all. And one of my contacts has said it would be pointless to check at the Old Bailey in London—that they keep the same records here.'

Ranya didn't know what to think. 'Does that mean we shouldn't bother with the cemetery?'

'On the contrary, you will want to know for sure, I trust?' Larder asked. 'A manifest would not show people who died upon entry to the port, whilst if someone died once in Manchester there would be separate documents kept in the churches or graveyards…records of burial.'

'But the ships dock in Liverpool first,' Owen interjected, his voice gentle. 'Would the same process not happen there? Would we not need to go and see the graveyards there first?'

Larder shook his head. 'If people died en route, it would be easer to dump the bodies overboard and avoid any point of entry protocols. It is only once a ship passes into the canal that such things are documented.'

'Must you be so crass in front of a lady, Larder?' Owen reprimanded, his warm eyes on Ranya.

He must have seen her wince at the word 'dump'. Her heart squeezed. But she couldn't cry now—not before she knew for sure what had happened to Muhammad.

'Let us go, then, and begin to search the graveyards for my brother.' She hoped she sounded stronger than she felt.

'There is but one we need to bother with. Unless a stowaway is known and claimed by a particular church, people of all faiths are buried in one particular graveyard. I have asked for directions.' Larder looked at their bags. 'It's a short walk from here. Perhaps you can leave your bags at the inn and retrieve them afterwards? Unless you already have a carriage?'

'I sent the carriage back to Warrington, with a note for the Countess, but if Miss Radwan wishes we can obtain one now?'

'No, the walk shall be good for me.'

Ranya was reminded of funerals in Damanhour—how they involved walking to the burial site from the mosque. But here when the path narrowed it was with thorns and weeds, as if they were entering a forest.

'It is abhorrent that this pathway be so neglected,' Ranya complained.

'With none to visit, such things are often forgotten,' Larder commented.

Next to her, Owen bristled. 'Such things?' he said. 'Respect for the dead is not just a "thing".'

Ranya could have hugged him then. How had she underestimated him so? Seen his Iskander persona as something he took on or off at will? That young Egyptian man with a kind heart—he was there, inside Owen.

Ranya had argued with him yesterday, but though he was her employer on this trip he wasn't her enemy. He had brought her here. Done all she'd asked. She had treated him like an earl to abhor, not understanding that her own pride and shame at needing him stood in the way of her *seeing* him.

But walking towards a graveyard to look for her brother, who might be buried here, of all desolate places…that had a way of killing Ranya's ego. Breaking her heart.

Her knees were shaking by the time they reached the

gate. The sight of a family of finches, maroon-breasted and tweeting a song far too light for such a sombre place, dizzied her, so that she had to clutch at the wrought-iron with both hands and breathe heavily until she calmed herself.

Seeing this, Owen whispered to Larder, and the latter left to find the office of the sexton or a graveyard attendant. 'I will search the records there,' he told them.

When they were alone, Owen turned to her, sympathy in his eyes. 'I could follow Larder, so you can be alone, or I can stay with you—whatever you need.'

'Stay,' she blurted, before thinking better of it. She did need him.

Slowly, deliberately, Ranya walked up and down the rows while he trailed close behind.

'In Damanhour,' she said, 'it is not traditional for women to go to the graveyards, but my mother often visited loved ones who had passed. *Allah yerhamha.* She used to say that a graveyard is a place of reminder, that it prompts us to live and to make the most of our time.'

'She sounds like a wise woman. How did she die?'

Ranya hadn't talked about it since it had happened, and refused even to think much about it.

'Baba told us she'd had trouble catching her breath in the middle of the night, so he'd brought her lemon and honey water, waited until she fell back to sleep. When he woke, she was gone.'

'I am sorry, Ranya. Losing you mother so suddenly… the shock of it. For you. Your father and brother.'

Owen took her hand, intertwined their fingers. Once again, he was showing her how he cared. How he was there for her hurts.

Most of the names on the graves were marked in the stone in English, but a few had words painted on in languages she couldn't read. A few were in Arabic. On one, she read: *To Allah we belong and to Him we will return.*

She and Owen were meticulous in ensuring they checked each one. Ranya counted fifty-three gravestones, seven of which were labelled by the name Muhammad, but none was a Muhammad Radwan.

Larder was waving them over to a makeshift shed that was probably the most tended thing in the whole graveyard. He showed them to a table and explained, 'No sexton attending, but there is a record book full of names. The last burial here was three months ago. An American woman from the Carolinas. Nineteen years old. Pregnancy complications whilst crossing the Atlantic. Black. Unmarried. Female offspring stillborn. Grave number fifty-three.'

Larder iterated the details indifferently, as if the poor woman and her child were merely lines of ink on parchment.

Ranya bent and read the name. 'Susan Cheraw.' She felt an affinity for the girl, her age, who'd died alone. Unclaimed. In a foreign country.

'There is no Muhammad Radwan,' Larder said.

Owen moved to check the pages himself before nodding in confirmation.

Ranya should have felt relief, even *hope*, but there was none of that. Her brother's absence was like a wound that had stopped bleeding but was still open. Festering. Aching.

'We will keep looking for him and we will find him, I promise,' Owen said.

She nodded, too spent to speak.

Larder checked his pocket watch. 'I should be catching my train to London. I have a meeting later. Do visit me there. My practice is always open for the Earl of Warrington. And his friends, certainly, Miss Radwan.'

He bowed, before rushing off and leaving them alone.

'Strange he did not ask if we should need his assistance in London to continue the search…'

Owen spoke more to himself than anything else, but his expression alerted Ranya.

'Do we?'

Owen shook his head. 'No, but it is strange. It stands to reason that if Muhammad is not buried here, nor appearing on any manifest, maybe he found a way out of here undetected. He'd have fled to London. I have a house there, and know people we might speak to.' He rubbed the back of his neck. 'And it is high time to find the deed I promised you. It's not anywhere in Warrington, so it stands to reason that is in London.'

It had gone eerily quiet in the graveyard, the family of finches flown away. 'Get me out of here, please,' begged Ranya.

Owen took his duty seriously and they spent the day wandering. He mostly let her silently brood, once stopping to offer his handkerchief when the stream of silent tears turned into louder sniffles. Ranya had always hated to cry in front of anyone, but somehow it was getting easier to do it in front of Owen.

'I must be keeping you from your duties,' she said.

'Me? I have not ever been accused of putting in a full day's labour, my lady.' Owen feigned indignation.

She knew he was trying to lighten her mood and she appreciated the effort.

'Yet there you were, the first time I met you, dressed like one of the hardest working class in Egypt.'

'I suppose I do strive for my art—the grandeur of the theatre, my dear.'

He twisted and bowed with a flourish, and she had an uncontrollable urge to kiss his cheek.

She found herself surrendering to it.

The peck took him by surprise, but before it could turn into more she put a gloved hand over her mouth and bolted away.

They stopped for a meal at a small pub.

'Only leftover hash,' shouted a stout woman from the back kitchen, wiping her sweaty brow with the hem of a checked apron as she emerged to greet them.

'Give us some cool water with it and that'll suit,' Owen shouted back.

The place was empty and dark, being between meals, but he led Ranya to a corner table for extra privacy. Soon after, the woman from the kitchen set two plates before them, and brought a pitcher of water and two glasses.

The bustle outside and in the kitchen felt far away. When Ranya wasn't catching his eyes on her, Owen was catching hers on him. He swiped at his plate, barely eating his meal. Neither did she eat hers. The potatoes were gluey, the meat salty. But the water was refreshing, cool and earthy, as if it had just been drawn up from a well.

'It's good water. I'm glad you asked for it.'

Her rush of gratitude for Owen was so intense, Ranya's eyes welled up. She wanted to explain how much she appreciated his support all day, his quiet strength and decisiveness, but the words wouldn't come.

Again he offered her a handkerchief from his shirt pocket, and discreetly pushed away her plate while she blew her nose and tried not to feel embarrassed. It was good to cry, though. She felt lighter afterwards. As if she could at least move past the matter of her brother for a little while.

But Owen wouldn't let her. 'We'll find him.'

'If Muhammad made it to London, *how*? It is a big city. And what will I say if I do find him? My brother doesn't even know my mother died six months to the day after he left.'

'Only six months ago?' He traced the rim of his water glass for a moment before speaking again. 'Is that why you insist on getting back home within three months? Because your father is alone?'

She thought of confiding in him about Baba's imprisonment, but what difference would it make? Owen was going to search for the deed anyway. And maybe she needed to retain the little pride she had left. She was a cotton pasha's daughter, wasn't she?

'I simply do not wish to remain in England.'

'Is there nothing at all that might keep you here?'

He teasingly pointed to himself, moving his finger from his glass to trace the outline of his face. His very handsome face.

Ranya's stomach jumped with the urge to grab his finger, pull it towards her mouth and watch what would happen if she put it to her lips.

To quell it, or enflame it, she found herself leaning forward, so close she could hear his breath hitching.

'The birds are pretty.'

'Birds?'

'Did you not see those with the red breasts earlier?'

His gaze shifted to her chest when she said 'breasts', and though it was so dark Ranya swore his cheeks flushed.

'*Acanthis cabaret* is their Latin name. Their song's quick pace is distinctive amongst others in the finch family.' He shrugged. 'My father was an avid birdwatcher.'

'Tell me about him.'

Owen had a faraway look in his eyes, but then he smiled. 'He tried his best to be a good father, mostly by letting me be. We tiptoed around each other. I was hurt after my mother left, and maybe he felt guilty for it. He felt guilty about a lot of things, my father. Lived with lots of regrets.'

Ranya was pleased Owen was opening up her, but she knew he was holding back his hurt too, trying to remain stoic.

'When I used the name Iskander to Madame Hala…her face. I could not describe it then, Owen. But now I know more, it think it must be her feeling great regret too.'

He swallowed, watched as the pub door opened and a young man entered, calling to the woman who had served them to come and deal with a farmer trying to sell them a bushel of rotten cabbage. She cursed, then ran to follow him without a glance in their direction.

'Madame Hala left me. A five-year-old boy. Crying on the threshold of her house, begging her to come back. I have nightmares about it still, Ranya. And that blasted lullaby plays in my head. Her voice…humming a tune without words. I chase it, hoping it'll get louder, but it is like running with the wind, going nowhere.'

Ranya noticed his fists clench and unclench, so she covered them with her own palms. Owen shifted his hands to thread his fingers in hers, a sensation that left her breathless. Then he pulled them towards him slowly, gently. Easily. Held her hands to his chest.

'You pity me,' he said. 'But I am not so proud that I will not take whatever emotion you toss my way like a beggar.'

The words cut her to the core, but as much as she wanted to continue basking in whatever this was between her and Owen, Ranya felt a duty to Madame Hala.

'She named you Iskander. Maybe it was a call to you to come back to her. Find some kind of resolution.'

He tightened his hold on her hands, and she felt his pain as if were a part of her.

'My mother has a new husband. Another son. I have

watched them, and I know her family exists in spite of my own existence. It is as if to her I had never been born. Her kindness to you was out of her regret, perhaps, but...' He inhaled deeply. 'Let us not dwell on what happened between my parents. Let us think about the future. *You*, Ranya.'

He bent and tenderly kissed her fingertips. Ranya wasn't sure they had a future, but she knew that no matter what happened between them she'd have this memory. This tender moment after the heartache of looking for her brother in a foreign, neglected graveyard.

Ranya could shed her fears like a heavy coat worn too long, because she knew that Owen was behind her, holding out something lighter. More bearable.

If she would only step into it.

Chapter Eighteen

Owen

It was strange how light he felt after speaking to Ranya…
how unburdened. Ever since his father's funeral Owen had
avoided remembering that last conversation they'd had.
How his father had mumbled his regrets and his last advice through bouts of coughing.

*'Find your happiness. See your mother. Choose your
own life.'*

For so long Owen had been torn between being the
half-Egyptian boy so hurt by his mother's abandonment
and the man who would be Earl and manage both an estate and an enterprise. He had hidden behind costumes,
never understanding nor thinking too hard about which
part of him he identified with the most. Not even his father's death, nor seeing that his mother had her own life,
had pushed him enough to find out.

But for Ranya he wanted to—badly.

Maybe, he thought, *if I know myself, and am secure in
that knowledge, she will want to be by my side.*

'Ready for an adventure?' Owen asked Ranya when
they'd stepped off the train in London.

They had missed the last one out of Manchester the evening before and been forced to stay an extra night there. It wasn't that he minded keeping her away from Warrington, but he knew the Countess would be upset—and that nagged at his conscience. Certainly the inconvenience of protocol was one thing, but the more time Owen spent with Ranya, the less he cared and the more distanced he felt from Warrington. And that, he had to admit, was freeing.

'And a decent meal?' he added.

'That mash yesterday was not pleasant.' She laughed and her dimple appeared. 'But the conversation made up for it.'

It was as if someone was squeezing his heart and he felt doubt spike. He had never thought so deliberately about his choices. Or at least had never considered so many factors when he made them. He'd thought he knew where they were going when they got to London, but now his respect for her made him second-guess himself. Owen couldn't draw her into his secret games of pretend without her consent. Even if they *were* looking for her brother.

He knew London better than he knew the Warrington estate, and easily flagged down a cab amidst the bustle of others doing the same.

'Where to, sir?' the cab driver asked, and Owen handed him a fare he knew he couldn't make in two days of full labour.

'Trot eastwards and give us a minute to decide.'

Owen had to give Ranya the choice.

The sensation of taking her hands in his was a marvel. The clash between wanting to keep her safe and protected and wanting to undress her was nearly too much for his poor heart.

You've been with other women, he chided himself, in

the same way he had been doing since he met her. *Why should Ranya be any different?*

Whilst Owen had been able to use the past as a kind of armour for his heart before, he now understood that she had broken through his defences. Even though he knew the Percy Ball was upon them, and Ranya was set to leave soon after, he couldn't help but imagine what might happen if she chose to stay. How he might deal with the obstacles in their path. How, *if* she chose him, he would fight to choose her...

'Ranya, there's an area of London... If a lady were to be seen there it would ruin her reputation. But it's where those without proper documentation go. From all over the world. They work, live, are free there. I know you'll want to look there for your brother, but I can do it alone. Drop you off at my townhouse in London. See you safe there and then report back on what I find.'

Her smile dropped. She wriggled her hands out of his and folded them in her lap. 'And how do you know of this place?'

She was upset, but that meant she cared, so he almost felt happy as he told her, 'Englishmen go there looking for drinking. Debauchery. Women. Because of my interest in the theatre I have known of it since my schooldays. I discovered the underbelly of Middle Eastern life there. It helped me. It's where I learned to speak Arabic. Learned of Egyptian culture too. There, I am not the Earl of Warrington, but only a rake with an odd obsession.'

Owen fell back into his seat as she considered what he'd said. He watched the emotions flit over her face, thinking he should try to decipher them, but he ended up only admiring Ranya's beauty.

Finally, she answered. 'My reputation might matter in

Egypt, but here in London it does not matter so much. Although if I meet my brother there, he will not like it.'

'I will not let any harm come to you, but we will need to make sure that we aren't recognisable. There's a room I keep there, with a change of clothes for me. Were you to agree, you might need to let loose your Egyptian side...'

She grinned. 'You mean be myself?'

'If you weren't a cotton pasha's daughter.'

She hesitated. 'Is this the place where you become Iskander?'

He nodded.

After a moment of consideration Ranya spoke again. 'Then I want to see. I will agree to come.'

Owen gave the cab driver the exact location, and they rode the rest of the way in silence, with her staring out through the window at the passing sights. the sounds outside were loud, but not enough to quell the screaming in his head. He thought of making Ranya scream...with pleasure. Of all the ways he might seduce her.

It was always like this when he visited the East End. The basest part of him came out. The Countess, like much of society, would speak of the savage minds there, make it sound inferior, but he'd seen humanity in these streets. Happiness.

It wasn't strolls in buttoned-up clothing along tailored roads in parks under a parasol and cutting cold food with a knife and fork. It was dancing under the moon and eating with your fingers. Letting sweet drinks slop in your glass because your lips were otherwise occupied.

This was the only place in England where Owen truly felt the joy of life, and if that made him savage then so be it.

But could he share it with Ranya?

When the cab let them down in front of the three-storey building where he kept a small changing room, the driver touched his cap and eagerly proclaimed, 'I shall await you here, sir.'

Owen tipped him, to make sure he would, then led Ranya to the building's back door, away from the façade facing the street. They made their way through the sour, astringent stench of opium that filled the air. The people who lived in these rooms weren't particularly neighbourly, but today a couple were pawing each other in a dim corner at the top of the steps.

'Perhaps it would be better if you wait with the cab driver?' Owen suggested.

'I want to be with you,' she said, and he had to inhale deeply, so as to not dwell on what those words meant to him.

In front of his door on the second floor, he fumbled for the right key on his chain. Nervous, he ushered her inside.

'It isn't much. Little more than a cupboard.'

There was a mirror, a single chair and a rack of clothes. But there was a small window that let in some light. He pulled put the chair for her and, as she sat, her face twisted to one side, he set about changing, and messing up his hair to let the curls loose.

He was still shirtless when Ranya's voice—a whisper that filled the space—asked, 'How am I to ready myself?'

He stepped closer…until she had to look up at him. He knew how to make a woman want him, but he also knew he should be careful with Ranya. It wasn't only a physical yearning that, once satisfied, would pass. Even as he knew he would like to have her body he also knew he wanted more. Knew she deserved better. She was a pasha's daughter, had likely never been with a man at all and was only ever supposed be with the man who would become her husband.

She stood, taking the hand he offered, and they shifted

a few steps until they were standing before the mirror. She lifted her bonnet, but held it so that it wasn't off completely.

His hands dipped beneath it and hovered where clips held back her hair. 'May I?'

He met her gaze in the mirror. Discerned her slight nod before tugging. Like a waterfall set free, her hair tumbled, slowly at first, then all at once. It was coarse and knotted and wild—and so very perfect. It crackled against his chest like flint, and it was all he could do not to rub himself in it.

She readjusted the bonnet over it, covering only the top of her head.

'We'll have to loosen your collar,' he managed, slipping his fingers behind the curtain of her hair to the throat of her blouse. He felt her watching in the mirror, but focused on the hooks and eyes. It took all his strength not to tug them open. Her chest heaved beneath the material and her breath grew ragged, but he didn't dare comment on it.

The first hook.

The second.

Only on the third did he let his fingertip touch the skin beneath. Slipping and sliding, easing open her clothing.

He looked in the mirror, but Ranya's eyes were closed.

'You should not touch me like that.' It was chiding, rough. Indignant.

'Ask me to stop.'

She turned abruptly. He felt the loss of her hair against his chest for only a second before her hands replaced them.

'You touch me… I touch you,' she said.

'Fair…' he managed.

She was hesitant at first, but he kept his hands clenched into fists at his sides, letting her explore the terrain of him. Her fingertips grazed gently, trailing over his chest bone, spreading towards the ridges of his ribs, frustratingly circling up to his nipples. They were warming as they moved, and he couldn't steady his breathing.

It took all his might to stop himself from guiding her hands down to where he truly ached for her touch. He closed his eyes, tried to enjoy the sensation, relax into it, but when at some point her finger moved near his navel, he couldn't be a bystander any more.

'Ranya...'

Her name was a plea for more. He grabbed her shoulders, pulled her to him until she could feel his desire. The danger.

'We should not start something we can't finish.'

Owen would have kissed her then, if she'd let him. But when he looked into her eyes he saw fear. The same trepidation he'd witnessed that first day in Alexandria. After her dress had been stolen.

She had planned to seduce him when she'd believed his father had stolen from hers. Before she'd known what seduction entailed or who he was. Before he'd known who he was in her life.

When he did have her—when he lowered his lips to hers and kissed her—he wanted her to see there was a future with him. Wanted her to want him for the long haul as much as he wanted her. She would have nothing to be scared about.

It took all his might to cup her face gently, place a chaste kiss on the top of her head. 'We won't have much time to look for your brother if we get...carried away.'

Ranya smiled, grateful. Then teasing. 'Then at least put on a shirt!'

The main street was dank and littered with strays. When Ranya rushed a little ahead, a down-on-his-luck man begging for pennies grabbed the hem of her skirt and nearly caused her to trip on a broken bottle no one had bothered to claim. She leaned into Owen after that, clinging to his arm like the women in Alexandria along the corniche.

'There are shops here you likely won't find anywhere else in England,' he said as they stepped into the market-place.

He pointed out a shop with brightly dyed bejewelled Indian saris, waved to the owner of a barber shop for those with African hair. He told Ranya that the owner there had taught him how to manage his curls.

'I'm grateful to him, otherwise the Countess might still have me shaving my head like a sheep.'

They strode past a Turkish café, where groups of men—and the odd woman—sat upon rattan chairs and tables, smoking hookah pipes and playing backgammon.

Finally, they arrived at their destination. *Sikeena's Egypt Experience* read the painted plaque on the lower wall. It was a strange structure, with a door built high off the ground and an external winding staircase so narrow only one person could go up or down at any given time.

'Elevated lest the Thames rise too high, this is a building that cannot decide what it wants to be,' Owen said to Ranya as they walked up. 'During busy hours it can take quite a while to get in or out. There is a back door, they say, but none are pressed to find it. The relaxed pace is part of the experience.'

When they walked in, they were greeted with an expansiveness that belied the streets outside, and bare windows that let in as much light as a typical London day might allow.

'Mr Iskander! It has been too long!'

Sikeena herself had responded to the chimes above the door. The former belly dancer blew kisses to his left and right in her typically animated manner, and when she turned to Ranya to do the same Ranya actually kissed the woman's cheeks. Happy, perhaps, to see a fellow Egyptian woman.

Sikeena was a stout woman in her forties, who did not talk of her past, but Owen guessed that, like his mother, she must have been brought here by an Englishman. The difference was that she'd stayed.

'Can we have a private room? And two plates of your famous *koshary*?' he asked.

'What else?'

Sikeena shifted her head, so only he would see her knowing wink, but if she thought he wanted to enjoy a show by one of her belly dancers whilst in Ranya's company, she was wrong. In fact, Owen was starting to doubt he'd ever again enjoy a woman in any capacity if she wasn't Ranya.

'Actually, bring one of the boys you employ. Kamal, maybe? We're looking for someone who might have found his way from Egypt and I know your boys know everyone.'

'Come this way,' she said. 'But you must take off your shoes before using the private rooms.'

As they crouched to do it Ranya chuckled and remarked, 'That request is the mark of a true Egyptian home!'

Owen was painfully aware of how Ranya's laugh, as charming as it was in its unmeasured spontaneity, brought a lump to his throat. It was a joyous sound, yes, but he was afraid too. Of doing or saying something that would silence it...

The room they were given was one he'd been in numerous times, with oriental carpets and ornate cushioned floor seating in red velvet. *Fanoos* lanterns hung from sconces at each corner, and a trolley held a pitcher of *qamar el din*, the thick apricot drink that was Sikeena's speciality.

She served them each a glass before leaving them to settle into their cushions.

Ranya sighed after her first sip. 'My mother never used to add sugar—said the apricots were sweet enough—and others in Damanhour could not afford sugar. The British are spoiled.'

Owen gulped his own drink, barely registering the taste and hoping that, despite it not being alcoholic, it would give him some liquid courage.

'All I want is to spoil you, Ranya.'

Chapter Nineteen

Ranya

Her mind was jumbled, as if she were trying to count cotton plants on a misty morning without enough sleep the night before. Ranya couldn't see, couldn't tell what was a dream or real, nor what she knew or didn't about Owen the Earl or Iskander the labourer. Earlier, she'd lost her senses at his touch, and the physical ache of it was akin to the devil himself whispering in her ear.

Let go...enjoy it. Slip off your clothes so your nakedness can know his.

Ranya had had infatuations before—attractions to men she'd seen in the *souq* or at community gatherings in Damanhour. One of her friends had even told her that her brother planned to ask for her hand.

But now Baba had failed to get the attention of the Earl of Warrington, and Muhammad had disappeared with the people's savings, she was no longer considered a good match.

No proposal had ever come. But even if it had, Ranya was changed from that naïve girl who had hoped it would. She knew she had to depend on herself. Understood that men could not always be depended upon. She loved her father, but he had been mistaken in trusting that the Earl would answer him in a timely manner. And, whether her brother was or was not guilty of running away from Egypt with Damanhour's money, Muhammad had acted on impulse. He had been undependable.

But Owen had thus far been dependable. She still didn't have the deed in her hand, but he had promised her. She was starting to believe she could trust him—but was that foolish of her? Perhaps it was the matter of his touch that was clouding her mind.

Ranya wanted to believe she'd have stopped him before he'd taken her virginity, but she wasn't so sure it was true. She might very well have given herself to him willingly. Even begged him to take her.

Maybe *she* was the undependable one.

'Why?' she asked now.

'Why do I want to spoil you?' he repeated.

She nodded solemnly.

'I suppose,' he started, taking the question seriously, 'it would be easy to claim that you deserve to be spoiled because you are so committed to your family, your people. More than that, though, I want to thank you for your presence. For coming with me here. When we first met I was struggling with my life choices…my inner desires versus society's expectations. Now, more and more, I find myself learning, getting clarity.'

'You owe me nothing, Owen.'

'What if I want to owe you everything?'

'You have been kind. Too generous. I have little hope of ever repaying you.'

Ranya knew it was the wrong answer to his question—but whatever he was asking, whatever he was proposing, she wasn't ready for it.

Owen let out a ragged breath. He set down his empty

goblet and shifted on his cushion, crossing his legs as he faced her. She stared at his knees, noticed how strong they were, stretching his trousers. She wished to see them uncovered. Like his chest earlier.

She felt a flush rise from her stomach.

What kind of person is so fascinated by knees?

'No more spoiling, then? Is that what you want from me?'

She managed a quick bob of her head.

'Tell me about your family while we're waiting,' he urged. 'I want to know you better by knowing about them.'

The sentiment was nearly too much for her, but she started talking quickly to curb her reaction.

'My mother was the only daughter of an elderly couple who were poor but loving. They died before my brother Muhammad was born. My father, a member of a large family with high status, whose own father had been a pasha under Ottoman rule, saw my mother washing clothes on the banks of the Nile and fell in love with her. His family were against the marriage, so Baba took his inheritance and invested it in land. He built a house, and Damanhour flourished around it. When Baba's family fell on hard times they came to live with us, and they were treated well by my mother, dutiful despite how they'd insulted her. She had taken their abuse, and knew they did not approve of her marriage to their son, but she treated everyone well. Served them even though she was now richer.

'I hated it. Hated my paternal grandparents for their arrogance. They died when I was ten years old, but I still felt insulted on Mama's behalf and did not grieve for them. They liked my brother because he was a boy, an heir, but they saw me only as the daughter of a poor laundress.'

'How incredibly unjust.'

Ranya had never told tell her parents' story like that—

admitting her own feelings and her childhood bitterness over her grandparents. She even found herself slipping in and out of Arabic, so knew that Owen might not have understood it all, but he smiled, encouragingly, like he always did, and so she went on.

'My father was a good pasha. People liked him. But they never really feared him. Never truly deferred to his judgement unless it was to their benefit. Financial or otherwise. Like the deal with your father. It was good for them. That's why they let him take the lead. But Baba was weak...'

'My father wouldn't have taken advantage,' Owen said.

He should have sounded sure, but Ranya saw how his hands gripped his perfect knees, his fingers flexing, the nails clean and trimmed.

Not like Iskander the labourer's would be.

'He had good instincts. I always believed I'd inherited that trait from him.'

'All I mean to say is that I grew to understand that Mama and Baba's kindness was often taken advantage of. Our house was always full, and so many wanted things from them.'

'You could tell that at so young an age? Our house was often bustling, for the same reason, but as a boy I simply enjoyed the entertainment of frequent guests.'

'I only wished to entertain ours with mathematical problems,' Ranya countered. 'But none were interested. I would end up arguing with people who I thought were taking advantage of my parents. Anyone who came complaining about a problem—I would offer a solution to it. This often angered them—they seemed to want problems. Wanted to complain and wallow. My brother was the same as me, though in his own way. Always seeking solutions, I mean. But he acted on impulse, complicating things sometimes. I was more deliberate.'

'Yet you came here. With me. On impulse.'

He was almost shy, speaking of it, and she couldn't help but laugh.

'I could not refuse you.'

His face still had that infuriatingly charismatic smile, but there was something more behind his eyes. He leaned forward, ever so slowly, and she found herself doing the same.

'So...' he mumbled. 'The numbers added up...correctly?'

She murmured her agreement, felt the fog in her mind become more like a flood. The *qamar el din* glistened on his lips...lips that were moving towards hers, then veering off to her left cheek while his hands remained on his knees.

'The dimple,' he said, before kissing her there.

Her hands flew to his hair, on a mission of their own to readjust his head so he'd aim for her lips. Instead, he dipped to her jaw. Kept his own hands still tight on his knees.

Music suddenly spilled into the space. Someone had opened the door to their room. Owen's head turned towards it, as did hers. Was he as frustrated as she with the interruption?

A girl stood there, pretty, with long, straight black hair and alabaster skin. She was practically naked, her ample chest barely contained in a bejewelled brassiere, and her legs were covered in silk trousers belted with bronze beads. A belly dancer.

'Ahlan wa sahlan,' she chirped in a false accent.

She lifted her arms, jutted her hip and swayed to the music that filtered in.

'No—' Owen started to protest.

But Ranya countered, 'I would like to watch.'

When the dancer came close to them and winked, Ranya realised that she and Owen knew each other. Jealousy flooded her, as it had that first night in Warrington when Owen had sung with Charlotte. And when the girls at the luncheon parties had talked of him as being one of the season's most eligible catches.

This was worse. Maybe because the dancer had what the others did not: the ability to appeal to both sides of Owen.

Ranya judged her as she danced and decided that, while she knew how to move her body sensually, it was being done in a way that was merely a show for the men who watched. Sikeena might have taught her the movements, but the girl did not understand that real belly dancing— true *raqs balady*—was a celebration of the feminine form, rooted in the earth, in history, and in the struggles of a woman's body. Celebratory. Powerful.

As the girl danced, Owen kept his gaze averted. It wasn't bashfulness, but could it be shame? Was he embarrassed by his desires? By coming here? Ashamed to know this woman?

Ranya had a sudden strong urge to prove she was better than any of the other girls who might throw themselves at Owen.

'You may go now,' she told the dancer. 'Tell them to keep the music playing.'

As the girl rushed out, Ranya rose to close the door behind her, then waited till Owen had lifted his gaze and was looking at her.

'I told you before… I know authentic *raqs balady*.'

'Show me,' he said, which was exactly what she wanted to hear.

Ranya closed her eyes. Though she didn't have the right outfit, she pulled off her bonnet and tied its strings around her hips, then waited for the music to flow through her body. She touched one hand to her left breast and pressed the other into the curve between her waist and her right thigh. Then she swayed. Shook her hips. *Slow. Fast. Slow.*

She twirled until she was close to Owen. Turned so her back was to his front and dropped gracefully to the floor. She arched backwards until her hair was in his lap, and it was as if she was sipping raindrops caught in large palm tree leaves.

When she opened her eyes Owen's head was over hers and he was groaning her name. In one quick move he'd taken her waist and spun her around so they were facing one another, and then he was lowering her head to the cushions, edging her back until he was over her.

Then he kissed her. Softly at first…his lips nearly quivering.

'Iskander…' she called, and his kiss deepened. Wild, hard. 'Owen…' she tried, and his kiss sweetened, became tender. She couldn't decide which kissing style she liked better—only that she never wanted to be deprived from either.

And then his weight was pressing on top of her—heavy, but not nearly enough. His lips left hers and she nearly cried from want, but then his mouth roamed near her ear, his arm holding hers above her head to quell any protest. Her breath was coming hard and heavy and she knew this could not end well.

'You shouldn't have danced like that,' he chided.

She felt strong, empowered, even with him so clearly desperate for her, but she answered innocently, 'I only wanted to show you real Egyptian dancing.'

'To be the death of me.'

His breath and hers vied for air, but neither surrendered to the need. And as she clutched his hair and let her hands roam the muscles in his back, he nipped and explored with his lips and fingers.

At one point his hands pulled up her skirt, desperately seeking for bare flesh above her stockings. Ranya knew how high those went, so when Owen's fingers were cold on her upper thigh, she yelped with how good it felt. Not just on her skin, but inside her. At the sound she made, he pressed down, his need hard and obvious against her own.

'We need to stop.' His voice grated roughly. 'I am supposed to be your chaperon, remember?' It was as if he were trying to remind himself. 'And this isn't right.'

'Someone might come in,' she said, worried, even as she sank her palms to the lowest part of his back. She fumbled to pull his shirt from his trousers, slipping her fingers forward to the button underneath his navel.

'Oh, God... Ranya.'

His tongue was in her mouth and it was torture, felt like a punishment. The desperation... The sensuality of it... Leaving one hand there, she moved her other to the rough stubble of his jaw, gripping his chin so his mouth wouldn't leave hers.

She could feel his desperate restraint. Worse, she could feel her lack of it. She wanted him in a way that wasn't measured, couldn't be deliberated upon. Purely instinct. But as he finally beat his need for her and was able to pull away Ranya knew she had to let him.

This was wrong. Immoral. Not the way she'd been brought up to act. Physical relations outside of marriage were forbidden in her faith, and she'd come too close to succumbing.

'You could have had me,' she said as he stood over her to tuck his shirt back into his trousers.

Then he turned, and she could hear him taking deep breaths to quiet his need.

'I want you, Ranya Radwan. Body and heart. But I won't take one without the other.' He stepped away, moved towards the door to put some distance between them. 'Concern for your brother... your thoughts might be affected by that and I will not take advantage. When we find Muhammad, and all is settled with your family, then... Just know that I would have you completely, traditionally and in all ways. If your father approves. If you would have me.'

Traditionally? If her father approved?

What did he mean by that?

He was supposed to marry a lady that the Countess would choose for him. Have an heir for Warrington.

She was too afraid to ask for clarification.

Too afraid that she was wrong.

She'd been loose with her morals. Maybe he only spoke out of pity for her, a pasha's daughter, acting like a common belly dancer.

As Owen turned to open the door—had someone knocked?—Ranya gathered up her hair, pulled the bonnet from her hips to cover it. A boy brought in two trays heaped with *koshary*. The sight of the lentil rice dish with its mountain of crispy fried onions and accompanying garlic and tomato sauce was enough to pause the passion between them.

She and Owen ate their meal in silence, a little too hungrily.

As they were finishing, a young man entered the door Owen had—cleverly—left open.

'*Assalam alaykum.* I am Fathi.' He was barely a boy, but his accent was thick, fully Egyptian. He looked as if he had just come from there, his dark skin that golden shade that reminded her of home. Of Muhammad when he'd worked too long in the cotton fields.

He answered Ranya's questions—a barrage of them—in Arabic. She learned that he was sixteen years old, an orphan from Aswan, who'd been working as a riverboat boy when one of the English tourists there had said he wanted to employ him as a servant to his new wife.

Ranya could see he didn't want to say much more by the way he looked at Owen and said, 'Englishmen who say they appreciate our culture only want to steal something from us.' Fathi put his hands across his chest. 'Now I don't move until they pay me first.'

Owen, who'd pretended not to understand anything he'd said thus far, surprised Fathi by saying in Arabic, 'As you should.' He offered him a few extra coins.

The boy smiled sheepishly before taking them.

'Why work here rather than the docks?' Ranya asked. 'I was told that is where the most abundant jobs for foreigners are to be found?'

'It is a fixed wage there. In London city, you have the opportunity to do other things…make more money.' He flicked at the coins Owen had given him.

'My brother has been missing for a year,' Ranya told him. 'Muhammad Radwan. I suspect he climbed aboard a cargo ship in Alexandria. For some reason he did not go through the proper channels when it arrived at the mills in the north. We have checked the records there already.'

'Which company's ship do you suspect he jumped onto?' Fathi asked.

'The Malden Trading Company,' Ranya supplied.

When he heard the name Fathi opened his mouth, then closed it. As if he had wanted to say something but decided against it.

When he did speak, he addressed Ranya directly. 'Never heard of a Muhammad Radwan.'

Ranya exchanged a look with Owen. He gave her a quick nod—he'd seen it too.

He said, 'Is there someone else who might have? I suggested Sikeena send us Kamal.'

'Kamal? That fool barely knows his own feet from his hands!'

Fathi did some calculations in his head. Ranya recognised the look people had when they were good with numbers but didn't have much occasion to use the skill.

'Thirty-seven Egyptians gone through the docks in the past eighteen months,' he said. 'I know where each is…the choices they have made. We help each other. We don't always keep in touch, but they are like my brothers. A few have found girls to marry, and aim to get their papers that way, or they have got jobs or started studying. Quite a few have returned home. The clever ones, maybe.'

'If they are like your brothers, then I am like your sister!' Ranya cried, a swell of emotion catching her at the knees even in her sitting position. 'There is no evidence of my brother passing through the docks, but if he didn't manage to make it here, where is he? We searched the *graveyard*, for Allah's sake.'

Owen sat next to her, concern in his eyes, wrapping his arm around her shoulders at this display of her emotion. He was trying to support her, but in the company of an Egyptian man, even a young one, she felt strange accepting his comfort.

Something shifted in Fathi when he saw them. And in his look between them Ranya saw what her own brother's reaction might be if he were to see an Englishman comforting her. Their proximity bothered him.

Fathi stared at Owen when next he spoke, his voice dripping with accusation. 'The Malden Trading Company, you said? I heard there was an incident there a year ago. I don't know if it was your brother, but…'

'What incident?' Ranya demanded.

'A stowaway murdered for the money he carried.'

Ranya turned to Owen, shocked. Could it be true? She read indignation on his face, but doubt crept into her mind. What if he was lying? He was an actor. He played at being

Iskander…at being the Earl. What if he knew more than he was letting on?

'Ranya, why are you looking at me like that?' he asked.

She couldn't share the questions racing in her mind, so she looked away.

He spoke, and all his words were for her. 'I would never murder anyone. And my father most certainly wouldn't—I can assure you of that. What reason would he have for it? He was a rich man, and your brother had no money. He only wanted the deed. Like you.'

Ranya knew she must finally admit what she hadn't been able to before because of her family's shame. People thought he'd run away with their funds, but what if Muhammad had been murdered for them instead?

'No, he did not come just for the deed. He came to enact the agreement within it. Muhammad carried with him the money to buy back Damanhour's cotton rights.'

Chapter Twenty

Owen

Owen didn't want to think badly of his father. He had been an honest man. Of that he was almost certain. But the way Ranya had looked at him, as if she didn't trust him to know better, hurt. It brought out his deepest insecurities, made him feel like that little boy on the threshold of the cottage, crying as his mother left him.

She is looking for an excuse to leave.

Her lips were still swollen from his kisses, their yearning and hunger for one another not yet sated. Maybe that was why. They'd got too close, too soon. He hadn't asked for her hand in the proper way. The traditional way. The way Iskander would have proposed and then waited for a wedding night.

Ranya's body might want him, but her mind and beliefs were pushing him away...

After Fathi left, Owen insisted on them going too. It took quite a while to get out of Sikeena's, with all the guests coming up the exterior staircase, and they waited wordlessly until their turn to descend came. Once on the street below, they marched back to the room Owen rented.

The path that had been empty before was filled now with the evening crowd, wilder under cover of night.

Men pawed at Ranya, and he had to growl at a few, take her hand and pull her along. But there was no warmth in her letting him. She barely looked at him.

They weaved their way past a bawdy clown doing somersaults, and heard the whooping sounds made by those watching, then a woman selling cardamom-and-pistachio-scented pink Kashmiri tea as an accompaniment to freshly fried spinach *pakora*, and finally between two buildings, where there was a clandestine cock fight. The practice had been prohibited by the Cruelty to Animals Act of 1849, but the only thing those in attendance cared about was making sure they weren't caught.

'I need to catch my breath,' Ranya said.

Owen stopped. He hadn't realised how fast he'd been walking, almost dragging her along. He pointed to the cab he had employed earlier. It wasn't far away.

'Go and wait for me inside. I will be down in a few minutes. I don't want him to see me dressed like this.'

'We need to talk about what Fathi said first.' She rubbed her temples. 'Is it possible your father—?'

'No.'

'He refused to answer my father's letters. What if he did something to my brother because he didn't want to sell back the rights?'

'I said no. Nothing of what you're saying about my father is possible! Will we even find a deed in London? What if your father is wrong and it never existed?'

She fumed. 'You are the actor—perhaps you have been playing *me* all along.'

'Why would I bring you from Egypt in the first place? Help look for your brother yesterday? Feel helpless as you cried over him?' And then, because that last sounded too raw, he added, 'I asked for three months of your time. For what, Ranya? To let you dress up and attend tea parties.'

She stepped back, turned her gaze so she was looking past him. 'You told me you wanted to benefit from my expertise. My ideas about the cotton industry.'

His frustrations churned into regrets. He sighed, 'Yes, and you have been instrumental. I cannot imagine my life, my business, without your influence…'

But she heard none of it. She was rushing ahead to the cab. Owen watched to make sure she was safely inside the carriage, then left to change. As he slicked back his hair with pomade and changed into his gentleman's clothes he thought of the Countess, that conversation they'd had when he'd first arrived.

When he's told her about the deed Ranya sought she'd agreed to sponsor her but made Owen promise that if he found out anything he would come to her first. Put it before their lawyers.

When he'd accused her of sending Larder on her behalf, the Countess hadn't hidden her desire to sell Malden Trading. But what if it wasn't just about getting funds for Warrington? What if she feared a potential scandal? An enquiry? Even if his father was proved innocent of any involvement in a man's murder it would lower the stock of the business, maybe even render it unsaleable.

He had to talk to the Countess. Demand she tell him what she knew. But it was too late to go back to Warrington now.

Owen locked the door of his room and rushed down to the carriage, desperately, irrationally thinking that Ranya might have disappeared. He heaved a sigh of relief when he saw her there.

Leaning on a nearby lamppost, the cab driver winked,

and wondered aloud if Owen needed a moment to 'smooth over' his tiff with the lady.

Owen ignored him, for he had a father to prove innocent of murder.

He gave the driver the address of their London townhouse. It was late, and the servants wouldn't be ready for them—they liked advance warning—but it was the place where his father kept his safe. Owen had intended to go there, search for Ranya's deed. But now he feared what else he might find.

As the horses clopped on and the carriage swayed, he stared at Ranya, grateful that the streets were dark.

'I will find out what happened to your brother. Prove to you that my father had nothing to do with it. That Malden Trading had nothing to do with it.'

'There are less than two weeks before I must sail.'

He hadn't been expecting her to remind him of the time they had left, the schedule she had not amended. He steeled himself, gripped the cab's bench until he felt wood shavings piercing beneath his fingernails.

'You would leave still? After everything that is happening between us.'

'Yes,' she practically spat. 'I have told you repeatedly: nothing will stop me from going home.'

Nothing.

He was nothing. His kisses were nothing. The way her body arched to his was nothing. The emotions he'd shared with her were nothing. His care and admiration of her was nothing. His love for her was nothing.

He'd been such a fool.

Owen fully expected to struggle to find any servants to set up their rooms in the townhouse, but the lamps in the windows were lit and when the butler answered the door the Countess herself was close behind.

His stepmother's scorn was apparent as she took in Ranya's appearance. In the light, Owen could see it too. How swollen her lips were from his kisses, the hair he'd tangled, the hooks and eyes on her blouse that she hadn't fastened well enough.

'Leave us,' she told the butler. 'Send tea and sandwiches to the drawing room at half-past nine.'

'Yes, my lady.'

When he was gone, she pointed to the drawing room. Owen moved to follow but Ranya refused to budge.

'I need to be alone. Please.'

The Countess huffed, then hissed, 'You need to answer for your wanton behaviour, young lady! It might be acceptable where you're from, but here we have rules. Civility!'

Owen positioned himself between them. Turned to the Countess. 'Enough.'

'Really, Owen? You at least should know better. Is this how I have brought you up? To run away from the house like a common criminal? To be seen alone with her by people in the village. Such callous irresponsibility!' The Countess stamped around them, forced herself to lower her voice. 'I had to rush here…pretend we'd planned to come. A little early for the Percy Ball…time to get a few waltz lessons and a properly fitted corset for Miss Radwan. Drivel—all of it!'

'It was my fault entirely. Your issue is with me,' Owen said.

'And you would be happy with ruining her reputation?' The Countess spoke of Ranya as if she was not in the room.

'I care not for my reputation in England,' Ranya answered, 'since I will not long be here.'

Ire rather than relief coloured the Countess's face. 'You

speak out of turn, girl,' she scoffed. 'And I am tired of it! Have a care for your sponsor, at least, who has so generously put you up in her home. Provided food and shelter and dresses to ensure you will uphold that reputation.' She scoffed.

'Please, Mama...'

Owen only ever used the word as a stiff endearment, a reprimand, but he could not tell if the Countess was upset by it because it was Ranya's reaction that felt like a punch. Her look of disgust. As if she were questioning why he should call another woman by his true mother's title.

He looked away from her before stressing, 'Miss Radwan is a guest of mine. And she is employed by Malden Trading. She has a women's committee meeting tomorrow in that capacity—'

'She has an appointment with the finest dance tutor in England tomorrow—you will not embarrass me, Miss Radwan! And you will not let her, Owen!'

This was getting ugly, out of control. He walked the length of the hall, called to one of the staff who might be a buffer for his stepmother's wrath. 'Can someone kindly take Miss Radwan to her room?'

'Get one of the maids to draw her a bath. Make sure she scrubs away the filth of her...*travels*,' the Countess said brusquely when one of the servants appeared.

Ranya gripped the banister hard as she followed the young woman up the stairs. She did not turn around once nor even bid them a good night over her shoulder.

It was something the Countess couldn't wait to comment on when they were alone. 'Ungrateful wench.'

Owen stared at her, his head still blaring with Fathi's accusation and the concerns he had about the Countess knowing more than she was letting on.

Unsure how to ask her in a way that wouldn't further

rile her, he moved down the corridor to the office his father had kept when he was in London, only to find it locked.

He had to call the butler for the keys, and the man gave the Countess a look before fetching them, as if he were asking her permission to do so.

This was Charles Malden's house. It had belonged to Owen's father, separately from Warrington. And now it was Owen's. The butler might be new, but he should know who was paying his salary.

As the fellow opened the door, Owen asked 'Where is Mrs Horton?'

She had been the housekeeper here. Managed the house when his father had been alive.

'She retired, my lord. Lives with her sister in Cardiff now.'

'I had no word of this.'

The Countess put a hand on Owen's arm. 'I arranged it.'

'But this is not Warrington.' Owen could barely contain the frustration in his voice. He twisted his shoulder to extricate himself from her grasp. 'I will be taking the key. Thank you.'

'Yes, my lord.'

This time the butler didn't look at the Countess as he dropped the key in Owen's open palm.

He hadn't been here since his father's death, but the office looked undisturbed. *Good.* The furniture was covered in sheets, and the darkness of the room practically gothic. He grabbed a few lanterns, and because the room was small they lit it up well. A few paintings—all landscapes, no former Earls. It would be easy to search it, were he alone. But, despite the dust and dankness of the cloistered room, the Countess had followed him inside.

He sank into the Chesterfield, the cloud of dust raised bringing on a cough.

'You cannot be in here until it is given a good cleaning,' his stepmother said. 'Clearly things have fallen off without Mrs Horton.'

Funny how she made it sound as if that was *his* fault.

'The house is small,' he told her. 'There are only a few rooms upstairs and, as you might appreciate, I must think about Miss Radwan's reputation. I will keep my distance, since the staff are servants I do not know and cannot trust not to gossip amongst our society friends. Particularly as London will be my home base if I take up the Warrington seat.'

'*If?*' the Countess rasped as she shut the door behind them. 'The Percy Ball is upon us. You know what is required of you—what you promised. Yet you've insisted on not making any decisions, avoided the season's activities. Placed that girl as a pathetic replacement.' She waved her finger in the air.

He rubbed his temples and scrubbed at his face. He needed to be alone, think, search this room. 'What would you have me do?' he asked.

'Choose.'

She marched behind his father's desk, took a slip of paper from one of the drawers. It was odd that the desk was the only piece of furniture that wasn't covered with a sheet.

Has she already checked the desk's false bottom drawer?

Why was she even here? The Countess had used to pester his father about this house, saying it was too far away from the parliament buildings, where the Earl of Warrington *should* have a residence, and often repeating the fact that this was a side of London that was neither hither nor thither. That she was embarrassed to have her friends call on her here. On occasion, the Countess would even rent a townhouse in a more prestigious area when she was in the city for an extended period.

'Choose,' she demanded again.

He must have looked confused because she pointed to the list she'd stuffed into his hand and sighed in frustration.

'Potential wives. I have numbered them by order of my preference. Miss Charlotte Parker, you will see, is at the top, but there are others that might appeal more to your physical tastes.'

He skimmed the names, but the script blurred. He focused on the desk. Not only was it not covered, it had been cleaned and dusted.

'You've been sitting there?' he wondered aloud.

'Just occupying myself while waiting for you.'

Her voice wavered, as if she had been caught in a lie.

'How did you know we would come here? I myself was not even sure.' He struggled to remember the message he had sent to Warrington and was sure it hadn't been detailed—especially after their day at the cemetery.

'I had a message from Jarvis Larder.'

'*You* sent Larder to Manchester? To the mill owners' meeting with the union?'

'You had not told me *you* were going,' she snapped. 'You were focused on the estate, which was as it should be. Then you went and ran off with Miss Radwan.'

She stifled a yawn—one that Owen, the stage actor, would have sworn was fake.

'It is late. You should rest,' he said.

'What will you do? At least go to the drawing room. Have some tea and sandwiches.'

He nodded. 'In a while, perhaps. I just need a moment to rest.'

What he needed was her gone, so he could search the office on his own. If he didn't find anything, then he would confront her, find out what she knew about Muhammad Radwan.

The Countess pointed to the list, still clutched in his hand. 'Study it. Prepare to waltz with each one at the Percy Ball. But have someone in mind to offer an informal proposal to by the night's end. Hopefully it will be Charlotte. I am made to believe that she will eagerly accept.'

'Very well,' he lied.

Owen could not imagine ever having a woman besides Ranya in his mind again.

With a last furtive glance towards the desk, the Countess left. He waited until her footsteps upon the stairs subsided and then shut himself inside the room to begin his search.

He went through every inch of the room first. It was easy enough—there wasn't much there. A small bookcase, the safe behind one of the paintings that used the same key as the room. Then Owen sat at the desk.

He heard his father's words like a ghost whispering in his ear. It was the lesson he'd imparted to him as a boy, when he'd first shown him how a false drawer worked.

'It is a successful life if you can go through it without any secrets, but if not there has to be a place to hide the things you don't want to keep near, even from yourself.'

Owen stooped. Of course everyone knew the desk had a false bottom, and the Countess might have checked that. It was empty. But it was under the loose floorboard beneath it where the *secret* secrets were kept.

And this space bulged with them.

Letters. In his father's hand. All of them for Owen's mother. Had they been sent to Egypt and returned or never sent? He couldn't tell.

He chose one at random.

Dearest Hala,
Iskander is ten now. He misses you still.
   As do I.

Owen stopped reading, set them aside. They were private.

But amongst them were letters from the Pasha. *Ranya's father*. These were open…read. In postmarked envelopes. They told his father that they needed to enact the clause in the deed. That he would pay the agreed amount to buy back Malden's interests in Damanhour cotton.

Owen pulled out money adding up to that amount. Bundles of it. All in Egyptian pounds.

And finally there was the official document, signed by both their fathers. The reason Ranya had come to England. The deed that would, were he to keep his promise, send her back home.

Chapter Twenty-One

Ranya

When she woke, Ranya had a hard time believing she had actually slept. It must have been the bath, hot water and clean towels. Or sheer exhaustion. After weeks of relative boredom in Warrington, going to Manchester and then coming to London in the span of a few days had taken a physical and mental toll.

The sounds and smells of breakfast wafted from downstairs. Fried eggs and toast. Coffee. The Countess ordering everyone about.

Ranya did not want to see Owen, or Iskander, or whoever he decided to be that day. Was he the good man who devoted himself to her, to helping her search for her brother? Or was he the man trying to cover up his murder?

It was the Countess herself who all but dragged her out of bed. 'There is much to do if you are to attend both the women's meeting and the dance instructor's lesson. Hurry, will you? It is near noon.'

'If you will permit me privacy,' Ranya said, fixing her gaze ahead. She added sourly, 'My lady.'

The Countess had something to add herself. 'You will

have no engagements with the Earl. Not until the Percy Ball. Is that understood?'

'Should you not be making that clear to *him*?'

'I merely wish to gauge if it disappoints you, Miss Radwan.'

'It does not.'

But Ranya found the words were a lie. She remembered the days without him at Warrington. How it had felt when he'd appeared at her cottage door with a tray and a proposition. How it had been in his arms yesterday. His kisses. How she'd wanted him with her entire being.

Before she'd found out he would rather protect his image of his father than face the truth that he might be wrong.

If Ranya had thought that after readying herself and having breakfast she would be free of the Countess, she was sorely mistaken. She had taken it upon herself to act chaperone for the entire day.

'I will convey you to your little meeting with the women's committee, and then ensure you go to your dance lesson. The next few days will also be occupied. You can rest assured I shall be taking my duties as your sponsor very seriously. Until the Percy Ball is over, all will progress as it should have done.'

Ranya wouldn't ask where Owen was, nor whether he had left her a note. But when she saw the cab driver from last night she knew he must have employed him. Left him for her disposal—or rather hers and the Countess's.

The driver bowed as if he couldn't believe his luck in driving a carriage for a countess. He barely acknowledged Ranya, and made no mention of the prior day or night and where he had taken them.

Were Owen there, she wouldn't have cared. He had made her feel wanted. Special. She didn't need anyone else to do so in his presence. She didn't feel lonely or like a foreigner when she was with him.

She might be angry with him for being stubborn about his father's role in her family's fight for Damanhour's rights, but she knew he wanted to find her brother. That he had been sincere in opening up to her about his feelings for his mother. None of that had been an act.

And he cared about her. Truly. He could have taken her—she had been swept up in the moment after her dancing—but he had been the one to stop them.

Because he respected her.

When she and the Countess were seated in the cab, and the horses were galloping at a steady pace, it was almost as if the Countess could hear the thoughts in Ranya's mind and wished to quell them.

'The Earl of Warrington does not take interest in many things. At least not for very long. I know him as only a mother can know a son. I also know the look of women who fall in love with him. Whatever pursuits you have here, it is best that you do not drag Owen into them, for when he loses interest, your heart will be broken. Your journey back to your own country will be a sad one. Best to enjoy your remaining time in England, take in London's sights. Have a pleasant story to tell, call it a season.'

Ranya swallowed back her tears. Owen must have spoken to the Countess, told her she was talking to people on the docks and looking for her brother. It felt like a betrayal. The woman was cruel and unfeeling about it, dismissing the most important aspect of her life and time in England as of temporary interest to the Earl of Warrington.

Ranya could not let either of them get to her. She was a proud woman and had to remember that. She drew her back and sat up straight to take in the sights of London. Not to take the Countess's advice, but as a distraction.

It was huge. She'd had a sense of it when they'd arrived yesterday, but in the morning light, and without Owen's physical presence to distract her, she could see it better now.

Boy in caps sold papers to men in suits, women strolled with parasols over head, uniformed officers under tall hats wove between traffic—carriages of all sorts, and bicycles. There were no donkeys and carts, like there were in Egypt, but London felt like Alexandria with its bustle. Here, there was no sea, but a river they trotted alongside called the Thames. And a large green manicured space called Hyde Park.

She knew from her reading and conversations with Mr March when she had been learning English that it was a park where thinkers with political ambitions and ideas would speak to gathered crowds. It was also the place that had housed the Crystal Palace for the Great Exhibition. Ranya had been only a girl in 1851, but she had a memory of her father and others across the Nile Delta gathering their finest samples of cotton for it. It was why she too had always carried pieces with her.

Her home.

It took them a little longer to pass through the square in front of some golden gates and a regal white building. A mansion? A castle? Ranya wasn't sure what to call it. It was apparently Buckingham Palace, because there were people demanding to see the Queen.

'Queen Victoria is at her summer residence,' someone shouted. 'Returns in September!'

How remarkable it was that people should be able to see their monarch—that she would see them too, and hear their complaints directly. The actual act of ruling would not necessarily happen in this square, but her subjects would feel they had access to her and were making their voices heard. It was incredible, and Ranya was sure the Egyptian government would benefit from realising such a thing.

There was discontent back home, and the people's interests were never at the centre of government policies. Even if she returned with the deed for Damanhour's cotton production, that didn't mean there weren't other towns and cities along the delta that the Egyptian government would exploit so that their profits were higher. It would be the people, the *falaheen*, who would suffer for it. There was no union to protect them. No queen to stand before and complain to.

Ranya would have voiced her opinions to Owen, were he here. She could even admit that she was sorry he was not.

Finally, the carriage came to a stop at the women's meeting house.

It was a two-storey building with a low gated fence and a large stone fountain where the birds could gather.

'I cannot be seen here,' the Countess said disdainfully. 'I will return in one hour. Look to the clock and make sure to come out then. You are not to leave that building before—understand?'

At least Ranya would get a reprieve from her company.

But it was a reprieve that, when she saw the ladies gathered in the meeting room, did not seem to her would be well-spent. Strange how the Countess should not deign to attend when everyone there looked as though they had come from her set.

The woman she had sat beside in the meeting at Manchester was welcoming people by a refreshment table.

'Mrs Johnson.' Ranya remembered her name.

'Ranya? I did not expect you to attend.'

She had been nice enough to her in Manchester, but here amongst the other London ladies she seemed to her more aloof.

Before Ranya could answer, the man who had mediated the meeting in Manchester approached.

'Miss Radwan is entirely expected,' said Mr Tisdale. 'She is come from Warrington. She is the Earl's Egyptian heiress.' He smiled at Ranya. 'His Lordship tells me you have a wealth of knowledge and fresh ideas from your father's cotton fields in the Delta.'

The Earl's Egyptian heiress.

He ushered Ranya forward, barely noticing the fuss he'd caused with the phrase, but she heard the gossip at her back.

'The Earl of Warrington is the talk of the ton, but he has been cloistered thus far this season.'

'He was more involved last year—dancing with many at the Percy Ball but choosing none.'

'His father was alive then. He has responsibilities now. And an estate that requires an heir.'

'While most think it a ploy, word is that the Countess has sponsored a pasha's daughter.'

'Why a ploy?'

'To deflect attention and then emphasise the big announcement she will make about Sir Henry Parker's daughter, Miss Charlotte.'

'Ah, but that would be a fine match…'

Ranya bristled with anger—but whether it was because they were talking about her as if she weren't there, or because they were talking about Owen with someone else, she wasn't sure.

She reminded herself that *he'd* ensured she was here. Ensured she would be listened to by Mr Tisdale. And, Allah help her, she wanted to do him proud.

'Perhaps we should get started, ladies?' Mrs Johnson threw her a sheepish look and smiled placidly at Mr Tisdale.

As the women settled into their seats and platters of

cucumber sandwiches were circulated some shared their ideas, which Mr Tisdale diligently recorded in his notebook. One suggested building a shelter for the families who'd come from Ireland, still reeling from the famine. And, though it was noted by Mrs Johnson that the famine had been over for a few years now, it was agreed that a collective home was a good idea. A different woman offered the idea that 'worker women' should take off a piece of their clothing—nothing indecent or improper, only symbolic—to get attention.

The woman giggled when Mr Tisdale asked, 'Whose attention?' perhaps, thinking it was a joke, but the man was clearly asking seriously. 'Do you mean at the protests?'

The woman didn't stop giggling as she said, 'Men never listen to us women unless we are undressed—begging your pardon, sir.'

Overall, theirs was a good cause. They were demanding rights for women workers. Nevertheless, Ranya got the feeling that this was only a passing phase with which the rich might occupy their time. Mr March had told her that the school in Alexandria had been started by such a committee. She wondered if these were the sort of women to dirty their hems in a mill and truly experience the workers' suffering, or volunteer many hours of their time to teach a child their letters?

Ranya didn't want to judge them, but in that moment she appreciated her mother—A woman who would have absolutely done both those things and given money to the cause as well.

Ranya had been too proud to see the work her mother had done with humility. But this journey had been humbling. She'd had to be at the mercy of Owen and the Countess. However, he'd been gracious, and she would repay him here and now, put herself on a more equal footing with him, by sharing her ideas as if they'd come from Malden Trading. And when it was done, and she had gone back home, Ranya would use the experience to be more like her mother—may Allah have mercy on her soul.

She stood. 'In Egypt, we grow the cotton and harvest it. The British companies who buy it demand we ship it raw to your factories. But I have recently come from a mill tour and seen the harm the process does to the workers. I wore a mask, and was there for only a short time, but the coughing fit it brought on—'

Mrs Johnson chimed in with her agreement. 'It is terrible.'

'Because we do not have such mills in Egypt,' Ranya continued, 'the cotton we keep for ourselves undergoes a more natural process. It is labour intensive…slower. Those who do it are women—many of whom would be willing to do it for others if they were paid well. That way the cotton would come to you clean, and ready to be sewn into garments of your choosing. A chance for the innovation you pride yourself on to find alternate, more humanitarian positions for your workers.'

Ranya looked around the room, met the gazes of each of the women without balking. She was a cotton pasha's daughter on a mission, no matter what they might say behind her back.

'I have come on behalf of Malden Trading with a simple proposition. Be willing to buy higher quality cotton at a higher price. Support other women.'

'Egyptian women?' one asked.

'Yes, women should all be supportive of each other. By helping Egyptian women, you help your own. We will give you good cotton and create better conditions for your mill-workers.'

'Am I to understand that your idea would be to convert parts of our factories? How?' Mr Tisdale wondered.

'The product would be made in England still, only the process would have been cut by one step. Eliminating the need for those terrible machines. The profit could be made by giving a higher price to the goods.'

'But why punish the consumer?' one of the woman asked, and Ranya thought that she looked a lot like the man who'd opposed her at the Anglo-Egyptian Bank opening party.

She'd been angry with Mr Gray then—had it been nearly three months ago already?—but now she answered calmly. 'The higher-quality cotton lasts longer, resists tearing, and doesn't reduce in size upon washing. It is more absorbent, and feels smoother on the skin. Consumers would pay less in the long run because there would be no need to replace their cotton clothing quite as often.'

'Is there such a difference in quality between the different processes?' Mr Tisdale asked.

From her travelling case, Ranya pulled the piece of cotton she'd brought from Egypt, a piece that had been processed in Damanhour, and samples of both the raw material that currently reached the mill and the finished product from her tour. She laid them out in a triangle.

'Will you leave these with me?' he asked. 'It will be a hard battle to convince businessmen to invest more for quality cotton, but I will know to contact Malden Trading should we require further clarification. If you see the Earl before I do, please inform him that the union is most grateful he has allowed us to meet you.'

Ranya's piece had been said.

She'd fulfilled her end of their bargain.

Now it was time for Owen to fulfil his. Give her the deed.

And, Allah help them all, find her brother.

Chapter Twenty-Two

Owen

Getting out of the house unseen by the Countess meant that Owen had had to sneak out earlier than usual and leave his bedroom door closed, as if he were still sleeping. In truth, he'd barely slept at all over the last few nights. He had been fretting over Fathi's accusations about Malden Trading, the amount of money he had found in Egyptian pounds, and the deed he had agreed to give Ranya months ago.

Owen needed answers, but he didn't want to get them with the Countess in listening proximity—and nor was he entirely confident that she would provide honest ones.

He'd heard news from the cab driver and the butler. Ranya had gone to the women's committee meeting and the dance lesson, and he guessed that in the next few days it would be the seamstress and the salons for the ladies' final preparations before the Percy Ball.

He was eager to hear about the meeting with the women and Mr Tisdale, but even if Owen could ask Ranya, he knew they wouldn't be alone. The Countess had been refusing to leave Ranya's side.

Maybe she was avoiding him too. The Countess stepmother had been elusive ever since he'd come back from Egypt. Or had she always been that way and he hadn't noticed? She'd hammered into him the fact that he needed to choose a wife, focus on ensuring the future of the estate, and all the while she'd been scheming. With Jarvis Larder.

Larder would have answers for Owen...

Even so, he'd avoid seeking him out until he could check the records at the Old Bailey himself.

He'd spoken to a man who had referred him to the copies of the manifests they would have from Manchester. He'd looked through all those, and some from London, even. Owen wasn't hoping to find a record of Muhammad Radwan's death, but he had to make sure Larder hadn't lied to him.

There had been nothing.

Now he had no choice but to talk to Larder. Get to the bottom of matters himself.

Owen made his way in the early morning to Larder's address, closer to the poverty-ridden Dorset Street than it was to the Old Bailey. It wasn't even an office, really, more like a terraced house with a plaque on the door—one that Owen might not have noticed if the carriage hadn't dropped him off at the perfect angle, so that its faded silver etching caught a ray of sunlight:

Jarvis Larder, Notary at Law

Owen knocked on the door once, then louder when he heard a child stamping about inside and Jarvis Larder, shouting, 'Take him to your ma's. It's working hours, woman.'

The child's screeches were muffled, then came the distant sound of another door slamming. A woman came from the back of the house. She was not much bigger than the child she dragged in her wake. Owen was too occupied in watching her to notice that Larder had now opened the front door and was watching him, watching her.

When he turned to him he smiled placidly, as if nothing were amiss. Owen remembered Larder in Egypt, wanting to join him in the season, to be his—what had he called it? Ah, yes. His 'first mate', so that he might secure himself a woman of some means.

'Your wife?' Owen asked.

'The whore mother of my bastard son.'

Larder spoke brazenly, as if it were not something he should be ashamed about. Indeed, he appeared to believe that even if he were to ask for the hand of a woman this season, having a child out of wedlock wouldn't necessarily be something to ruin his chances.

But Owen remembered how he'd dared to intrude on Ranya in his drunken state. Thank God he'd got there before he'd been able to do her any harm.

'I did not come to discuss personal matters,' Owen said, although he pitied any woman who chose to get involved with a man like Larder, 'only one related to Malden Trading.'

Larder's lips thinned. 'Where are my manners? Come in.'

When Owen stepped over the threshold he noted how the house needed an overhaul. The flooring was nubbed to the brick beneath, the walls more watermarks than paint, and the furniture sparse and unfashionable, as if it had been pilfered from a medieval fort. The place doubled as a home and an office, but it was clear that the former had taken on the bulk.

Larder picked up discarded clothing and forgotten trays as he led Owen down a narrow corridor into a sitting room.

'What happened to Muhammad Radwan?' Owen asked, wanting to get out as soon as possible.

Larder calmly took his seat on a Chesterfield...didn't invite Owen to join him. 'Has the Countess finally confessed?'

He said it with such a superior air that Owen suddenly understood. 'You are blackmailing her.'

'I thought *you* would be better, to be honest. More enamoured of your dear papa. But she was right—you don't care about your father's business.' He shrugged. 'Or at least you did not until the Egyptian wench came upon the scene.'

Owen would have defended Ranya's honour, but he needed answers first. 'What could you possibly blackmail us about? My father was upright. Honest.'

'Does an honest man cover up the death of a stowaway? One Muhammad Radwan who fell ill en route? No one found him till they were docked in Manchester. Some of the crew had seen him making a fuss in Alexandria, trying to get on board and saying something about a deal with your father in Damanhour. Then your father tells mine to put him on a boat in the dead of night, sail back through the canal and dump his body in the sea. No one any the wiser.'

'My father wouldn't do that!'

Larder laughed. Owen grabbed him by his collar, made him stand, pushed him against the wall while he tried to calm himself. The anger he felt towards him had been simmering since that night with Ranya.

'Touch me and I'll ruin you too,' Larder whispered.

Owen pushed him back, paced the room, his mind racing. He couldn't believe it. He had known his father, believed him a good man. But what if he'd been wrong? What would he tell Ranya about her brother?

If this were to come out, Owen would lose Malden Trading and he would also lose *her*.

He could see why the Countess had let herself be blackmailed. He was contemplating terrible things then too.

'What proof do you have of this?' he demanded. 'Your father is dead and—'

'You think him dead?'

'You told me he was—back in Egypt. The day before we sailed.'

Larder tilted his head, threw Owen a *poor dunce* look. 'I said he'd had an accident—and I lied about that too.'

'What? Why?'

'You thought *you* were such a good actor, with your peasant garb and curly hair.' Larder sniggered. 'But I had a fun time playing taskmaster, *Iskander*. And I think I did a good impression of being drunk that night in France. You *had* to intrude—selfish, wanting Ranya for yourself alone. Tell me, is the cotton pasha's daughter a good knocking?'

Owen punched him.

He'd never been so angry in his life and his fist seemed to act on its own, meeting with the fellow's jaw. Larder only chuckled as he pawed the spot.

'Guess I was owed that. You'll pay for it, though. Or the Countess will.'

Owen stepped back, pacing with the kind of frustration he didn't know where to place. On Larder? On the Countess and her concern for Warrington at any cost? Or on his own father for being so utterly deceptive?

Something struck Owen. 'Your father is alive, then?'

'Thriving, lives near the sea. Fit as a fiddle.'

Well, that was something.

'If he didn't blackmail us, why would you?'

'The Countess was eager to sell Malden Trading. I saw an opportunity.'

'I need to talk to him…find out what really happened.'

'I'm telling you now,' Larder insisted.

Owen's head pounded, 'My father was friends with the

Pasha. He wouldn't ignore his letters—cover up his son's death!'

Larder stared at Owen for a long minute before answering. 'He would if he was trying to make Malden Trading more successful. According to my father, yours was determined to make the company as rich as possible in order to allow you choice, your own path in life. Not be subject to the Countess's wishes.'

There was some truth in that, Owen knew.

Charles Malden had wanted his son to learn the business. He had never forced it upon him, but he'd wished it. But Owen had been idling his life away. Not taking anything seriously.

His father had wanted him to be happy.

'My father was not on that last trip,' he insisted. 'The consumption was setting in by then.'

'He might not have been on the docks in Egypt or in Manchester,' Larder countered. 'But news would have reached him. A stowaway turned into a dead body.'

'Why not declare him, then, and bury Muhammad at the graveyard we went to?'

'Come on—that should be obvious even to a fool like you! Because of the money carried. Who he was. Son of a pasha…heir to one of the largest Nile Delta holdings. He was no regular stowaway. And the letters from Damanhour were damning. Your father kept them hidden, but an investigation would have proved they went through the post. It would have been a mess for Malden Trading.'

'You might have told me! I could have made amends whilst I was in Egypt. Visited the Pasha…begged for his forgiveness on my father's behalf. Why were you not man enough to let me know rather than blackmail the Countess?'

Larder shrugged, undisturbed. 'There was profit in one.

Nothing to gain in the other. Besides, you were ridiculous in Egypt. I watched you go after that poor girl who lost her scanty dress. I might have put an end to it then and there… But I'm glad I didn't. It made my value to the Countess rise. To have another Earl of Warrington fall in love with an Egyptian woman—heiress or not… Well, the irony of it was too good!'

Owen's stomach dropped. Larder had everything worked out. He knew the Countess was not his real mother. *Knew who he loved.*

'Leave Ranya out of it,' he snarled.

'She is of no matter to me. But what would she think of *you*? Of Malden Trading's role in her brother's death? The Countess has sponsored her during the season. Anybody doing a simple calculation would see that it doesn't add up, and Miss Radwan values mathematics. You will lose her good favour from any angle it is considered.'

Larder chuckled at his own pun, then faced Owen. He made a show of straightening his jacket by the shoulders, dusting off the arms as if he were a tailor taking measurements.

'Tell the Countess I will require one more payment and our account will be settled—for now.'

Owen had come wanting answers, but now he had them he could only feel regret and try to contain the helplessness of not being able to do anything to rectify the situation.

Larder was right.

Ranya would never understand.

Chapter Twenty-Three

Ranya

Over the next few days Ranya had a reprieve from the Countess. She had stopped breathing down her neck at every turn so she was somewhat surprised to find the woman already at the salon when she entered for her last dress fitting before the Percy Ball that evening.

The Countess sat at the very edge of a seat in the waiting area with the other ladies—mothers come to watch over their daughters. Against its bright velvet the Countess looked frightening, her thin-lipped smile just wide enough to expose her sharp incisors.

Ranya had the distinct feeling the Countess had only appeared to ensure the Owen was not with her.

Was that a sigh of relief she'd expelled?

The truth was that Ranya hadn't seen him since the night before the women's committee meeting. Even though they'd argued about his father's possible involvement in her brother's disappearance, she had yearned to talk to Owen about her success with Mr Tisdale. And as the Countess had stewarded her across London, keeping her busy with preparations for the ball, she'd realised she missed Owen himself. His smile. His touch.

The Countess excused herself from the other women and took Ranya aside. 'There has been word from the Earl,' she whispered. 'He has obtained the deed you require.'

Ranya's heart leapt, but it wasn't with the happiness she'd thought she would feel. If he had the deed, that meant she would be leaving. Maybe to never to see him again.

With a cold hand, the Countess twisted Ranya's chin to face her, prompting her to focus. 'I am made to understand you will be returning home shortly, since this deed is the main reason you came to England.'

She waited for Ranya to nod before continuing.

'Nevertheless, I will expect you to make me and my family name proud tonight. Show off your etiquette training under my sponsorship…what you have learned from my time spent with you. The tutelage.'

Ranya bristled, but tried not to let her mixed feelings at the news she would soon leave Owen affect her. She said, 'If correctly memorising a sequence of waltz steps and knowing which of three forks matches which course is knowledge which will make your family proud, then you can count on me to demonstrate it.'

The older woman's already cold smile fell away entirely. 'We are your benefactors. We have made you sound grand by allowing you to use the title of pasha's daughter. But I know the Egyptian government transgresses on your land holdings. In the grand scheme of global trade your city's role is but a minuscule one. You are heiress to very little.'

Ranya blanched, recalling the initial agreement she'd made with Owen as the Countess spoke. She had been tasked to distract the Countess with her presence, while secretly teaching him about the industry. That the Countess should know about any of it didn't make sense. Unless she was only saying it out of cruelty.

The Countess continued her lecture, pointing discreetly

to the seating area. 'It is all but agreed that my son should marry Miss Charlotte, but do you see that woman with the dark hair? Her daughter is also on the shortlist of brides Owen is considering as we speak. Her family's is a line connected to the noble side of the East India Trading Company. Her father continues to import silks and jewels from there. Cotton is the material of the poor and for undergarments, and when America's Civil War is over it will come to us as cheaply as it is worth. Your city will be nothing and your people will struggle to survive. You cannot rule yourselves. Even your titles such as "pasha" are owed to the Turks.'

'You do not know us.'

'You forget—my husband was an admirer of your country. I know you all too well. Know how you need us. Need England…our wealth. The sooner everyone knows their places and their stations, the better.'

Tears pricked at Ranya's eyes. At the injustice, the insult. Even at the truth in what the Countess was saying. Because hadn't Ranya seen the signs across Egypt? At home in Damanhour, where the people had turned on their loyal Pasha, sent away his son then imprisoned him to lure him back. She loved cotton—the industry. But had it ever loved her back?

Maybe when she returned home she would throw the deed Owen had found in their faces, convince her father to sell their land so they could start afresh somewhere else. Alexandria. Or somewhere further away, like Cairo, where they wouldn't have to witness how their countrymen toiled at the ports to please foreigners, only to be treated like rubbish by swine like Jarvis Larder.

A salon girl interrupted her thoughts. 'Are we ready to begin, Miss Radwan?'

'Ready,' the Countess said, in one beat, and then, with a lifted brow at Ranya, 'Are we not, my dear?'

There was a challenge, a dare in her voice. Ranya didn't know what made her nod…agree…but it felt like a duty, another thing she had to do. This Percy Ball was one last obstacle before getting the deed. Going home.

The Countess be damned.

Her brother's life forfeit or not.

And Owen? She would have to find a way to get over him. *Her love for him.*

Ranya's thoughts swarmed as she was stripped and strapped into a corset, her hair tugged and her face painted before the dressing process began.

The Countess's directions came in a blur.

'Wrestle that hair into a style so that it looks less like a lion's mane.'

'Can you hide the colour of her skin more?'

But Ranya's skin was too dark to be lightened with powder, her hair too curly to be straightened with pomade. They would have to burn her curls with an iron to achieve the result the Countess wanted. Or bleach her skin with creams that smelled like poison to make her look more like the women she would stand next to that night.

When Ranya slipped into her gown—a rich azure with golden threads that played up her skin tone—she knew that the Countess would hate it. It was a gown by English standards, certainly. But on Ranya it looked entirely Egyptian.

It came with a short veil that would cover her hair modestly and with its fitted sleeves and waist its silk fell perfectly over her hips. Ranya felt as if she was wading in the most still, most pristine waters of the Mediterranean on a bright day, and despite how upset she was with everything that had happened, she wondered what Owen would think when he saw her in it.

When she stepped out from behind the curtain for the Countess's inspection, there was a collective intake of breath from the other women who had been fussing over their daughters. They stared curiously at her.

For her part, the Countess examined the dress as if it hung on a mannequin and not on Ranya. She spoke to the dressmaker directly, lowering her voice so the others would not hear.

'It fits much too naturally. Almost as if there is no corset. Where is the cage crinoline? Or a tournure, perhaps?' She lifted one of Ranya's arms, then dropped it unceremoniously. 'Sleeves? Not gloves? No lace? No ruffles? It is at once too much in colour and material and too little in style and detail. I cannot fathom it.'

'It suits her figure and her colouring well,' the dressmaker offered.

She had merely received the gown. Its style, material and measurements had been ordered from a catalogue—a selection Ranya had made in Warrington weeks ago. It had not interested the Countess at the time, though she was clearly regretting it now.

'It will garner attention, to be sure.'

'There are some admirable kinds of attention,' the Countess snorted, 'but this dress will not produce that sort. Do you not have anything else we could procure?'

'At such short notice, my lady, the cost might not be justifiable and the fit might be inappropriate.' When the Countess looked away, the dressmaker winked at Ranya. 'Best to make the most with what one has.'

The Countess sighed and looked at the clock overhead. 'I have a few errands to run before the ball tonight. And I must get dressed myself. If you will come with me now, Miss Radwan, I'm sure one of the maids can help you finish.'

The dressmaker moved between them with a smooth smile. 'The salon has retained a carriage so the ladies might ride together to the Percy Ball. Make a fashionable entry, as it were. It is part of our services for this evening and it will allows us to take our time with the final polish. If you please, Your Ladyship, Miss Radwan is in good hands and will meet your party at the event.'

The Countess stared at Ranya, as if demanding she turn down the dressmaker's offer herself. But the choice to ride with the woman after her disparaging remarks earlier or get away from her nit-picking gaze was not a choice at all.

'I will stay,' Ranya declared.

'Very well,' the Countess relented. 'Maybe it will give you time to learn to slouch a bit. No woman stands tall like that.'

This was an outright contradiction to what the dance instructor had told her—Ranya's posture was the thing he'd praised her for most, and the Countess had even heard him doing so.

When she was gone, Ranya breathed a sigh of relief while the dressmaker watched from behind the curtain to ensure she truly was.

'Now, let us get that horrible stuff off your face—but, if pressed, you should know that I will deny that my powders aren't of the highest quality. Unfortunately they're only suitable for the skin colours that match them. Your complexion is lovely—you do not need them. In fact, I dare say that many of those who do wear it will be jealous of you for not having to.'

Then she pulled out the clips in Ranya's hair.

'Natural curls should be celebrated.'

Molly had told her a version of Cinderella that featured a fairy godmother. The Egyptian version didn't have one, focusing more on the shoes she wore to catch her prince. But at that moment Ranya could see the appeal of Molly's tale more, because she was sure the dressmaker was, in fact, her fairy godmother.

* * *

Ranya peeped outside the carriage as it came upon the entrance to the Percy Ball. It was a converted opera house, the carriage driver shouted, dating back to the days when Prussian architects had been commissioned to build fantastical buildings.

It was eye-catching, to be sure, and gothic, with its angles that seemed to reach for the sky, and as she admired it one of the other girls in the carriage said, 'It must be a marvel to you? Is it not bricks that make up Egypt's pyramids?'

'We have mosques, universities and palaces from ancient times—the Fatimid period. The Byzantines and Ottomans have left their mark too,' she said, prickling at the fact that she wasn't well travelled in her own country and hadn't seen them. She would do something about it as soon as she was home, but Ranya didn't want to think about that now, for it meant remembering that she would soon leave England.

Leave Owen.

Instead, she reflected on this, her last engagement in a fine gown. The party at the bank opening in Alexandria had not been a ball, with dancing, but attending it had helped to make this one less intimidating.

She thought of Madame Hala's dress, still in the cottage at Warrington. Perhaps she would tell her about this one someday. This dress was beautiful, but Ranya had no desire to keep it. And the Countess wouldn't insist on it, she was sure.

She wondered if Owen would compare her appearance today to hers that night in Alexandria, when he'd first proposed their deal. And then she wondered what he would be wearing tonight, and how it might differ from his suit on that day.

Her stomach leapt at the memory of what he'd looked

like with no shirt on. How it had felt when he'd held her. Kissed her.

When Ranya descended from the carriage after the other girls her eyes searched everywhere for Owen, but she couldn't find him.

Then her name was being called from a corner near the steps. Molly!

The maid hugged her warmly. 'I'd say I almost didn't recognise you, but you have a distinctive beauty, Ranya. Draws the eye.'

Ranya was glad to see her friend and warmed in her embrace. 'How can you be here?'

'It was the Earl! He sent me a note, arranged for my entry into the ball…money to buy a dress, and Tom's sweets! He said I would be a welcome companion for you in London. And that you'd convinced him to offer Tom a job too!' She twirled happily, in a green frock that complemented her red hair.

Owen was incredible. Each time something had made her feel unwelcome in England he had risen to make up for it. He seemed to know exactly when she needed one of his boosts.

'It was nice meeting Tom. He thinks only of you.'

'Oh, and you would know a thing or two about thoughtful chaps, eh?' Molly grinned for a second before her face sobered. 'Was Tom able to find anything about your brother?'

Ranya considered telling Molly what she knew, but was overwhelmed with a strong desire to protect Owen and not to think about where Muhammad was. If he actually lived…

'He helped as much as he could, but I am no closer to knowing anything for sure.'

'Oh, I'm so sorry,' Molly said. 'It's the not knowing that must be the worst.'

She squeezed her hand just as the Master of Ceremonies came to them. After taking her name, and comparing it to the list he held, he asked, 'Would Miss Radwan like to be announced singularly, as the Pasha's daughter from Egypt, the personal guest of the Countess and Earl of Warrington, or would you like me to call one of them to appear by your side?'

Owen and the Countess were already inside, then, and here she was, thinking that one or the other would surely meet her here.

She was eager to get this evening over with. 'You needn't call anyone. I can be announced on my own. Announce me as Miss Ranya Radwan, a cotton pasha's daughter.'

Before she could stand in the line behind the other girls, Molly told her she'd have to sneak in through the back, per Owen's instructions. 'He told me to seek out a contact of his with the caterers, pretend to be with them until I am inside.'

Always pretending. At least now it was for a good cause.

Ranya nodded to Molly, then stood in the line behind another of the girls who had come with her from the dressmakers. They were the last to arrive. As they entered, the sound of violins was lovely, and the scent of burning candles and myrrh was potent.

The Master of Ceremonies waited for a lull in the music before proclaiming the ladies. Standing there alone, Ranya suddenly felt nervous. Announcing guests was a such a strange tradition, and to have all eyes on her... She clutched her veil with both hands as if it were a hood.

When the man stumbled on the word 'pasha' she didn't really mind—because her father might not be a pasha any more, but she would always be the proud daughter of a man who'd sacrificed more for the honour of that title than anyone in Damanhour ever had.

Ranya would have stories to tell Baba about her adventures in England, but only when he'd got over her not finding Muhammad while she was here. Because suddenly she knew that she would not find him. That he had never reached London.

How she knew, she was not sure. But as she stood there, Ranya felt her mother's spirit rise in her.

Maybe it was the good deeds of her mother and her love for Allah that gave Ranya clarity. Had her believing, without a doubt, that the night her mother had died, seven months ago now, was the night she had seen Muhammad's soul in her dreams.

'Allah is the best of planners,' her mother's voice constantly whispered to her.

And now Ranya heard her again, confirming what she had known herself. *'Muhammad is with me now.'*

Remembering them steadied Ranya's back, made her stand straighter despite what the Countess would have wanted. Despite not having Owen behind her.

Much had changed in the last couple of months. She was no longer that girl on the Alexandrian harbour who'd felt the crowd's harsh judgement so plainly when the thief had shown them her dress. She was stronger for all the experiences she'd had since then. She was a proud woman and she would walk like one.

As she descended the stairs and the music grew louder, her eyes scanned the room, but there was one corner that they were drawn to almost against their will.

Him.

Owen.

He strode towards her, as if he and she were both magnets and he too couldn't resist her pull even if he wanted to.

Chapter Twenty-Four

Owen

He had to reign in his emotions, the pounding in his heart…the way she seemed to reach into his chest and clench it until he felt he could hardly breathe. He had to slow his pace and not run to her.

Because people were watching, and if they saw, they would see it too.

Owen Malden was completely, utterly and hopelessly in love with Ranya Radwan.

He stood before her for a long moment. Took in the regal gown. The blue that made him feel as if he was drowning, the golden threads in the veil that hid her curls and framed her cheeks in a way that highlighted her brown eyes set high in her face.

He had a strong desire to slip his hands beneath the veil, cup her face and bring her lips to his. One he couldn't fulfil because of what he now knew with certainty had happened to her brother.

'I always forget how beautiful you are, Ranya,' he whispered. 'Until you walk into a room and I am taken by surprise all over again.'

'Perhaps it is a good thing,' she answered. 'When I am gone you can forget me easily.'

It was a cruel thing to say, and he would have despaired, but then she smiled, showed him her dimple. 'I have missed you.'

'There is something I need to tell you.'

She shook her head. 'A gentleman is supposed to ask me for a dance.'

It was a gentle chide but a demanding one too. As if he were in a trance, Owen remembered the two things in each of his coat pockets.

From the right one he pulled the dance card he'd snatched from the Countess before she could fill it with her choices of partner for Ranya, and tried not to think of the deed in his left pocket.

Unable not to stare into her eyes as he did it, he wrapped the ribbon of the card around her wrist, letting his fingers linger in her palm. 'I have taken the liberty of being the first on your card,' he whispered. 'But I am not sure you will want to dance with me once I tell you what I know.'

'Owen, please dance with me.'

As the music started again, he watched a look of recognition pass across her face. As if she knew instinctively what he had to tell her.

'It is the Viennese Waltz,' she said.

'Are you familiar with it?' he asked.

'I have memorised the number pattern, but the instructor kept saying one must *feel* the necessary beats. With a partner for whom one…*feels*.'

His heart swelled. He hated to accept the reprieve, but was unable to deny her power over him. 'Then let us try. See what you *feel*.'

They bowed and curtsied, as per tradition, but Ranya did not go low. 'An Egyptian woman curtsies to no man.'

'I know that.'

He took the small of her back in one palm, and though he longed to pull her close, it was not the way of the dance. He spread his other arm outwards and waited for her to take his hand. Relaxed only when she did.

'Especially to a man who is a *homar*,' she whispered.

It was hard not to laugh out loud as she used the common Egyptian insult to refer to him as a donkey.

They separated, and he watched her counting her steps as he went through his own. When they came together again, he teased, 'Did the teacher not discuss arching your heels?'

'Yes. But you are not so much taller than me that I would seem less graceful.'

He pulled her so close he knew people would think it scandalous. 'I have missed you.'

He winced when she stepped on his toes. On purpose, if the lift of her brow was an admission.

'You groan too loudly, my lord,' she said.

'As you did when you were showing this *homar* how belly dancing is done?'

It was foolish to remind her of that day, knowing he would soon have to tell her what he'd found out about her brother. Even as he thought it, he made eye contact with the Countess. He would have to deal with her tonight as well. Though he might talk to her first. But there were too many people around and she, like Ranya, seemed to be avoiding the pressing matters. Letting the Percy Ball be an occasion, even though the expectations of all three of them had of it would soon be dashed.

They danced silently, as if they were alone in the ballroom, and Owen was struck by how incredible Ranya truly was with the steps, the measured way she twirled and held herself, somehow both vixen and ingénue.

When they drew close, she said, 'You have not asked about my meeting with Mr Tisdale.'

'Because I have already heard. You were a stunning success. He has told me he would like Malden Trading to have more of a stake in negotiations. Couldn't stop talking about your brilliance. It was all "your Egyptian heiress this" and "your Egyptian heiress that".'

Owen saw the flush in her face.

'The term caused quite a scandal amongst the other ladies,' she said.

He pulled her closer, spread his fingers to encompass more of her back and her curves. The hand he held he squeezed gently, intimately. 'Ranya, we can't keep pretending. I have to tell you—'

She hushed him, her chest rising and falling in a way that matched his own heartbeat.

'Please do not say anything. Not here. Not yet.'

He didn't know how long they stood there, staring at each other, but it was the Countess who practically pushed them apart.

Owen realised the music had stopped. The waltz was over. The other couples had drifted away. People were staring.

'Owen, we have an agreement,' the Countess warned.

He perceived the threat in her face. She knew more than she was letting on about Muhammad Radwan, and his father's role in the man's death. Owen had travelled in search of Larder's father, to talk to him directly, but he hadn't been able to find him. What if the Countess had done the same before she'd allowed herself to be blackmailed by his son? The elder Larder had been friends with the Countess's brother, had served in the navy with him. Of course she would know where he was.

Ranya was staring at him, and repeated what he had

missed the Countess saying to her. 'Lord Denham is on his way over to ask me for a dance.'

He saw the question in her gaze. Denham was a professional bachelor who had been frequenting the season's balls and social scene since Owen was a boy. And he needed to talk to the Countess.

'There is no harm in His Lordship.'

When Lord Denham bowed and swept her away, Owen felt regret. A twinge of frustration that had absolutely nothing to do with all that was in his mind about Malden Trading and the death of Muhammad Radwan.

He wanted to be the one to dance with Ranya. Him alone. For always.

He turned on the Countess. 'We need to talk. Now.'

She answered Owen out of the side of her mouth and with lips that barely moved. 'I have nothing to say to you until you have danced with Miss Charlotte. Lady Elizabeth has kept her daughter's card free for you. On my bidding. Do not embarrass me, I beg you.'

He relented against his will. 'One dance. Then you will meet me in the gardens?'

She inclined her head, acquiescing. She must know that he knew Jarvis Larder had been blackmailing her.

He scanned the floor for Charlotte, but his eyes kept snagging on Ranya. The way she had her hand on her partner's shoulder...the way he cupped her waist with his meaty fingers. She was out of earshot, but she suddenly smiled at something Denham said. Not enough to bring out her dimple, but...

'For heaven's sake—to your left. Charlotte is there,' the Countess directed.

Owen trudged over to the girl and bowed. 'Miss Parker, may I have the honour of the next dance?' He tried to sound enthusiastic, but his acting ability had suffered of late.

Charlotte seemed too eager to notice anything but his keeping the promise the Countess must have made. She curtsied low, extended her gloved hand with her dance card dangling from it. He couldn't remember if etiquette dictated he should fill in his name before or after their dance so he simply led her to the floor.

Owen knew he should not sanction her hopes. Charlotte was a pretty girl who would be a catch for any of the season's most eligible men. Just not him. He was not eligible.

They made awkward small talk between steps, with Owen trying to be polite and keep his glance away from Ranya and Lord Denham.

'The Countess has said you will marry this season,' said Charlotte.

'Has she?' He tried to sound non-committal.

'Is she wrong, my lord? I do not mean to be forward, but I trust you will be honest as to where your intentions rest.' Tendrils of Charlotte's hair barely covered the frowning lines of her brow. 'The ton's young ladies might choose to direct their devotions elsewhere.'

It was a strange thing for Owen to want to be honest. There had always been lies surrounding him. Secrets all his life. But he was tired of it.

He said, 'All my hopes and intentions, indeed my whole heart, lie with Miss Radwan.'

It was a good thing the dance ended then, giving them both the excuse to part amicably. Owen bowed as gallantly as he could, and bade her a lovely evening.

Before he marched over to the Countess and demanded she follow him to the gardens he took one last look at Ranya. She had accepted another dance.

As soon as he was finished with the Countess Owen would find her and confess all, be at her mercy. He would tell Ranya the truth about her brother. Then he would tell her what he had just told Charlotte.

That he wanted to be the only man she would ever dance with. And that if she stayed with him he would give everything up for her. The title. The estate. Even the Malden Trading Company. He would be Ranya's Iskander, or her Owen, or whoever the hell she wanted him to be.

If she stayed after he had told her everything.

The gardens were well lit with lanterns, to dissuade couples from finding dark corners and getting to know each other beyond their chaperones' watchful eyes. This had been implemented a few years ago, after a particularly colourful ball that had resulted in a half-dozen duels, three rushed marriages and, most scandalous of all, one premature child. The brightness, Owen found, was a good deterrent. Save for a few of the ousted fathers smoking and playing card games in the gazebo, he and his stepmother were alone and could talk freely.

Behind a particularly tall azalea bush he paced around her, tried to choose his words carefully, but she didn't give him the chance.

'Larder has sent word. He told me you know,' she said.

'Why didn't you tell me?'

He hated it that he sounded like a little boy waiting for her approval.

Though she wasn't actually shouting, Owen could hear how irritated the Countess was when she answered.

'I didn't tell you because I knew you would want to come clean, confess—live an honest life, sleep soundly at night. All that nonsense. Just like your father.'

If his father had been honest, it made no sense.

'I found the letters from the Pasha. But my father was already sick when the Pasha's son came as a stowaway.

Died. He couldn't have known about him. Couldn't have demanded his death be covered up.'

But it was almost as if the Countess didn't hear him. She scrunched a bundle of the flowers in her hand, watched them fall to her feet. 'I used to think it would have been better if Charles had left your mother in Egypt, kept her a secret wife by their laws which have nothing to do with ours, visited her on his trips there. Many men did it in India. But he had to be honest with me. He never asked me what *I* wanted! I swear it would have been easier to find out about Hala and his son after he was dead.'

Owen was taken aback by her confession. 'You cannot mean that.'

'Please Owen, let this go. I will pay off Larder. He won't bother us again. You'll marry, take up the Warrington seat in Parliament. Just as you promised.'

He shook his head vehemently. 'Ranya has to know what happened to her brother. I will tell her tonight.'

'And your father? His name? His legacy? You would drag it through the mud? She could ruin us!'

'She left her home to search for him. Made a plan to get here, travelled the seas and dealt with prejudice. She went from grave to grave, looking for him. Crying. I watched her. Then came here to London. Ranya loved her brother. Her family has suffered. Their letters could have been answered by Father! I don't even know if he knew and it's killing me. But no matter—I will not keep a secret from the woman I love!'

The Countess seemed to miss the point of all he was saying. 'Take her as a lover, if you must, Owen. All I ask is that I don't have to watch it. It would bring back too many memories of your father bringing another woman to live here. In my face. A woman who had given him what I could not. A son.'

She stepped towards him. Put her hands on his cheeks. 'You were the sweetest boy and you did not deserve Hala's abandonment. But I was there for you.' She lowered her hands to clutch his. 'I will withdraw, Owen. You may rip up the list of young ladies I pushed upon you, the demands. Forget Charlotte, and your promise to me. You don't have to marry anyone this season. Let us work together to sell Malden Trading. When everything dies down we can negotiate what will make you happy—and *whom*.'

Chapter Twenty-Five

Ranya

Ranya refused to dwell on what Owen wanted to say to her. Only wished she could dance with him again. Have his arms around her, his smell, the feel of his breath near her ear. Even as she danced with the stiff Lord Denham, or the next gentleman whose name she didn't catch, she thought of Owen. Of the cravat he wore high on his neck, how she'd like to unknot it. Push off his jacket. Lay kisses along his chest as she slowly unbuttoned his shirt.

He looked especially handsome this evening. Something in his demeanour surpassed all the other men here. She'd heard it from the women at the union meeting, seen it in their faces here. Owen was the season's most eligible bachelor. And easily the handsomest. He was suave and graceful, but the pomade in his hair had not done a good enough job, and with the slight stubble at his jaw he looked a little wild too.

She flushed with the thought that he looked as if he belonged naked, under bed sheets. The things they could do together… She might never want to leave his bed!

Contrastingly, the dance she was currently in the middle of was something she couldn't wait to get out of. The man's hand felt limp in hers, and the way his leg brushed her gown with each step was off-putting. He spoke as they spun, but his voice did nothing for her—not like Iskander, speaking in Arabic with its unique cadence, grimacing at how terrible he knew it to be, or Owen's English, a deep, assured baritone.

Even the dance steps of Lord Denham and this man were too stiff. Ranya had started to lose count. Unlike being in Owen's arms, when the numbers had seemed natural, as smooth as taking a felucca across the Nile when the breeze was so perfect it sailed on its own.

Her mother had told her she would know—*feel*—when she was with the right man.

Owen was the right man.

Ranya had never felt so sure about anything.

She curtsied to the man she was dancing with and rushed off to the side if the room, hiding behind a group of young women lest another asked for a dance.

Although she wasn't sure she was yet ready to hear what he wanted to tell her, Ranya searched for Owen. But he wasn't in the room. Neither was the Countess.

She did, however, find Molly—by the refreshment table.

'Oh, but that's good punch,' she said, swaying uneasily towards Ranya when she appeared by her side.

Her face was flushed, but green-tinged rather than her usual red.

'You need fresh air,' Ranya said, helping her friend out to the terrace. She set her down to rest on a bench while she marvelled at the lovely gardens, bright with lanterns.

Owen's distinctive voice came to her, carried on the perfume of freshly manicured grass. Ranya had compared it with those of the other Englishmen who had held her while dancing, and she knew she was right. It did affect her—reeled her in as if she was a fish caught in a net.

'I will be back soon,' she told Molly, and started walking towards it.

But as she neared it was the Countess's words that became clearer.

'Send Miss Radwan back with the deed, Owen. It's the only way she will not accuse your father of murdering her brother.'

Ranya stepped from behind a bush, her head pounding. Her knees were ready to give up on her, and internally she was screaming, but somehow her body moved of its own accord. The anger she clung to was the only thing she could find in the darkness around her. Dark despite the garish lights.

She'd known it. Muhammad was dead. She'd realised it earlier, when she'd felt her mother's strength within her, but hadn't wanted to face it.

When Owen had insisted on speaking to her, she'd insisted on dancing first.

She'd thought he wanted to tell her that Muhammad had died in the sea. But murdered?

Fathi had been right.

She shouted at Owen, 'What do you know of my brother's murder?'

Chapter Twenty-Six

Owen

'Eavesdropping is decidedly unladylike,' the Countess rebuked her. And when Ranya turned to her with a blank expression, she persisted. 'It means listening to other people's conversations.'

Owen knew it was the unkindest, most insensitive thing to say. Ranya had heard. She knew her brother was dead. And he didn't know what to say to that.

It took him a second but he reached her. Caught her before she fell.

'Muhammad?' she whispered.

He nodded. 'I am sorry, Ranya. He...he died en route from Egypt. I have only just found out.'

'Not murdered,' the Countess insisted. 'Make sure she knows that.'

Ranya looked at his arms around her as if wondering what they were and how they came to be holding her. Owen couldn't read her face exactly, the range of emotions moved over it quickly, but he felt them in his very core. Her shock. Her disbelief.

She twisted out of his grasp. Then she spun, pointed to the gazebo rather than the ballroom. She swallowed, spoke in Arabic, then translated it into English with a shout. 'Did you know my brother was murdered by your father while you were waltzing with me in there?'

'Really, Miss Radwan. Lower your voice, please!' The Countess stepped between them. 'Is this how you repay our generosity? All we have done for you?'

'All you have done for me?' Ranya shouted. 'You horrible, wicked woman!' She pulled away from him and pushed her back so hard Owen had rush to the Countess's side.

'My brother is dead!'

The Countess huffed angrily. 'No amount of etiquette training can teach her how to be a true lady.'

'Go inside,' Owen commanded her. 'Let me talk to Miss Radwan.'

'I should go inside and call a police officer.'

'Please do,' Ranya seethed, 'that I may tell him what you have done to my brother!'

Owen led the Countess behind the azalea bush. He summoned his Earl voice. 'Don't do anything. Go inside until I come and find you.'

She took a steadying breath. 'Deal with her, Owen, but do not, under any circumstance, allow her to jeopardise your future.'

When she had gone, he could only look helplessly at Ranya. She'd pressed her palms to her cheeks as if trying to stop the tears. When she'd succeeded she dropped her hand and her face went slack. Owen saw that the gazebo had emptied, so he guided her towards it, taking her arm in his, surprised when she actually let him. But she was moving as a sleepwalker might. Someone who knew they were in the midst of a nightmare but could not act on the knowledge.

The gazebo was pretty, with its latticed wrought iron

painted a bright white and the seats still warm from the gentlemen, their pipe smoke lingering in the air.

If circumstances had been different, he might have brought Ranya here after the ball…declared his undying love for her.

It was as romantic a place as any to ask a woman for her hand in marriage.

He sat down, patted the seat across from him and hoped she would take it. When she did, he clenched his knees, rubbed his hands against them, trying to warm them. It was a perfectly warm late summer evening, but he was cold from the inside. As she must be.

He took the envelope from his pocket. Placed it in her hand. 'It makes up for nothing, but I have found the deed agreed between our fathers. And the money Muhammad brought to buy the rights back for Damanhour. It is all there, untouched.'

There were several moments of silence…only the distant music from the ball and the envelope between them.

'How?'

It was barely a whisper, but Owen pushed forward with his answer as if Ranya had opened a door.

'I found it stashed under a floorboard beneath my father's desk. Maybe he planned to send it back, but then he was taken ill and…and didn't get the chance. For what it's worth, I don't believe he knew your brother was on that ship. Or even that he'd died. Over and over, I try and recall everything about his last moments—the things he said to me on his deathbed. If he knew about Muhammed he would have told me. Asked me to make amends, somehow. I'm sure of it. I will talk to everyone on that ship—find out how the money come into my father's possession. We will have the whole truth, Ranya, I promise.'

Owen knew he was right about his father, that his uprightness was not a lie, even if this affair with the Radwans made Charles Malden look like a liar of the worst sort.

Gingerly, Ranya brought the envelope to her chest, held it there for a few minutes with her eyes closed. Then she dropped it onto the table as if it was on fire and rushed to stand at the gazebo's edge. Her movement reminded Owen of that first day on the Mediterranean.

He went to hold Ranya's head here as he had there. Nothing came up—only an empty gagging. He moved to stand at her back, wrapped his arms around her so that they hovered over her clenched fists.

She threw her head onto his shoulder then. Permitted herself one scream that came from somewhere deep in her chest. He hugged her tightly from behind. He whispered how sorry he was as she cried.

She kept repeating her brother's name and an Arabic invocation. *'To Allah we belong...to Him we return.'*

When Ranya finally turned around, he pressed his lips to her forehead, at the top of her veil.

'I am here. Whatever you need, my darling.'

'I need to go home.'

He nodded. 'You'll want to see your father, certainly. Tell him in person.'

Owen wanted to tell her he was determined to right the wrong done to Ranya's family. He had plans he wanted to share with her if she was ready to hear them.

'When you return, we—'

'Return?' She pried herself away from him, moved to snatch the envelope from the table. 'Return to what? To those in this cursed country who have stolen so much from me? To a family who killed my brother?'

'My father didn't kill him, Ranya. Muhammad chose to sneak onto that cargo ship. I understand that he was desperate, but—'

'Desperate?' Her anger burst like rain from a heavy cloud that had waited too long for thunder. She pointed to the ballroom. 'You are like her, that witch of a countess. Like those people inside, the rich and the noble, thinking you know better. That you are cleverer than us! That my people and all those on the docks and in the back lanes of your East End should serve you. Pick your cotton… carry it till our backs break. You force us to sneak onto your ships to get your attention, to take back what has always been ours—' Her voice cracked, her lips trembled, but she didn't stop. 'You want us to cook you spicy dishes and dance, dance, dance to satisfy your exotic appetites.'

She shook her hips the way she had in that room at Sikeena's, reminding him of how it had been between them. But this wasn't the same. This was hateful, accusatory. Meant to shame him.

'Is that what you want from me, Mr Earl of Warrington? My body? Are you *desperate* for it?'

She'd thrown the word back at him and he was sorry. He hadn't meant it like that.

He tried to reach for her, reason with her, 'Ranya please—'

She cut him off with a slap. 'You are a *ghashash*. A cheater! A boy who likes to play and dress up!'

'I never cheated you…' he managed—but her voice had been too loud.

Behind her, the people from the terrace had gathered. Some of the men who'd been in the gazebo earlier. A small crowd from inside too. And a young woman who looked familiar. Molly. Yes, he'd sent her a note…thought it would be nice for Ranya to have her here.

Molly called to her and they hugged as Ranya confided that her brother was dead. Molly rubbed her back, muttering that she was so sorry.

Owen was glad they had one another, but his frustration was taking hold of him.

This gazebo wasn't his mother's cottage in Warrington, but suddenly it felt like it. He was no longer the little boy who'd cried on its threshold as she left, but he might as well have been.

'Is this how a pasha's daughter behaves?'

The Countess spoke to the gathering, trying to contain the damage, while Owen clutched his smarting cheek as if it might contain his breaking heart.

'I want to go home.' Ranya's sniffled as she separated from Molly. She waved the envelope and repeated her declaration—louder. 'I have what I came for and now want to go home. To Egypt.'

'That can be arranged,' the Countess answered. 'This is London and there are many ways to leave it. I will secure your passage myself.'

'Are we finished, then?'

Ranya had turned to Owen. He should have known this would be how it ended. It didn't matter that he'd fulfilled his promise of finding the deed, or even that her brother's death had had nothing to do with Malden Trading.

It had always been going to end this way between them.

And if he was disappointed he only had himself to blame. From the start Owen had known that truly loving a woman was a dangerous thing. Those he loved would leave. It had always been that way.

'We are finished,' he said.

Chapter Twenty-Seven

Ranya

All the way from England to Egypt, Ranya cried until it seemed her tears were competing with the land's mud, the sea's water. She travelled as an automaton—catching ferries and trains, sleeping, waking, eating—repeating the process every day like the workers she'd seen at the Manchester mill.

Still, there was healing in the routine. Ranya knew she was returning to Damanhour with terrible news, but was grateful to have the strength to deliver it. She carried the deed that would free her father, and the money that would shame any who had ever spoken badly about her brother.

Occasional letters exchanged with Molly would be enough of a reminder of the good that had come out of the trip to England. And as for Owen… It would be hard, but she would eventually move on with her life without him in it.

In the end, he'd been the man she'd thought all along. A *ghashash.*

But he didn't cheat you, went the argument in her mind.

Maybe not about the deed, but he did cheat me out of my heart. Made me love him then left me to leave on my own.

Sometimes that was the argument that won. And that final image of him, next to the Countess, telling Ranya they were finished, seemed proof of it.

Other times, she remembered the good. How kind and respectful he had been with her. The way his curls fought against the pomade that tried to keep them at bay. His mischievous secret smile. The fire his touch lit in her. How the sound of his voice spread like wings in her soul.

No other man would ever make Ranya feel the way Owen had. She loved him, yes. She also had to forget him.

Ranya decided not to disembark in Alexandria. She might have if her trunk had held the dress that Owen's mother had given her three months ago. But she'd left London in such a hurry she had forgotten her promise to Madame Hala to return it and pay her then.

Ranya would write to Molly, asking her to send it to Egypt instead.

Owen would hear of it, perhaps offer to pay the shipping fee. Maybe it would be a means to bring him closer to the mother who still loved him.

When they'd first landed in France and she'd heard Owen humming the lullaby that night in Chateau Canebière, she'd prayed he and his mother would find peace. Reconciliation. Madame Hala should know how her Iskander had grown and fared.

It was after Fajr when Ranya made out her home from the Nile riverboat she'd boarded in Rasheed. The dawn's orange and yellow sun rising over the cotton fields of their *izbah* in Damanhour stole her breath in its beauty.

The irrigation for the winter crops had begun, and the fields would soon be swarming with workers. Children, mostly, because they could bend easily to distribute the smaller channels of water, which their fathers and mothers would rake around. The smell of the earth, wet with the river's water, was heady, thick—like *moolohia* left too long to boil when it should only be allowed to 'kiss the heat', as her mama had used to say.

A lone grey heron stood alert, one spindly leg angled, the other straight, as if he had no intention of moving. He saw Ranya, though, and tilted his head stiffly, let his beady black eyes corner her.

'If you're lost,' she whispered, 'I can't help you find your way.'

But now the home she'd known and lost in the past year stood before her.

Baba.

She had missed him. He'd be happy to have her back, to know that even though she hadn't found Muhammad she could confirm that he had done for their family and their city all he could. That her brother had given his life for them. Baba had served as Pasha. Mama had been like a mother to all. And Ranya too had struggled in ways the people of Damanhour would not know.

It had to be enough.

Seeing before her the house that had used to be theirs, as she'd predicted, soured the memories she had of it. The villa, despite its welcome familiarity—the gorgeous white veranda and the large second-storey windows with shutters that matched the tall palm trees flanking them—had been transformed into a house of mourning. Her father was imprisoned there now. It was the last place she'd seen her brother alive, hugged him. And her mother had died here.

'Annisa Ranya!' the *ghafeer* greeted her when she neared. 'Welcome back!'

He scrambled to his feet, knocking back the last of his tea and what looked like a sandwich. He hadn't been the caretaker when she'd lived here, but he was a nice man, appointed by the city council. Poor, with too many children to feed.

'They said you wouldn't come back, but I knew you would. I told my wife the other day to raise our daughters to be like you. Strong as boys. Better than sons.'

He meant it as a compliment, and Ranya's lip quivered with what she had to tell her father about Muhammad. But she couldn't cry before then. *'Shukran.'*

'Most mornings your *Baba* comes and sits here with me, waiting for you. He counts the days, but he wonders if he's doing it wrong. He says, "I gave her six months, and Ranya knows her numbers better than anyone in the whole world."'

She nodded, happy to let the *ghafeer* talk, relieve her of her luggage, call for her father.

'Hajj Radwan! Guess who is here?'

The upstairs had been closed off, as had most of the house. It was better that way—for now at least. She wouldn't have to wallow in the memories.

The *ghafeer* led her to a room off the kitchen, one where their housekeeper had slept when the house had been in its prime. A lifetime ago.

'Ranya!'

Baba stood in the doorframe, thinner than he had been, his brown *galabaya* hanging on him in a way that scared her. As he hugged her, she felt it too. She would need to make sure he ate again. A lot. Maybe she would finally learn how to cook.

'Alhamdullilah ala salama!'

He welcomed her back with kisses, and though his stubble was not as sharp as it had used to be, the feel of it broke something in her. Ranya had thought she had no more tears, but her father dug them up with the smile beneath that thick moustache, mostly grey now.

'*Wa'Allahi*, I have good news, Baba. Not all good news but some good news, *Insha'Allah. Abshir.*'

'I am *mustabshir, habibti.* My daughter is home. That is all that is important.'

Ranya bent to kiss his hands out of reverence, but he pulled them away to grasp the top of her head, press his nose to her scarf.

They were both crying while the *ghafeer* stood apart, giving them some privacy but trying to make them both feel better by boisterously urging them to praise Allah. He told them that God was merciful, reuniting them. He asked what greater bond in the world was there than between a girl and her *baba*?

'*Khalas! Khalas!*' he pestered until both father and daughter's tears had stopped flowing.

Ranya sat on the lone small bed while the *ghafeer* ambled off to get a chair. He apologised for not being able to let them outside. 'The guard will be coming soon. I don't want either of you to get into any trouble.'

'There is no more trouble!' Baba shouted. 'My daughter is back. *Allah Kareem.*'

'Ask the council to come,' Ranya said. She retrieved the package with the deed and the money from her bag and placed it on the table. 'I have all they asked for and more. They will release my father today!'

The *ghafeer* clapped and ululated, making the happy sound reserved for weddings and other joyous occasions. 'I will run to bring them here this very minute!'

When they were alone, Ranya gave her father an account of her last six months—not the part about falling in love with Owen, but how his Egyptian roots had brought out kindness in him—the need to help her.

'He found the deed. Gave me all the money Muhammad had with him.'

'Charles Malden was a good man, too,' Baba said, nodding his head. 'I did not know he had an Egyptian wife...'

'Baba,' Ranya began, 'about Muhammad... he tried—'

'Muhammad was a good son. Allah have mercy on him.'

Her father knew. Maybe he didn't want to face it, but he felt it. As Mama must have before she'd died.

'He didn't always think before he acted, but we all loved him. And you, all the way to England and back again!' He kissed her head again, his eyes glistening with tears of pride. 'Tell me, were they kind to you, these other Maldens? His mother named him Iskander, you say? Like the city she wanted him to return to, find her there?'

There would be another time to talk of her brother, the details of what had happened to him. For now they spoke of Alexandria, and what it would mean if they moved there.

'We should spend some time away from here. From the *izbah* and the cotton,' her father agreed. 'The sea air will do us good. We'll come back to my land renewed. *Your* land, to do with as you see fit. You are the heiress, after all.'

When the village council came and found them there in each other's arms, the deed and the money on the table, they let them be. They were ashamed of themselves. Of the loss the Radwan family had faced because of them.

Baba's voice trembled as he spoke. 'Know that my son was ever in your service, as I and my daughter and wife have been. But not any more.'

'Forgive us, Pasha,' they answered in unison, taking turns to shake his hand and kiss his head.

'The house is yours, undoubtedly, and we are trespassing,' said the eldest amongst them. 'You are free to come and go as you like. The *ghafeer* will be sent back to his family. Or if you need him to stay, we will arrange that too.'

Baba looked at Ranya. 'No. I will not ask my daughter to remain in this house. We will go today to Rasheed, to stay with cousins there. Then on to Alexandria. The council can take up the *izbah* work, of course, but leave me out of it, *khalas*. I will shut up the house until I decide what to do with it.'

He was frail, but determined. *The Pasha.* Ranya had never been prouder of her father.

When he went to pack his things, she followed the councillors outside. She inhaled deeply. She could name every scent in the air. Remembered the childhood games she and her brother had used to play.

'I want a *janaza* prayer for Muhammad. A funeral. A marker for him next to my mother,' Ranya said. She let her gaze circle the council, so that they knew they owed her family this at least. 'Maybe Allah, in his mercy, will allow my brother's soul, lost at sea, to find its way to hers.'

'We would be happy to do that, of course,' one of the councillors answered. 'Did you bring a certificate of death from England? We will need it to be authorised, but it should be easy enough to do.'

Ranya hadn't thought of that. But she'd walked through that graveyard in England, knew how the Countess had covered up her brother's death.

There would be no death certificate for her brother.

And without it, Muhammad's tombstone couldn't be erected in Damanhour either.

Chapter Twenty-Eight

Three months later

Owen

The bells overhead chimed lightly when Owen finally managed to gather his courage and push open the shop door. It was early in the afternoon, when he knew his mother's shop would be at its emptiest, with her working while her family would be upstairs for the city's siesta time, before the second half of the day would start.

A voice came from the back room.

'Sanya wahda.' One moment.

Her voice.

Owen wasn't sure how he knew it was his mother's voice, and wondered if perhaps the body contained a phonautograph that held sound memories from childhood. Like the tune of that lullaby he still didn't know the words to. Ranya had said they were sad. And Owen didn't want any more sadness.

It had been almost twenty years… His mother probably wouldn't recognise him. He wasn't dressed as Iskander, but he had found a balance between his English upbringing—

his father's side—and the Egyptian blood that flowed in him like an ancient river. Blood he couldn't deny.

It didn't mean that Owen wasn't scared to face Hala after so long a time. To ask why she'd left him. She couldn't regret it entirely—Owen knew that. She had a husband and another son. But maybe there could be some healing for them both.

Ranya had written to Molly about it.

Please ask Mr Malden to ship the dress to Madame Hala's shop in Alexandria.

He hadn't asked Molly if she ever wrote about him, but that sentence had kept him afloat since she'd left. Ranya was thinking about him!

When Molly had asked what she should write back, he had known what he must do.

'Tell her Madame Hala will have it in her shop in seven weeks' time. That she should call on her there and make sure it has arrived.'

It had been a deadline for him, more than anything. There had been matters he'd had to attend to in England before he travelled here. A visit to Jarvis Larder's father. Affidavits collected and presented to a judge. A serious conversation with Malden Trading's employees and Mr Tisdale. A town council's duties outlined at Warrington.

'Iskander.'

His mother stood in the doorway, eyes wide, the lines around them deep. She was older than he remembered from when he'd been there a few months ago—or maybe he just hadn't seen her clearly and up close then. Her back was hunched with what he presumed were years of seamstress work, and her curls were thinning and grey.

She tiptoed towards him as if he were a fragile, timid animal who would scurry off if she got too close.

He greeted, *'Ahlan, ummi.'*

She took the box from him, put her hands on his cheeks. Then he let her take him into his embrace, marvel at how 'grown and handsome and tall' he was. And for a few minutes he was that five-year-old again. Basking in his mother's love before it all went terribly wrong.

It would never be completely right again. Too much hurt had transpired. But he would be here in Alexandria for a while, trying to get to know her better. To claim what had been lost.

'Every day I regret leaving you, but I was dying there, Iskander.'

She kept stopping to wipe her tears and reaching out to squeeze his hands. He did the same. She sat him down at her work table, brought them both one of the handkerchiefs she sold—lovely cotton ones, embroidered with flowers that reminded him of Ranya.

'We don't have to talk about it all now,' Owen said, but he needed to hear some of it.

'I'm happy that you understand the Arabic, my son. Let me tell you—please. It has been on my heart for too long. I wanted to take you with me, but…much conspired against it. Even though your father had married and divorced me here, I'd had an Egyptian birth certificate issued for you, hoping you'd come and live with me. The Countess fought it—saying you wouldn't have a future here and, because your parents' marriage was never recognised in England, none there either. But as her son you would be rich, have power. Become an earl. I was young, foolish. I had nothing to provide you with here and I refused to further burden your father after I had broken his heart. Charles agreed with Vivian to keep you there…wanted you near him.'

'He didn't love her,' Owen said.

He knew now all that the Countess and the Larders had done behind his father's back. He'd always suspected she had only ever cared about the estate, and he knew she'd only ever claimed him as her son because it would be his.

'No, he did not,' his mother agreed. 'But Charles had a pure heart, and she…knew how to manipulate it. Me? I did not know my own mind then. I'd had a difficult life before I met your father. I needed him, but even before you were born I knew I did not love him. Could not live away from my home land.'

At this she laughed, waving to what was beyond the window.

'The sea hasn't always been kind to me, but I need the salt in its air like one of its fish. It is why I named you after the city—so you would come back to it. Find me.'

She kept on talking and Owen thought it might be out of nervousness, or the fact that she was scared he'd leave and she wouldn't get another chance.

Maybe she wouldn't.

He was still hurt. Still in many ways the boy she'd left. He wasn't sure he could ever forgive Madame Hala. Not completely, at least.

'Your brother, Issam, keeps asking when he can go to England and know you! Will you come up and meet him now? And my husband? They're sleeping after lunch. I have food left—but let me cook something fresh for my son, come all the way from across the sea.'

'They know about me?'

Owen was surprised. He had convinced himself that his mother had replaced him and his father. Made a new family to forget about her old one.

'Yes, *habibi*. I am not one to keep secrets. Only by talking about you did I alleviate some of my suffering.'

It was refreshing, to know that she was living her life in an open and honest manner, and Owen found he quite admired it.

'It would be my honour to meet them.'

Before she led him upstairs Madame Hala opened the box he'd brought. 'I had a feeling that evening, when that beautiful, lovely, proud girl came into my shop, that this gown would bring me my son. It is why I told Ranya to take her time with it. I had waited for twenty years—what was a few extra months?'

'You haven't seen her since then?'

Owen asked it in a way he hoped didn't sound desperate, but he was sure it did. If she noticed, Madame Hala didn't let on. She was too eager that all the men in her life should know each other. And so, for now, Owen swallowed his disappointment when she shook her head.

He spent a lovely afternoon with his mother and her family.

He left with a promise to see them again soon, not realising that if he had lingered only a few minutes longer, he would have come face to face with Ranya.

Chapter Twenty-Nine

Ranya

It was seven weeks to the day since Molly's letter had been written, and Ranya thought she would wait until the end of the afternoon to finally visit Madame Hala. She was embarrassed to be doing so without having the dress she had promised in her hand, but she thought that even if it hadn't yet arrived, she could at least say her son had promised it would.

And Owen—Iskander—if nothing else, was a man who fulfilled his promises.

Time had given her the chance to put distance between herself and the hurt that lingered when she thought about the times she and Owen had spent together. Ranya missed him. She loved him.

That was the truth she'd decided she would finally share with Madame Hala when she talked to her about him.

She had no one else to do so with. Baba would look at her oddly when she spoke of Owen, and she couldn't very well talk to him about what it had felt like to be with a man she desired with her heart, body and soul. Especially when she knew that, like her, Baba still harboured resentment over the fact that he wasn't able to get a death certificate for Muhammad.

Baba had asked his new friend Mr March for insight, and Mr March, always ready to help in any way he could, had promptly taken it up with the British Consulate. But they said that even under the simplest of circumstances records for foreign nationals who had died and been buried abroad, or had been lost in British waters, were frequently lost in governmental bureaucracy. And without the aid of those who'd last seen him it would be next to impossible to find them.

When she entered Madame Hala's shop, she was disappointed to find the seamstress wasn't alone. A lady was looking at some material, another was buying a handkerchief. Ranya wasn't even sure that the woman would remember her, but at the sound of the bell chimes she had looked up, and recognition blossomed into a wide smile.

'Ranya! What a blessed day for me, seeing those whom I love!' She rounded the table and came to hug her, tightly, as if no time had passed between them and they knew each other by virtue of more than one—albeit, special—encounter. 'May Allah reward you, *binti*.'

Over her shoulder, Ranya saw the dress in an open box. 'It is delivered, then. I am glad to have fulfilled our agreement, Madame Hala.' She patted her satchel. 'What do I owe you for borrowing it for so long?'

The older woman pulled back and chided her, 'Nothing. It is I who owe you, for bringing Iskander back into my fold.'

Ranya swallowed. Hoping, but barely believing. 'He delivered it himself?'

Madame Hala's eyes twinkled at whatever she perceived in Ranya.

'You just missed him. But he is coming back tomorrow. Shall I fetch the kaftan you left as collateral?'

Owen had been here.

She could run after him, look for him. All Ranya knew was that she had to see him.

'It belonged to ummi, I trust you to keep it! Did *he* say where he was staying?'

Madame Hala's mouth twisted in the same way Owen's did when he smiled. 'The hotel by Cleopatra's Needle—'

Ranya was already out through the door as she called, 'If I cannot find him, I will return tomorrow, early morning, to wait, if that is all right by you. Tell him, please!'

She didn't hear the woman's response—could barely contain her run.

She planned to barge into the hotel, demanding his room number, but as she dashed through the crowd collected along the corniche she thought of trying the place where they'd first met. The rock from which her dress had been stolen.

There was someone there.

A man in a blue tunic, with a back that looked strong. Familiar. But the hair was different. Not a mass of loose curls nor slick and pomaded.

Owen had shorn it close.

She watched him for a minute, forcing herself to still, catching her breath. He was looking out at the waves. His arms flexed by his sides.

He was lost in thought.

From Ranya's vantage he looked…lighter, free. And her heart swelled so much she was sure it would burst right then and there.

People walked around her, nudging her. She was standing in the middle of the corniche, blocking their way like a statue.

At the last possible second, doubts riled her. What if was already married? What if Miss Charlotte Parker was nearby?

Ranya should go before he saw her.

But even as she thought it, that magnetic connection between them had him turning, catching her gaze. There was relief in his eyes, and love, when he saw her.

Ranya.

He mouthed her name and she moved towards him as he stood up. Then they were standing opposite one another, each absorbing the other. Up close.

'I… I went to see Madame Hala. She told me you were in Alexandria,' she managed.

'Yes,' he answered. 'I counted the days from when Molly sent the letter. Knew that you would do the same. I concluded that my mathematics must be wrong for yours couldn't be.'

Owen smiled and it was too much. She'd missed him so. She'd known it, of course, but having him before her was something altogether different than an intangible equation done in one's head.

He put out his hand and she shook it awkwardly. She thought he might lift it to his lips, but he let it go, ever so gently.

He gestured to the rock. 'I would be honoured to have you join me.'

She sat down and he resumed his seat beside her. His hand came around her hips, not touching her, but close enough for her to know that the fire that burned between them had not diminished in the slightest since they'd been apart. At least not on her part.

'You're here with the Countess?' Ranya stared at her lap as she asked.

'Vivian would never make such a trip.'

'I meant the new Countess. Your wife?'

He chuckled, and it was infuriating to think he might be mocking her when she was clearly not in a state to be mocked. She spun on him to tell him as much. And seeing his breath hitch, his gaze steady on hers, made her want to cup his chin and kiss him. Hard.

As if knowing what she was thinking, he let his eyes fall to her lips. Ranya shook her head. They weren't alone. Her father might even see them from the water. He'd taken to fishing in the late afternoons with Mr March on occasion.

Owen said, 'I do not know if I will even retain the title. There is a petition with the Committee of Privileges. If there is anyone who can prove his claim, Warrington might have a new heir. In the interim, the estate is in the hands of a very capable town council. Headed by a sheep farmer and assisted by a good chap named Tom—fiancé of a friend of yours, I believe?'

Ranya did not fully understand the rules of the British peerage, but before she could ask questions, Owen continued.

'Turns out Vivian's deceit with Larder and his father had been ongoing for years. She didn't have your brother murdered, but it was her idea to cover up his death because she *did* know about the letters from your father. She hid them from mine, knowing they could be traced in an investigation. She planted them for me to find, along with the deed, so I would trust her and doubt what I knew of my father. That he was an honest man.'

Ranya put a hand on Owen's knee. He had been through too much. He smiled at her gratefully before continuing.

'Luckily, the elder Mr Larder isn't as bad as his son. He was ready to come clean about it all when my private investigator found him. When I confronted them with all I knew, the Countess and Jarvis Larder threatened to expose me as a bastard and not the true heir, but I had already presented my case to the Committee of Privileges. The Consul here found my Egyptian birth certificate. Remember him, the man who helped with your travel document?' Owen chuckled. 'I don't think he'll be getting that promised tour of Warrington, somehow.'

The ramifications of his words were jumbled in her mind, and Owen still hadn't answered her question. 'So, no wife?'

'No wife.'

He lifted her hand from his knee and held it in both of his. He stared at her fingertips as if they were a meal he wanted to devour, but his touch was infuriatingly gentle. With the sound of children playing on the sand and laughing below them, and the city's pedlars shouting their wares behind them, Ranya and Owen were definitely not alone, but it felt like it. As it had so many times before.

Would so many times to come.

'The Countess is banished from Warrington. She may be made to answer for her lie about my being her son if it is called to court or another heir comes forward. In any case, she is gone from society. I suspect she is in hiding at Larder's house in London. He himself has fallen into ruin. I will tell anyone who will listen of his dishonesty. How his acting shamed even me, a one-time theatre aficionado.'

Owen locked his eyes on hers.

'I am glad that both of them are punished because of what they did to Muhammad…to your family. And for their ill treatment of you, my darling Ranya.'

She had to keep reminding herself not to do anything stupid. Like throwing herself into his arms, pressing her lips to his. But she wanted to. Desperately.

'What about Malden Trading?'

He smiled brightly. 'It has new life, actually. I have

made some exciting deals, inspired by a certain very brilliant advisor and a labour dispute that came to a head at the mills in Manchester. Malden will be smaller, but the owner,' he said, tilting his head sheepishly, 'being me, thinks the company will weather the global conflicts. Maybe even be a beacon for others in future.'

'I have put aside my father's title too,' she said. 'I'm no longer a cotton pasha's daughter. Baba and I have moved here to Alexandria.'

Owen didn't seem surprised at this, only echoed her earlier question to him. 'No husband?'

When she answered in the negative, he blew out a long breath.

'Ranya, I have been to Damanhour and met with the city elders. Molly told me you were having trouble putting your brother's memory to rest in the cemetery there. You should have written to me about it.'

It was her turn to hold her breath. She'd written to Molly in complaint that first week…hadn't realised Molly would tell Owen.

'What could you do? I could not ask more from you.'

'I got an affidavit from Larder's father, who was there when your brother's body was found. And I called in favours before the hubbub with Warrington. I have the certificate.'

Ranya dared to hope that this chapter of her life would be concluded—that her brother's name, his sacrifice, would be honoured in both memory and in stone.

'You did that for me?'

'I would do anything for you, Ranya. Love for you…*my* love for you, it runs deep and…' Owen stumbled on the words. 'Well, I had to learn it could not be bound to the fear of you leaving when the three months had concluded.'

'It was not that I did not want to be with you. I had a duty to my father,' she explained.

He nodded. 'Yes, they told me everything in Damanhour. They regret imprisoning him, forcing you to travel to England to get the deed. They asked me to convey to the Pasha that the whole city is ready to attend your brother's funeral and pray for him. They are calling him Muhammad the Martyr. Whenever your father returns, the tombstone is ready.'

Ranya couldn't wait to tell Baba. This would please him—that he could visit his wife and son together in the graveyard at his home.

'I was ashamed to tell you my father was being held prisoner. Afraid that you would cheat me...that I couldn't trust you.'

The tears came freely then. Owen waited a moment and then his fingertips gingerly touched her face, wiping them away. When her cheeks were dry, his lips brushed her hand, kissing it anew with every word he said,

'Darling, you can trust me. My heart, my soul—they belong to you, Ranya. And all I ask in return is a glimpse of that dimple of yours. For now...for ever. For infinity. Is that a mathematical probability you can believe in?'

She didn't care who was watching. She took his cheeks in hand and brought his face to hers. She let her lips melt into his in a long, deep, hard kiss that barely did anything to satisfy the fire he'd lit in her soul.

When they came apart it was because somebody was whistling much too loudly. She and Owen laughed at the older couple passing by, the woman tutting and the man chiding his wife with the comment, 'We were like that when we were newly married.'

Owen waved at him gratefully, before turning back to Ranya. 'Which reminds me—please lead me to your father. There is something I need to ask him. I seek his permission for his lovely daughter's hand.'

'Ask me first,' Ranya said, trying to rein in her excitement. 'I am, after all, a modern Egyptian woman. I have even travelled to England, you know.'

'And you took the ton by storm, I hear. They will be talking about the cotton pasha's daughter for seasons to come—the Earl's Egyptian Heiress…who became his wife.'

'Yet I still do not hear you asking me the question,' she teased.

He lowered himself on the rock so he was crouching before her. Behind him the sun was setting, coral over the sea's prancing waves.

'Will you marry me, Ranya Radwan?'

It was not a customary Egyptian proposal, but she knew Madame Hala would teach him how to do it properly… how their parents should speak together, be a part of the marriage process. But she would bask in this English proposal for now, because Ranya knew that she loved both Owen and Iskander.

The Earl and the labourer. The son and the heir. The emotionally scarred boy and the man who could parry the toughest of his sex. The man who sought out her ideas, believed in them, and worked to see them implemented.

Ranya loved every aspect and every inch of him.

'Yes,' she promised. 'Yes, *lil abad*.'

For infinity, indeed.

* * * * *

The Earl's Egyptian Heiress
is Heba Helmy's debut.
Be sure to look out for her next book,
coming soon!

COMING NEXT MONTH FROM

⊕ HARLEQUIN
HISTORICAL

All available in print and ebook via Reader Service and online

THE LADY BEHIND THE MASQUERADE (Regency)
A Family of Scandals • by Diane Gaston

Marcus can't forget the mysterious woman he met in Paris or the passionate night they shared! A year later, he meets Juliana again, and Marcus must uncover who she is...

TOO SCANDALOUS FOR THE EARL (Regency)
Cranford Estate Siblings • by Helen Dickson

With her reputation ruined, Tilly must leave London! Only, her escape to Devon leads to a series of encounters with the insufferable yet dangerously handsome Earl of Clifton.

THE GENTLEMAN'S CINDERELLA BRIDE (Victorian)
by Carol Arens

When Andrew discovers his brother has cheated Clara out of her wealth and that she's now almost destitute, he feels obliged to offer the only thing he can—marriage.

A LAIRD WITHOUT A PAST (Georgian)
Secrets of Clan Cameron • by Jeanine Englert

When Royce wakes with no memories and suddenly blind, his situation seems dire. The only thing he remembers—the beautiful woman who came to his rescue.

THE VIKING SHE LOVES TO HATE (Viking)
by Lucy Morris

In a competition to prove who's the better boatbuilder, Astrid and Ulrik know the stakes are high. But soon their rivalry turns to a heated passion they can't ignore!

HOW THE DUKE MET HIS MATCH (Regency)
by Sophia Williams

Alexander, Duke of Harwell, couldn't stand by and let a rogue ruin heiress Emma—so to save her reputation, he shocks himself by announcing their engagement!

YOU CAN FIND MORE INFORMATION ON UPCOMING HARLEQUIN TITLES, FREE EXCERPTS AND MORE AT HARLEQUIN.COM.

HHCNM0623

Get 3 FREE REWARDS!

We'll send you 2 FREE Books **plus** a FREE Mystery Gift.

FREE Value Over **$20**

Both the **Harlequin® Historical** and **Harlequin® Romance** series feature compelling novels filled with emotion and simmering romance.

HARLEQUIN
PLUS

Try the best multimedia
subscription service for romance
readers like you!

Read, Watch and Play.

Experience the easiest way to get
the romance content you crave.

Start your **FREE TRIAL** at
www.harlequinplus.com/freetrial.